Victoria Dimmock began writing her debut   1
2009. She was inspired by numerous years s   d
by an assortment of interesting characters which fuelled her over-active imagination
and her love of an apocalyptic scenario.

She lives in a small village in Bedfordshire with her husband, Charlie, and their three
daughters, True, Faith and Anna.

This book is dedicated to my husband, Charlie. Your support and enthusiasm are both inspiring and motivational.

Victoria Dimmock

EYES DOWN

AUSTIN MACAULEY PUBLISHERS™

LONDON * CAMBRIDGE * NEW YORK * SHARJAH

A CIP catalogue record for this title is available from the British Library.

ISBN 9781528919883 (Paperback)
ISBN 9781528988056 (ePub e-book)
ISBN 9781528988049 (Audiobook)

www.austinmacauley.com

First Published (2021)
Austin Macauley Publishers Ltd
25 Canada Square
Canary Wharf
London
E14 5LQ

I am and will forever be grateful to the following people for their c_ this book:

My husband for being my muse, my rock and my greatest critic. I apol_ for my over-use of commas.

My daughters for celebrating and encouraging every little victory regardless understanding.

My sister for her attention to detail as my acting editor. I hope you enjoy the en

My brother for keeping me on my toes and constantly igniting my imagination. Y_ positivity is always appreciated.

My mum for believing in me enough to help get this book published. I can't tell you how grateful I am for your endless support.

My dad for his extraordinary ideas. Our Sunday morning conversations constantly remind me of why I love to write.

My sister-in-law, Jade Thomas, for her amazing artwork on the front cover. You captured exactly what I wanted to convey. Thank you for your hard work and dedication. I am truly grateful.

My friend of seventeen years, Daniel Humphreys, for answering my tedious questions and for your helpful advice. You were one of the first people to believe in me, so it just seems fitting that you have contributed to the completion of this work.

And finally, thank you to all of the character inspirations I worked with during my fourteen years in the bingo industry. At some point, you have all played a major role in my life. You know who you are. Thank you for all the years of fun, friendships and frivolities. We were all a band of misfits together.

Friday, 19th April 2019
8:30 am

"So, not only do we have to worry about this virus that could potentially wipe us out, but there is also someone going around killing people in their homes once they've been told they don't have that virus?" Matt slammed the newspaper onto the bare table. "What the fuck's happening to this world?"

The room was confined and the unexpected collision of folded newspaper onto a hardwood table made its inhabitants jolt upright. The topic of conversation matched the dreary interior of the staffroom. Its faded yellow walls which once promised a positive atmosphere now served as a washed-out version of its former self, much like the attitudes of its employees. It used to house five small tables, surrounded by chairs provided to encourage socialising between shifts. If the walls could talk, they would reminisce about untold bouts of laughter and numerous inspirational presentations. To look at it now could bring a tear to the eye of anyone who might still care about days gone by working for the notorious Heaven Bingo Club.

Sitting in the lacklustre room, boasting its solitary table with two accompanying chairs, the two men indulged in a final pre-shift lounge around while a third sat on a beaten-up couch beside the doorway trying to ignore them.

"It's all going to shit, mate. And, apparently, it's not just one person killing these people. It could be a group, like a cult or something," Darius added.

"Where'd you hear that?" Matt leaned forward; his interests spiked. He was tall, thin and regimented in his actions. He'd had a tough upbringing which led to him joining the army at a young age. He served for ten years, then was sent home with post-traumatic stress disorder. It had taken him a further five years to recover which was when he met his wife and decided to start a family. He rarely spoke about the nightmares he'd had to endure but on occasion, you could see the pain in his eyes.

"It's been popping up on social media, everywhere you look. The victims had all been to the hospital displaying symptoms resembling the rabies virus. Within twenty-four hours of them being released, they were murdered." Darius was an upbeat individual covered in tattoos, equally as tall as Matt but almost double in width. He liked to refer to it as relaxed muscle, but his joviality exposed his imaginary armour. He had a lip piercing and a scar through his left eyebrow where a piercing used to be.

"A cult for what though?" Matt loved a conspiracy as much as the next theorist, but he required more evidence than social media propaganda.

Darius thought for a minute, but his acquired knowledge was actually quite limited, and he struggled to think of a motive since he hadn't been offered one in any of the stories he'd read.

The clock ticked in the silence of their debate, reminding them that they only had twenty minutes until they needed to start work.

"I've got it! I've bloody got it. They must be a vigilante group." Darius was so excited by his revelatory conclusion, but by the look on his friend's face, he could tell he was alone in his supposition.

"Mate, they've killed kids and old people. What kind of vigilante group does that?"

Darius was convinced. "They, obviously, do it for the 'greater good'. Think about it. These people are given the all clear from the hospitals. Look, right here." He began poking the newspaper article vigorously.

A Dr Terence Eastwick had examined six of the victims himself and told them that they didn't have the virus and because they hadn't been bitten, their symptoms pointed elsewhere. Although the symptoms were similar, they lacked the contraction bites to prove it.

"He's not taking into consideration an airborne version of the virus. It's not officially been proven yet. Maybe these people are experiencing the symptoms because they've contracted rabies from someone who had been bitten without being bitten themselves. This cult or vigilante group or whatever you want to call them could be tracking down the patients they've sent home because they know more than the doctors do and they're trying to prevent an outbreak."

"How would they know more than the doctors do?" Matt was still not convinced. "And while we're on the topic, surely the doctors would be aware if this virus had any threat of becoming airborne."

"Who knows? They could be MI5; they could be renegade agents or maybe just people who are crazy smart and clued up about zombie apocalypses." Darius was getting far too carried away and Tyrone (the third man over on the couch) had had enough.

"Zombies? Are you fucking joking? Can you even hear yourself?"

Darius became defensive. "Come on Ty, is it insane to think that it could've happened before on a lesser scale? All this zombie paraphernalia had to have come from somewhere. Maybe it's happened before and was covered up before it became a pandemic. The government can hide all sorts of things now."

Tyrone didn't bother to hide his frustration. "No, Darius. It came from someone's imagination. You know, like vampires and werewolves? It doesn't mean they're real, not enough to make some group of psychopaths kill a bunch of innocent people with the flu."

The tension in the room could've been cut with a knife and the silence quickly became unbearable.

"You know what, carry on fellas. I can't listen to this shit anymore."

Tyrone excused himself from the awkward atmosphere that engulfed the now claustrophobic staff room and headed for the open door. He hadn't meant to snap at his soon to be former colleagues. It wasn't their fault and he felt bad instantly but was too stubborn to apologise in the moment. He would make a point of clearing the air before they said their final goodbyes later on. He would be glad when this day was over. He had had a rough night's sleep and there were plenty of places he would rather be today.

On his way down the stairs, he reached into his pocket and pulled out a bright red lighter that he had acquired after a night of heavy drinking at a strip club in Leicester Square. The lone cigarette behind his ear would be put to good use soon enough. He kept promising himself he'd quit, but recently, it just seemed so easy to create reasons as to why he shouldn't. The fact that he had another fifteen minutes until he was on the clock was as good a reason as any and the topic of conversation in the staff room had also riled him to say the least. He'd watched the news and read the newspapers and everything had been explained in such depth, yet he couldn't help but think that it was all just an exaggeration, a ploy to divert attention from the current pressing matters of the country. The government always loved a scapegoat. Still, his unnecessary outburst with the guys was exactly that: unnecessary.

According to the media, they'd found a new strain of the rabies virus which they believed carried the genetic traits capable of mutating into an airborne disease. They were busy taking precautions and running tests in the areas where cases had been reported which were mainly in Central London and Manchester with a couple of cases in Hertfordshire and Cambridge.

Over the past ten years there had been numerous scares like Foot and Mouth disease and Swine flu and although they were real diseases, an outbreak of rabies? Could they really make that stick?

The closest incident to Enfield was in Islington, a mere ten miles away. It was the first known human rabies case in over a century so, needless to say, everyone had gone into a blind panic. Apparently, this patient hadn't visited a foreign country in five years and had not been in contact with any dogs or bats in months. Tyrone had also read all about Dr Eastwick, the supposed expert. They were waiting on him to give his opinion before the patient could be properly diagnosed. Tyrone was no scientist or doctor, but it all sounded like scare mongering to him. Religion was no longer the opiate of the masses. No, the media had commandeered that role, social media, in particular. However, the murders from this past week were more terrifying than any virus in his eyes. Those murders meant that there were maniacs out there willing to end other people's lives because of a superstition. The doctor had said the released patients weren't infected. Why wasn't that enough for them? Maybe it was a personal vendetta against Dr Eastwick.

Tyrone didn't want to think about it anymore. He walked through the quiet deserted bingo club. Part of him was glad he wouldn't have to set foot in that room ever again once the day was over. The club was shutting down after thirty glorious years because customer footfall had dropped and over the last five years, income had plummeted due to online gambling sites growing in popularity.

Heaven Bingo was to close its doors to employees for the final time that afternoon, fruit machines and any property of the company were due to be collected after the bank holiday weekend, and customers had enjoyed their final session of bingo the previous evening. Staff had either been offered positions in neighbouring clubs or had taken a redundancy package. Tyrone had opted for the latter in a hope to move past the gaping vortex that was the bingo scene.

There was never a more solitary atmosphere within the workplace than there was right now. It was his favourite time: no customers, barely any staff and no annoying arcade noises. It was a tranquil surrounding. They could take their time this morning since they didn't have to be out until 2 pm.

The General Manager had been in his office for the last half an hour, but he would procrastinate with 'paperwork' so that he didn't have to help them with the machine collection which was a Godsend really. He didn't have a clue as to what he was doing so they would be able to get on with things without having to talk him through how to empty a machine, or where they would enter figures onto the system, or hell, even how to switch on the computer. It was frustrating working under a manager that had to be talked through every tedious task, but that was the way the company had always worked. The managers relied on supervisors to be around to hold their hands.

Luckily for Tyrone, his supervisor was in today too. At least Grace knew what she was doing, she was that guiding hand. Kathryn, the other supervisor, was also in and was just as competent, although she wasn't as generous with her knowledge. She enjoyed being the person who knew the answer and as much as she liked to boss people about, she didn't delegate much because she liked to be the one taking the credit when the job was well done. She also had difficulty trusting anyone to do a job as well as she could and was, of course, severely put out if they ever did.

As Tyrone reached the entrance, he slipped his key into the double doors at the front of the building heading out into the retail park. The unexpected brightness of the morning sun caught him off guard and he shaded his eyes until they could adjust. Working in a building for hours on end with no windows was absolute torture.

There were only a handful of cars parked on the bingo side of the car park and those mainly belonged to staff. He did, however, spot the familiar red Nissan Micra. He gave a wave to the little old lady it belonged to. Jean Saunders was an elderly woman who had been playing at Heaven Bingo since the day they'd opened. She was always pleasant, asking after the staff, and inquiring about their families. She didn't have any children of her own and no siblings to speak of, so she liked to think of the Heaven employees as her family. She was an easy woman to warm to and the staff cared a lot about her. She must have forgotten that they were no longer open.

The DIY shop and the supermarket seemed quite busy already. People panicking, he bet. He could recall a few years previously, when the car park had been jam-packed with easily influenced clientele, barging past each other because there was a 'horrendous storm' approaching. In British terms, that literally translated to heavy rain with slightly strong winds. Yet people imagined a tsunami was heading their way and intended to stock up so they wouldn't need to go out in it.

Needless to say, the 'horrendous storm' lasted for eighteen whole hours and disrupted next to no one's day.

It was 8:48 am as he stepped outside into the surprisingly hot April sun. It was the hottest spring they'd seen in England for a long while and he couldn't wait to take advantage of it. For as of 2 pm that day, he was temporarily a man of leisure.

The air was warm, but the shade offered a slightly cooler resting place. He perched against the wall that was neighbouring the entrance doors and lit his cigarette, drawing in deeply on its relief. Leaning his head against the cool concrete supporting him, he exhaled slowly. That was just what he needed to prepare himself for the day's work ahead of him. He looked around at the retail park that he had watched grow over the last eight years.

It used to consist of the bingo hall, a night club and the DIY shop but two years previous, the night club had been shut down due to its heinous clientele and the violence they brought with them. It had stood derelict until last year when they had remodelled it into a supermarket. It was a shame because staff used to enjoy going to the nightclub to unwind after work. They got in for free which was handy. It was just unfortunate that Enfield was known for its rising crime rates. He remembered one night when one of the doormen had been shot in the face. Luckily, the bullet just grazed his cheek, but it was one of the numerous attacks the nightclub had seen and was undoubtedly the straw that had broken the camel's back.

Tyrone sighed. A lot had changed in eight years and he found himself wondering how he would fare since he had decided to leave the company. What would he do now? He'd mused breezily over his options when he'd first made the decision to leave the bingo industry but now that the crunch time had rolled around, he was nowhere near prepared.

He banished it from his mind as that was not a thought he wanted to consider before 9 am on a Friday and following a much-needed stretch, he dropped the cigarette butt to the floor and stamped it out. Jean began to exit her car and as Tyrone chuckled to himself, he went to meet her halfway.

It was then that he heard the screams.

8:50 am

At that moment, Tyrone turned his attention to a crowd of people running towards him. He froze, trying to assess the situation. These people were crazed and screaming, throwing their shopping bags to the floor and running for their lives. Small children were being hoisted into the air by frightened parents and older ones were being dragged along.

In the distance, he could see figures launching bins into shop windows, hysterically shouting unfathomable words. They didn't look real. Their movements were exaggerated and sporadic. He wasn't sure what he was actually seeing and his mind kept flashing back to the discussion he had so rudely disregarded mere moments ago.

He lunged forward and grabbed Jean's arm, escorting her hurriedly inside the club's open side door.

Before he knew it, the frenzy of people had reached him too. He beckoned to the doorway and ushered the frightened crowd inside the building. Some followed his directions, but others chose to push past him, knocking him to the ground. He felt a knee collide with his jaw and his fingers were trodden on multiple times. He yelled out in pain as the rush of people slowly subsided.

Through the stampede of feet, he noticed a woman lying on the floor, a few metres from the door. A red-headed woman and a small child were struggling to move the fallen young woman. He scampered to his feet and ran towards them, pushing through the oncoming herd, keeping his eye on the tormenting shadows behind them. His athletic build aided him in his mission towards the damsel in distress but as he reached her, he felt his muscles beginning to seize. He hadn't sprinted like that in a long time and he fought to maintain his stamina. He peered down at her not fully acknowledging the extent of her injuries. The unconscious woman's shirt used to be white with a yellow duck pictured on the front which was now covered in dirty footprints. He then noticed that the side of her mouth was bleeding. Without a further thought, he looked at the woman with the red hair. "I've got her."

He attempted to lift the woman but underestimated her dead weight. He tried again, and fuelled by adrenaline, managed to struggle to his feet with the woman nestled in his arms. It took every ounce of strength he had to get them back to the building. As he ran, he could feel his deafening heartbeat throbbing in his ears and he had an overwhelming sense of nausea take hold of him. The distance was short, but panic had set in and with every step he took, their combined weight appeared to increase. As he made it through the doorway, her body acted as an anchor and he collapsed onto the tiled floor, holding onto her small frame as tightly as he could. He heard himself screaming for help and it came in the form of a teenage boy who had been steered into the club with his friend. He helped lay her down as gently as possible but before he could thank the young lad, Tyrone realised the side door was still open.

He ran outside to retrieve his key, but the threatening figures had loomed closer and he could see the fury and blood lust in their eyes. They looked to be salivating. Their bodies jerked forward, uncontrollably twitching and jolting. They had him in plain sight and were heading straight for him.

His body switched into survival mode. He locked the door from the outside, took the key and ran around the corner of the building hoping to lead them away. If he could activate the emergency hatch, he could lock them all inside the building. They would be safe inside away from the terror. Dropping to his knees on to the paved floor, he yanked the hatch door open and forced the key into the slot. With one swift movement, he turned it to horizontal, entered the six-digit code, withdrew it and ran for his life.

8:55 am

Grace sat at one of the fruit machines awaiting Tyrone's return. As she sat on the revolving chair, she was snapped into action when she heard the harrowing screams of the people rushing into the building. Amongst the noise, she focused on the frantic incoherent shouts coming from Tyrone. He was calling for someone to help him and something about locking the door. She had no idea what was happening, but the urgency in his voice told her it was serious.

In the foyer, an injured woman lay motionless and as Grace reached her, she saw the shutters going down at the front of the building. She desperately looked around for Tyrone, but he was nowhere in sight. She lost herself for a moment. The whole situation was surreal and her head was spinning. She had to help these people. They were all so scared, yet she had no clue as to what they were scared of and that, in itself terrified her.

The commotion became accompanied by deafening bangs threatening the outside layer of the shuttered barrier. The people in the foyer screamed and darted further into the club, away from the horrifying howls. Grace's imagination was going crazy at the prospect of who or what could be making those sounds. The barrier was practically impenetrable without heavy-duty power tools, so they needn't fear anything getting inside. Regardless, the screams and noises were horrific. It sounded like they had already compromised the outer glass.

She began tending to people, the first being the unconscious young woman who looked to be in her mid-twenties. Her dark, curly hair drooped limp aside her pale pretty face and she was breathing strenuously. Grace thought back to her first aid training two years previously and she searched her memory in order to recall what to do. Her search was interrupted by the woman sitting next to her.

"She's my sister. Her name's Vickey." The trembling red-headed woman began to explain whilst rocking a small child who Grace had failed to notice before. "We ran and she fell. I didn't even notice. When I did, I went back but we couldn't move her. People were treading all over her. No one stopped to help us until that guy came over."

The young woman's face was drawn and pale like her sister's and Grace couldn't be sure whether it was the colour of her hair or the tears clouding them that made her green eyes stand out so much. The child in her arms was small, around three years old Grace guessed. She resembled her mother with her dark hair and Grace could only imagine that Vickey's eyes matched her daughter's mahogany brown.

"Is she breathing?" The words came from the taller of the two teenage boys.

"Barely," Grace replied.

He knelt down beside her. "You might want to check her for marks or bruises or something."

The sister became defensive. "They didn't touch her. They didn't get that close."

"No, no. I just meant to find out why she's unconscious. You said she was trampled…"

Out of nowhere, a pair of hands reached in and ripped open Vickey's shirt, in one quick motion as if the material were made of tissue paper.

"Hey! What are you doing?" The redhead shouted at the giant of a man and forced his bear-like hands away.

"Her rib's been broken and there's probably some internal damage." The man towered over all of them. Grace instantly recognised him by his sheer size. He was their security guard, Winston. He had nodded his hellos when he'd first arrived that morning but had begun checking all the entrances to the building straight away, so few people had clapped eyes on him. He'd been working at the club for a few years and had quickly formed friendships with the majority of the staff. He had an amazing gentleness about him despite his stature and it emanated as soon as he spoke. He looked like he knew what he was talking about. Grace preferred to think that he hadn't been the cause of any broken ribs, but she couldn't be sure. She quickly realised that this was a guy she wanted on her side in a bad situation.

"You're not a doctor." The red-haired woman was still trying to maintain her sister's dignity by covering her bare torso with her own jacket. She had felt, before leaving the house that morning that it was too hot for a jacket but thanked God she'd decided otherwise.

"No. I just know a broken rib when I see one. She might have punctured her lung by the way she's breathing." The security guard turned to the redhead. "I'm Winston. I'm the security guard here."

She looked at him uncertainly. "I'm Rosie."

Grace ushered the group into the main hall where they could seal the doors shut, away from the horrors and noises that were outside. The two teenage lads helped Winston carry Vickey's limp body into the hall even though he could probably have lifted her on his own in one arm.

9:05 am

Panic and confusion burst through the entrance to the main hall. The crowd of people rushed into the building that had stood empty and peaceful only moments before. The three men carried Vickey toward the General Manager's office to the left of the stage. They were led by Grace and closely followed by Rosie and her niece.

Michael Pearce read his newspaper completely unaware of the hubbub that was occurring outside his office door and stood brusquely when that door was barged open by Grace.

"What the hell is going on? Don't you knock?" he demanded.

He stood with his hands placed firmly on his hips in a pose of presumed authority. It rarely worked in his favour and he was well aware of how his employees viewed him. He'd only got the job because his cousin had called in a few favours and, before he knew it, he was running a bingo hall without having any experience in management and an equal amount of knowledge about bingo, hence the staff's fair opinion of him.

"We need the couch. This woman's been hurt."

Grace was not about to take the time to explain the urgency of the matter to Michael. As far as she was concerned, this was not a work-related issue; therefore, his authoritative pose wasn't going to achieve the expected response.

She began throwing files and mountains of accurately stacked paperwork onto the floor to clear a space for the injured woman. It wasn't the most comfortable couch, but Grace managed to fluff up the pillows before the men rested her upon it. She carefully placed a couch cushion under Vickey's lifted head and lowered it down gently.

Michael tried to rebut but his efforts were ignored as he was outnumbered in his lack of concern for the woman's comfort or wellbeing. He was still confused. Why did they have a responsibility to help her? Who was she? How did all of these people end up inside his club and, with a child no less? No, he was not okay with this situation at all. His office had been invaded and he struggled to maintain his anger as he pulled Grace to one side.

"Why the hell have you brought her in here?"

"It's not just her. There are others in the hall," Grace answered, dismissively.

He grabbed hold of her arms with a little more aggression than intended but Michael wanted answers, real ones and now he had her attention.

"Well, yes, I can see that," he spat with a frustrated tremor, pointing towards the CCTV monitors. "I want to know why they are inside *my* club."

Grace had no answer. She was still unclear on exactly what had happened herself. The club had been breached and Grace had been bombarded with people who needed her help.

"I have no idea, Michael. Tyrone was outside…" She struggled to fabricate any explanation that could justify what had just happened and Michael was clearly not satisfied with her response, getting angrier by the second.

"That guy, Tyrone? He told us to get inside, that we'd be safe in here. He basically saved our lives."

Michael turned to face the young man who had spoken. "I'm sorry, you are…?"

"I'm Charlie." The teen then nodded towards his friend. "This is Serhan."

"Safe from what?" Michael was looking at them all like they were crazy.

"The infected." Serhan wasn't about to join the club and pussy foot around the matter. He was a straight talker and an impatient one at that. "You've got CCTV, right?"

"Of course," Michael answered, offended.

Serhan pushed passed Grace to get to the monitors in the corner of the office. He was completely void of anything that resembled courtesy. "Rewind it."

Michael responded begrudgingly, spurred on by pure curiosity. He fumbled with the controls before moving aside to let Grace take control. She rewound the footage and watched in horror as they took in the scene that had occurred not thirty minutes ago. They witnessed terrified people running for their lives towards the building and she saw Tyrone hurry them inside, locking the door behind them. Grace put her hand to her mouth in fear for her friend. Switching cameras, they watched him run around the side of the building and activate the time lock. The figures were gaining on him and you could see that there was something abnormal about their eyes, but the grainy footage failed to convey the detail. They started throwing glass bottles at the camera and behind them, you could see Tyrone running away with a couple of them close at his heels. Then the screen went blank. One by one, the external cameras were sabotaged.

Michael backed away from the monitors. "I need to make a phone call."

Grace looked to him for some form of response. "Michael?"

He placed his hands behind his head as he shook it in disbelief.

"Make sure everyone is all right. Give them drinks: water, tea, coffee. Keep them calm." He walked behind his desk and sat down. "I'll be out in a minute."

"Are we going to be okay in here?" Rosie's voice was barely audible yet firm. Michael had completely forgotten she was there. She, along with the small child, had been sitting with the injured woman the whole time. He looked at them for what seemed to him like the longest of moments. They hadn't needed to watch the CCTV. They were out there. He had seen them, running scared. He'd seen Vickey stumble and he'd watched her get trampled by the dozens of other scared shoppers as her sister and daughter had tried to get back to her, like fish swimming against the current. He'd seen the hero that was Tyrone lift the woman and bring her to safety, bring them all to safety.

"It's fine." He gave a supportive nod as he sat down. "You stay there. I just need a minute."

He tried to comfort her with a smile, but a look of worry masked his intention, so he dismissed himself for more privacy in the toilets behind his desk.

9:22 am

Grace, Winston and the two boys re-entered the hall as she tried to comprehend the scene before her. Charlie and Serhan grabbed two seats on the first row of chairs and tried to get comfortable. It had been an unbelievably manic morning for everyone involved and they needed time to gather their thoughts and figure out a plan of action.

Grace stared across the sea of frightened faces, not knowing what to do next. It was strange to see the way different people reacted to things. Six of them were staff members and felt at ease inside the familiarity of the club, but the others were strangers who had probably never set foot inside the building in their lives. Everything was foreign to them. Grace looked around the hall and counted twenty-two people inside the building, including herself and the people in the office.

She caught sight of Sophie (one of the club's cleaners) and Kristie, their receptionist. If Grace could enlist their help to settle people, the task may not be as intimidating. Kristie Burns had a naivety that was very alluring. It made you want to shelter her from everything that wasn't sugar coated and rose tinted. She thought a lot of Kristie. She was probably the most genuine person Grace had ever met. She always looked beautiful even today without any make up and her hair all scooped up into a messy bun and the best part was that she didn't even realise how stunning she was.

"Ladies, can I borrow you both for a sec?" She spoke the words quietly so that only the intended people would hear. Grace gave them a quick rundown of what had happened outside but deliberately left out information that would cause them to panic and assured them that everything would be explained once Michael had made his phone call.

"Would you both mind going around with trays of water, teas and coffees, while I go and make sure that everyone is okay?"

The girls nodded in agreement and turned towards the diner where the coffee machines lay in wait.

Grace noticed Kristie cradling her finger.

"Kristie? What's the matter with your finger?"

The eighteen-year-old looked down at her index finger with her naive expression. "A wasp stung me on my way to work this morning. I've never been stung before. It really hurts."

Grace was momentarily blindsided by this somewhat innocuous conversation in comparison to what she had seen on the CCTV footage. Nevertheless, she offered some kind words so as not to offend.

"There should be some antiseptic cream in my handbag."

Kristie nodded her thanks and skipped off to the diner to join her workmate. Kristie boasted a tall, voluptuous physique whilst Sophie was at least a foot shorter and extremely thin. She could easily be mistaken for an adolescent at a distance but up close, you could see the neglect in her eyes: a tell-tale sign of restless nights and a stressful life. Sophie was also very kind but much quieter than her co-worker. She kept to herself and rarely divulged information about her personal life.

Grace returned to the task at hand and followed an imaginary line that linked each person just to be sure that no one was forgotten on her mission of assurance. She decided to start with the people she knew, so looking at the right of the stage, on the first row, she decided to start with the boys who were sitting with Winston.

"Hey guys. Thank you so much for all your help in there." She motioned to the office behind her. "I'm Grace. I'm one of the supervisors here, not that that really matters."

"It's cool. We were just across the car park at the DIY shop."

Charlie was tall with scruffy brown hair and his baggy clothes hid his thin physique. His voice was deep and soothing.

"I can't believe we got stuck in a bingo hall because we chose to buy a nail gun today, of all days."

Serhan was slightly shorter than Charlie and a bit bulkier with jet black gelled hair and olive skin. His dark eyes didn't look impressed with the current situation. Whenever he'd imagined being in the midst of a zombie apocalypse (as most guys of a similar age had) Serhan had always seen himself hauled up in a loft space surrounded by supplies and necessities, not trapped inside a bingo hall, of all places, with a bunch of strangers.

24

"Let me know if you need anything." Grace smiled and turned to Winston.

"How you doing, G?" He smiled from the side of his mouth.

"I could be better. What about you, big guy?" She playfully punched his massive arm.

"I'm good. You're good. We're all gonna be good." His relaxed nature was a blessing.

"I admire your positivity," Grace joked.

"I'm just worried about the little lady in there." He gestured towards the office.

"Vickey?"

He lowered his voice. "The girl."

Grace looked confused.

"She's gonna lose her mum and that lady is gonna lose her sister."

"She's just unconscious. We'll know more once she wakes up, Winston."

Her words harboured no consolation as Winston was sure of the severity of the woman's injuries.

"No, that rib has punctured her lung and if we're all locked inside this place, she won't be going to the hospital. She's not going to make it."

Grace processed the information and placed a friendly hand on Winston's shoulder.

"I take back the positivity comment," she said, light-heartedly.

"Just keeping it real, G."

She continued on to the next aisle of colleagues, Darius, Matt and Kathryn. The latter was also a supervisor at the club and hated having her toes stepped on. She liked to use her authority to bully people and only a few could see through her façade. Grace had moved in with Kathryn the previous year and had seen a completely different side to her: a softer, more caring side but it remained at home. In the workplace, she had continued with her merciless rules and strict orders regardless.

"So, what's going on?" Kathryn asked, her blonde hair tucked annoyingly behind her ear.

"I'm not sure. I think someone should make an announcement in a minute, but I wanted to make sure everyone was okay first."

Kathryn rolled her eyes. She wanted to be in the know, and even more so now that she knew Grace wasn't. She'd be damned if she was finding out at the same time as every other Tom, Dick and Harry so she got up and made her way to the office. Grace watched her as she stormed off and fought the urge to smirk when Kathryn walked into a locked door, hitting her face off of the wood. She looked back at Grace who diverted her gaze as if she hadn't witnessed her friend's embarrassment and then stomped off to the toilets in a huff. Grace shrugged it off as pathetic yet classic behaviour for the twenty-eight-year-old and moved on.

Darius and Matt had also seen Kathryn's blunder and laughed about it between themselves. Grace stood within earshot of the two men.

"That woman irks me." Matt shook his head as he spoke, shooting proverbial daggers at his superior.

"Don't let her get to you. You know, she gets off on it," Darius chuckled. "Isn't that right, Jean?"

"Don't you bring me into it, Darius Newman, you devil." The old woman flashed Darius her look of mocking disapproval as she sat in one of the neighbouring seats.

Grace had no idea what she was doing here and prayed that it was a coincidence, not that she'd forgotten that the club was closing.

Jean turned towards Grace and using her usual soft tone asked the question on everyone's mind.

"What on Earth is going on, dear?"

Grace took a seat beside her. Jean held onto her Zimmer frame half-heartedly and looked around the room anxiously. As if answering Grace's unspoken question, Jean spoke again.

"I came here early to make sure I got my favourite machine and as I was walking to the doors to see Tyrone it was like a mad dash. They almost knocked me off my feet. Is that young girl all right?" Jean gestured towards the office. "I saw her on the floor, but it all happened so quickly, and I can't see Tyrone anywhere." She began hysterically searching the hall for him. "I don't know where he's gone."

Grace placed a hand on Jean's shoulder dreading the conversation that loomed. Jean wasn't aware of the happenings in the world nowadays. This was going to be a challenge.

"Jean, haven't you been watching the news?"

"No, dear. You know me, I don't bother watching television. There's never anything good on. I just read, darling, or I come here. Why? What's happened?"

Grace felt that familiar surge that rushed through her whenever she spoke to Jean. The feeling that she just wanted to cuddle her and protect her from the harsh reality of the world, even though she'd probably experienced more than enough of it in her many years.

"Jean, something bad has happened." Grace took hold of the woman's fragile hand. "I mean, really bad." Jean stared blankly at her, so she continued as if addressing a child. "There are dangerous people outside who want to hurt us."

"Oh, you don't believe all that rubbish, do you?"

"Jean, it's happening right now. That's why we're all locked in here."

"But Tyrone was outside. Where is he now?"

Jean had grown very fond of Tyrone and swore daily that if she was sixty years younger, she'd marry him.

"He's still out there. He locked us in."

"Oh dear. He's still out there? What if he's hurt? Someone needs to go and get him." She began hyperventilating. Grace rummaged through the old lady's bag for her asthma pump. It was like any woman's handbag, filled with crap she didn't need, or things she had forgotten about or thought she might have needed on a separate occasion but had never removed. Once she located the inhaler, Jean drew on it twice, shaking it in between breaths, trying to calm herself. She had a fleeting moment of anxiety and then faced the problem head on. Grace marvelled at the old lady's ability to handle a crisis.

"Those things can't get through the shutters." Grace tried to assure the now-trembling woman. "Tyrone saved us."

9:53 am

Michael slunk out of the office and headed towards the stage. It was then that he realised these people wouldn't see him as any form of authority. He was about to speak to a group of scared people with whom he had absolutely no control over. He focused his attention on the crowd of confused faces and encouraged himself to remain calm. He cleared his throat.

"Ladies and gentlemen," he announced with arms wide open, only slightly less theatrical than a ring master addressing his audience. His exaggerated confidence felt false in his own ears, but he carried on regardless.

"My name is Michael Pearce. I am the General Manager at this club." He took a deep, cleansing breath. "As most of you know, the front doors have been locked as a precaution. I'm now aware of what has happened outside and I can see that those of you who were out there believe you are safer in here."

"Are we *not* safer in here then?" The words were louder than she'd intended but she stuck by her question, all the same. The woman's name was Lorraine. She was in her late fifties and was with her husband, Lewie. They had been shopping next door when the chaos broke out. She was blonde with stunning blue eyes and was slightly taller than her husband who had messy grey hair and a friendly smile.

"If it's not safe, why are we still in here?" This came from Claire. She was what Michael referred to as a 'Statement Girl'. She was possibly in her thirties. It was difficult to tell from where he stood. Her skin was pale, her hair was a vibrant green and her make-up was elaborate and pristine. Instantly, he could tell that Claire was going to be a handful by her smug expression and defiant attitude.

"No, no. You misunderstand. You're much better off in here. We closed the shutters to make sure people in here were protected from the rioters."

"That wasn't normal rioting. That was different." The voice was quiet but familiar as all eyes turned to look at Sophie. "There was something wrong with them. They were acting crazy."

28

"What do you expect rioters to act like?" Her boyfriend, Craig, seemed agitated and resembled a caged animal, jittery and hostile. His hair was greasy and he reeked of an unidentifiable odour. Sophie recoiled at his remark and didn't respond.

Most of the staff had never met Craig before but rumours had circulated throughout the workplace inspired by Sophie's mysterious bruises and apparent curbed demeanour. Studying them now, it was easy for one to believe that Sophie was the victim of an abusive relationship.

"She's right." A man from the back of the hall stood up in order to be seen and introduced himself as if he were at an AA meeting. "I'm Tom. I work next door. Those people weren't normal."

He avoided eye contact with Craig and shifted his position nervously as he remained focused on Michael. "They were dangerous. Their eyes were crazy and they were just attacking everyone and everything."

"So, what you're saying is that they were infected?" asked Kathryn. "With this virus they're talking about on the news?" Her question was blunt and demanding which prompted Tom to fidget with his clothes as his anxiety rose.

The hall was filled with aisles upon aisles of seats and tables. Tom guessed that it could probably seat about 800 people comfortably. So, why did it seem so small all of a sudden?

"I can't say for sure," he stuttered.

Kathryn could be very intimidating when she wanted to be. Unfortunately, sometimes she just forgot how to turn it off and sound in the least bit caring. It clearly took a lot of effort as she took a deep breath and deliberately lowered her tone.

"I'm just asking you because you were out there. Did they look like they had that virus?" Tom was troubled by how daunting she still sounded and the walls seemed closer to him than before.

He took a rushed breath and answered Kathryn. "I'd say so, yes."

Panicked rumours erupted throughout the hall.

"Well, this just got real pretty quick." This came from Matt, sarcastic as ever but straight to the point.

"What about you two?" Kathryn continued. "What's your story?"

Charlie and Serhan looked uncomfortably at each other as everyone in the hall fixed their eyes upon them. "To be honest," Charlie began. "I didn't see the crazies. We had left the store and were almost out of the car park when we heard screams. Then we just got caught up in the panic, I guess."

"Yeah, I had no idea what was going on," Serhan agreed. "Everyone was running so I ran with them. That guy told us to get inside the building so that's where I went."

Matt stood, gathering his keys and phone. "I need to get home. Ashley's there with the kids. I can't sit around here all day."

He got up to leave and was furiously dialling on his mobile phone. He wasn't the only one. Hands had already reached into pockets, retrieving their lifelines only to become frustrated and further confused when their phones lacked reception. Staff members and customers knew that if you were inside the club, your phone signal was non-existent and Heaven Bingo did not have the luxury of Wi-Fi.

"Why aren't our phones working?" and "There's no signal," were among the questions and statements launched at Michael. Terrified people swiftly became irritated and stranded terrified people.

"Don't worry. It's something to do with the roof. We never get signal in here and we don't have Wi-Fi." Michael's attempt at consolation was met with criticism and judgement.

"You don't have Wi-Fi? What age do you live in?" Claire pressed.

"There was no need. The company knew we would be closing soon so they never bothered installing it." Michael's retaliation wasn't the answer people had expected and people began cursing amongst themselves about how ridiculous it was in this day and age to not have Wi-Fi especially in a building that didn't allow you to even have a signal.

"I have a question. If those people outside know we're in here, won't they try to get us, or wait for us to come out? Like zombies?" The angelic voice was immediately recognisable as Kristie's.

"I don't think they're like zombies," Charlie comforted Kristie.

"Yea, I doubt they want to eat your brains," Serhan scoffed. "After what I've seen on the news, they might beat you to death, but they probably won't eat you afterwards."

Sadly, he didn't possess the charm that Charlie did. He was not considered a tactful man, but he was a good friend. Charlie just gave him a look and shook his head. This was the common reaction Serhan received. It warned him when he'd gone too far with a joke or had said something that was out of place. Most of his mishaps were unintentional however factually accurate.

Charlie rubbed Kristie's shoulder reassuringly.

"I have a boyfriend," Kristie abruptly pointed out. Charlie removed his hand from her shoulder and nursed his shattered ego instead.

The crowd was becoming restless as crowds usually do when there are too many questions and not enough answers, and Michael seemed to shrink slightly.

"We can't stay here either. I have to get my sister to a hospital." Rosie clutched her niece close to her chest.

Winston held onto her arm gently. "You can't go out there. It's not safe."

"Winston, you said it yourself, she has a broken rib. It could have pierced her lung. Maybe that's why she's not waking up."

"How can you tell it's broken?" Kathryn loved to think of herself as the Queen bee and in this club, she knew her stuff. She also liked to be the centre of attention.

Winston became defensive as if Kathryn was accusing him of a murder he did not commit.

"I used to be a wrestler. Heavyweight."

"Yep, that makes sense." Charlie wasn't surprised and had quickly developed an admiration for Winston.

"As I said before, I know a broken rib when I see one," Winston repeated.

"Or when you've caused one, you mean!" Yes, Claire was definitely going to be trouble. "Do you expect us to stay in here with a violent man? He belongs out there with those monsters. There are children in here, for God's sake."

"He doesn't need to be violent. Wrestling's, mostly, fake anyway. Any injuries are caused by accident." Charlie defended his new hero.

"That's right. And there's only one child in here and she's not scared of Winston." Rosie knew it was better to keep this mountain of a man as a friend rather than a foe.

Claire scoffed at the defendants. "This is no place for children. Isn't it illegal to have them in here?" She aimed her absurd comment at Michael this time.

"I'm sure the rules can be bent, considering the circumstances." Michael was a lot of things, but he would not see that child outside the walls of the club regardless of the gambling commission's laws. He wouldn't tolerate it. Desperate times call for desperate measures and, by God, now was a desperate time.

Claire snorted her obvious distaste for the club and all that it stood for.

"Would you rather she took her chances outside?" Grace had heard enough of Claire's illogical accusations.

Claire revealed an evil expression. Her eyes didn't seem so dark before and her head was lowered intending on putting the fear of God into everyone looking at her. "Children don't last long in situations like this. They're normally the first ones to go."

Everyone just stared at the woman in disbelief that people like her even existed. Everyone seemed concerned by her last comment, and her cronies nodded and agreed like melodramatic puppets. She had three companions with her: two men and a woman, all looking to be in their late thirties. Danny and Mark were brothers and didn't seem too clever. Both had dark hair and predominant bags under their eyes like they'd spent too many nights glued to their television screens playing video games. Kim had bleach blonde hair and half of her teeth were missing. She was taller than Claire but shorter than the two men, yet she looked like she could take either of them in a fight. She stood closely behind Claire, clearly a follower. She rarely took her eyes off of her leader.

Michael had, also, heard enough and announced, "Anyone who isn't comfortable staying here is free to leave via the back exit if there aren't any more of those…people out there."

The majority began hurriedly reaching for any belongings they had with them. They didn't want to stay in a building away from their families no matter how safe it was. There was only a handful who were quite content to ride out the proverbial storm inside the bingo hall. Grace stepped onto the stage, as everyone made a dash for the doors, and pulled Michael to one side. She held his arm tightly as she whispered to him. His eyes turned from concern to worry and then to blind panic in a matter of seconds. The exchange didn't go unnoticed by the few onlookers who alerted the rest of the group to their possible cause for concern. Grace held his stare and loosened her grip as his body seemed to deflate. Having witnessed his reaction, the crowd demanded to know what they weren't being told. Grace foolishly looked to Michael for a response.

"If this is really happening, my mum's at home, alone. I need to be there with her." Michael was a coward and was clearly in some state of shock. His legs gave way as his body slowly sunk to the floor resting against the back wall of the stage in plain view of the already panic-stricken crowd. He began muttering to himself causing Grace to turn on him.

"You saw the CCTV. Ty activated the time lock. You saw him do that. How can you not have known this was the case?" She was dumbfounded. He had watched the same footage she had. It took all of her might to not shake him vigorously.

"I didn't know." The words were inaudible. He mouthed them to Grace with a look of sorrow on his face that she had only previously seen children wear. She had no time to console him. She shook her head in disbelief that this guy was in charge of everything. She then realised that everyone was staring at them, waiting for an explanation. She stood up and begrudgingly embraced the sudden yet inevitable shift in authority, and primed herself, ready to address the occupants of the hall.

"Nobody can leave this building. We're locked inside for seventy-two hours."

10:02 am

An angry chorus of questions and demands were shot in Grace's direction like a tidal wave, lacking empathy but fuelled by conviction. She watched the mass of reactions ranging from silent disbelief to full blown emotional collapses. She felt the pressure hit her all at once and she realised that she was the one who needed to calm these people down.

Before she lost her nerve altogether, she shouted at the top of her lungs.

"FIRE!!!"

Grace's mother had always told her that if a lone woman was being attacked, she stood more chance of drawing attention to the situation if she screamed "Fire!" rather than "Rape!" or "Help!" Apparently, people responded more to a fire as a chance to show heroism. Grace knew this wasn't the same circumstance, but it was the first word that came to her head and so, she screamed it. Thinking about it as she yelled, she could be in the midst of causing an unnecessary panic in an enclosed space with no exits. Fortunately for her, the people in the hall just stared at her in shock and confusion, so Grace took advantage of the coerced silence and began her explanation.

"When the people from the other stores were attacked outside, they were let into this building by one of my colleagues. He must have panicked so he locked us all inside. Obviously, those doors are made of glass so if those…things out there wanted to get in badly enough, they could. But as most of you know, before we brought you into the hall, the metal shutters were coming down. This means, Tyrone switched on the emergency time lock from outside the club. We're locked in here."

"Until when?" Craig's agitation rapidly turned to aggression. Grace felt immediately intimidated by this change and she wasn't the only one. The whole hall felt it. He was unstable and put everyone on edge.

"Around 8:55am on Monday." Grace stared straight into his swollen red eyes and began to realise the cause of his sudden mood acceleration. He was on some form of narcotic. It was a reasonable assumption which, alone, meant they were occupying space with a ticking time bomb.

He walked away from the crowd with his arms raised high. He placed his hands on his head and pulled at his hair in frustration, all the while groaning. It was difficult for Grace not to imagine him as an animal, the dangerous kind. He was fidgety and restless and his overall appearance looked unclean.

Other questions flowed in a stream towards Grace, and she felt herself brace for the onslaught.

"Can't anybody let us out?"

"What will we do for food?"

"What about our families?"

Grace tried to answer each question honestly without causing any further unwanted dismay.

"This club is only ever time locked at midnight on the 23rd of December and can be reopened after midnight on the 26th of December. The club isn't open for those three days and we need to ensure maximum security because of the amount of cash that accumulates. It's locked from the outside so that no one can get in or out to access that money. It was never supposed to be activated other than on those days but clearly Tyrone thought we were in danger and he saw an opportunity to help us and keep us safe from whatever is going on out there.

"As for food, you don't have to worry. We have frozen goods that can be cooked, vending machines which can be opened and a fridge full of sandwiches and desserts. We can last three days. We just can't afford to be greedy."

She paused for a few moments to let some of the information sink in before she continued.

"Where your families are concerned, the only comfort I can offer is that you will be able to call your families. Mobile phones, you've probably noticed, are completely useless in here. It's something to do with the roof but it blocks phone signals and internet connections. You can all use the club phone, one at a time but we need to be civilised about this. You need to form a queue and that will be the first thing we do just to try to put everyone's minds at ease."

"What are we supposed to tell them?" Matt was getting a bit irate. Grace wasn't used to her colleagues not supporting her, but she was very aware that this wasn't a club issue. They were as scared as the other people in the building. They didn't have the inside scoop that they normally held over the customers. She also held onto the knowledge that Matt's girlfriend had given birth to a baby girl only three months before and had three other children, all under the age of seven. He was having a rough time leaving her at home without all this drama to add to it.

Grace rushed down from the stage and headed straight for him. "Matt, I'm so sorry but there's nothing we can do. You know what the time lock means. Ring Ashley and explain to her what's happened. She won't blame you and as long as she stays inside, they will all be fine."

"But you heard what they said on the news, Grace. The virus has spread. The most recent case was in Islington. And if what those people say is true, it's already spread to Enfield. Pretty soon, the towns going to be like a Danny Boyle horror film." He dropped his head, trying to stop the oncoming surge of tears but gave up. "Ashley can hide inside from a disease but how is she going to protect herself and our babies when the diseased come crashing through her window?" He took a deep breath in an attempt to curb his emotion. "I'm meant to be the one who protects them, Grace."

Her heart went out to him as she thanked any form of higher entity that she didn't have children. She couldn't imagine the fear that every parent in the hall would be experiencing. For once, she thought herself lucky. She had no close family. She lived for her work. In Grace's mind, that alone, made her a survivor.

Out of the corner of her eye, she saw Michael crawling towards his office, and she marched forward in a determined pursuit. She reached him just as he entered the room and closed the door behind her.

"What the hell are you playing at?" She was beyond caring about his laughable superiority over her.

"What are you talking about?"

"You said you needed to make a phone call. Who were you phoning?"

"That's none of your business, Grace. Remember who you're speaking to," he threatened.

"Are you kidding me?" Grace released her grip on the door handle. "I thought you would phone for help. Tell someone we were in here. You couldn't have done that if you didn't know we were trapped. Who the hell did you call?"

Michael burst into tears at the thought of being undermined by one of his inferiors.

"It was my mum. I called my mum, okay? I needed to make sure she was okay."

Grace stood back, harshly judging the sobbing man before her when she heard movement coming from behind her. She turned to see Rosie cradling the tot.

"I forgot you were all in here." She bent down and stroked the little girl's head. "Will you look after Michael for me, please? He misses his mummy and he needs a big, strong girl like you to take care of him. Will you do that for me?"

The little girl nodded her tiny head looking at the man cowering across the room from her. Grace then turned to Rosie. "I'll come back to check on you guys in a bit. Can I get you anything?"

Rosie shook her head.

Grace grabbed the phone from the desk and forced it into Michael's hands. "Sort yourself out and make the call to the Regional Manager or anyone who might know how to override a time lock. I have an angry group of people to deal with and I don't have time to hold your hand."

10:30 am

Grace assembled everyone in the centre of the hall by the cashier's unit. They were all talking amongst themselves about who they were going to call. The crowd formed an orderly queue which Grace was rather impressed by. She'd envisioned pushing and shoving in the least.

She flashed back to the traditional free bingo session on a Thursday evening and shook her head slightly. Heaven employees often compared their free bingo customers to money hungry zombies, lurching towards the counter, grabbing as many free books as they could possibly play, sneering at any optional flyers that would require payment. This queue was nothing like that. Claire and her three sheep sat to one side, watching and whispering about the people they shared the hall with. They had no intention of falling into line at the command of Grace or anyone else, for that matter. Claire wouldn't entertain it.

Grace reached for the retriever and punched in the outgoing call code. Handing the phone to Matt, she turned her head to give the impression she would not be listening to his conversation.

He listened intently for the connection to be made. The ringtone resounded in his ear and seemed to drag on forever. With every ring, he grew more and more uneasy. After six excruciatingly long rings, the phone line went dead.

"Hello Ash? Ashley?" There was nothing. He hung up and put the phone to his ear once more. Not even a dial tone. "No, no, no, no, no. What's happened?" He held the receiver to his face, listening, hoping for some sort of sound but when one didn't come, he crumbled. He slammed the phone onto the holder several times, until Darius grabbed his arm, pulling him away in an attempt to calm him.

Mark commented from his seat. "Maybe they've cut the phone lines." He trembled sarcastically and Matt lost it.

"Do you think that's funny; you prick! My wife and kids could be fucking dead!" It took Winston and Darius to hold Matt back.

Darius pulled Matt over to a set of chairs as he stared unforgivingly at Mark. "Nice one, dick." Mark stared right back at him unapologetically.

"Calm down, man. The phone line is dead, that's all." Winston spoke with an amazing sense of serenity about him and Matt deflated in his arms.

"That's all? That's all…" The gate had been opened and the tears poured unabashedly down Matt's face.

Back at the unit in the centre of the hall, the orderly queue was slowly regressing into a panicked mob, once more. The phones were down and they had lost their last contact to the outside world, her one bargaining tool.

"Everyone, please calm down. I'm not sure what's happened but the phones aren't working."

"What are we supposed to do now?" Lorraine shouted from halfway down the line.

"Look, we're all in the same position here. It's not Grace's fault. There's nothing else she can do," Charlie said.

She smiled her thanks as people exchanged worried glances. The atmosphere had shifted dramatically and everyone was feeling the pressure. The unimaginable fear they felt for their friends and relatives outside the building, the infuriating lack of knowledge as to what was actually happening outside, and the uncontrollable reactions from the other occupants.

Serhan began biting his nails furiously as Tom sat on his own taking deep, controlled breaths. Matt was drumming his fingers on the table and twitching his leg into a spasm. Everyone was feeling somewhat claustrophobic and a few of them had ventured away from the majority just to take advantage of the space. Needless to say, they still felt just as trapped.

Grace called Kristie and Sophie over, and suggested they start taking orders for food. "We have to make people as comfortable as possible. We don't want to upset people any more than they already are."

Michael ran up behind Grace holding the phone in his hand. "The line went dead. I think the phone lines are down."

Grace sighed and pleaded, "Tell me you made the phone call before we got cut off."

"Yes. They have all the information they need. It went dead as I was finishing up."

"Thank God." Grace struggled to hide her relief. "What did they say?"

Michael shuffled on his feet, transferring his weight from one foot to the next as if realising he was about to be horribly belittled.

"Not much." His voice shook undeniably as he spoke. "I had to leave a message."

Grace awaited a further explanation.

"Well, Steve's not answering his phone and he normally goes away over bank holiday weekends. I'm sure he'll check it at some point though."

Grace studied the man standing before her and couldn't believe that she'd left him with such an important, if not idiot proof task. He retreated back into his office whilst Grace glanced around the hall. She caught sight of Craig a few rows in front of the stage. His stare was burning straight through her. She must have caught him off guard as he seemed to shift his gaze to Sophie. He clearly didn't want her to leave his side and Grace became increasingly concerned about his behaviour. As Sophie passed by him, he grabbed her arm and threatened her to put the tray of beverages down.

"You ain't getting paid for this. You don't owe these people nothing. Just sit down and let them take care of it." His words dripped with venom.

Sophie tried to make a case. "Grace is my boss. I'm just doing as I'm told."

He slammed his fist onto the table. "You do as I tell you."

Grace edged forward, ready in case it turned physical. He saw her react and eased up slightly. Sophie quickly nodded and fought back tears, looking around to make sure no one was watching. To her dismay, most people were.

Craig leaned forward onto his elbows with his eyes fixed on Grace in the centre of the hall. "I don't trust these people one bit."

"Why not?" Sophie asked nervously.

"There's something they ain't telling us. They're hiding something." His eyes were swiftly moving from person to person all around the hall. He didn't like the look of any of them.

She didn't understand. "Like what?"

He leaned in closer to Sophie putting his mouth to her ear, his breath rancid on her neck.

"Like why the fuck they have a fox in here."

12:07 pm

Rosie was sat next to Vickey rocking True in her arms. Michael knelt down beside her and offered her a drink of water. Rosie declined but handed the cup to True. She was still unsure about Michael. Her first impression of him was that he didn't really care for anyone but himself and as the hours passed, he seemed to become even more cowardly.

He sighed loudly, "I really hope she's going to be okay."

Rosie held his stare and acknowledged his attempt at sincerity. "She will be." Then she turned to True. "She's just tired, isn't she, little one?"

Michael smiled to himself. "Listen, why don't you get yourselves something to eat? Grace is out there. She can get you anything you want."

"No, we're fine. Thank you."

"Well, at least go and help yourselves to something from the vending machine. You must be starving." He handed her a small gold key. Before she could refuse, he put her mind at rest. "It's just outside the door to your right, not far at all. I'll watch over her, I promise."

The last thing Rosie wanted to do was leave Vickey alone with this guy. But they hadn't eaten since early that morning and her stomach was growling.

"I'm really hungry, Aunty Rosie." True's voice was like that of a weakened angel. Rosie peered down lovingly at the babe on her lap and admitted defeat.

"Okay, baby." She lifted the child with ease and moved to the door. She would be quick. Before she left, she thanked Michael.

"It's not a problem," Michael smoothly responded.

As soon as they'd left the room, Michael quickly began inspecting the unconscious woman's body. It seemed that his heroic routine was a façade after all. He had decided that there had to be more to Vickey's condition. She was showing signs of what they described on the news as the paralysed rabies victim. She could very well be infected and that would explain why she wasn't waking up. If so, they just needed to make sure she stayed that way. He felt around the back of her head but there was no blood. He then proceeded to closely investigate her torso. It seemed that the security guard was right about her rib. It would explain her laboured breathing. He re-covered her chest with her sister's jacket after stealing a quick glimpse of her cleavage. As he manoeuvred the jacket, he accidentally brushed her skirt revealing a mark on Vickey's upper thigh. It was a deep purple bruise with five dark red indentations. He pulled her skirt up to get a closer look but heard the door creak open, forcing him to post pone his investigation and resume his doting position.

"Any change?" Rosie asked.

"No, I'm sorry, ladies." Michael maintained his cool.

"We got you some treats," True said as she offered him a handful of snacks.

"Oh, thank you." He patted her awkwardly on the head and clambered to his feet. "I'll leave you guys alone. I should really check on everyone else. I'll make sure you don't get disturbed."

As he got to the door, Winston appeared.

"Hey, boss. Just came to see how the ladies are doing." Michael considered himself a relatively tall man but compared to this beast, he felt extremely emasculated.

"Hi Winston!" True waved her tiny hand at the friendly giant who returned the gesture.

"I'm going to leave them in your capable hands, Winston." Michael patted a hand on the man's shoulder and felt the rock-solid muscle beneath it as he edged past him, through the doorway. He then headed for Grace and took her to one side. He looked around for anyone within earshot, then once he deemed the coast clear, he spoke quietly to Grace.

"I don't want to alarm anyone, but I'm pretty sure that unconscious woman has been bitten."

"What? How do you know?" Grace was immediately concerned.

"I fucking saw it, okay. Stay calm. We can't let the others know. It'll cause panic."

"Have you spoken to Rosie about this?"

"Of course not, it's her sister. She's not going to admit that her sister's infected, is she?"

Grace thought he was being erratic. "Or she doesn't know anything about it. Maybe it's not even a bite. Are you sure?"

He looked at her with such animosity that she no longer required an answer.

"Look, she's unconscious so she's not going to be hurting anyone anytime soon. We just need to keep an eye on her. Have someone sit with her at all times. We don't know what it really means if she has been bitten. We're just going by what they've said on the TV. Don't say anything to anyone. These people are already scared. If they think there's a potential threat inside the building, God knows what will happen."

Grace hated to admit it, but Michael had a point. Any further panic would be unnecessary until they knew for sure.

Kathryn came up behind Michael, having seen the intense exchange between her two colleagues. She had only caught the end of the conversation, but it was enough to spark her interest. "What's going on? You look freaked out."

Michael didn't even look at her. "The mother's been bitten. Keep it to yourself and keep an eye on that office at all times."

12:19 pm

Winston entered the room quietly and Rosie could have sworn she saw him duck his head in order to fit underneath the door frame. Nevertheless, his physique didn't intimidate the little girl who had already welcomed him into their temporary abode.

True smiled up at him with her big brown eyes and offered him half of her Kit Kat. He gratefully accepted and took a seat on the carpeted floor beside her.

The room was quite cramped, and the walls were decorated with charts and targets and in the corner was a list containing staff member's names and phone numbers. There were no family photos on his desk, just a rubber band ball and a really fancy paper weight with an engraved message on it. "*Do what makes your soul shine. – Love Mum x*"

Winston wondered if Michael had truly found happiness in this place. He highly doubted it and then couldn't help but feel sorry for him. It was no secret that Michael lived at home with his mother. Winston worried that the staff judged him too harshly as he had accidentally overheard a conversation between Michael and what seemed to be an Alzheimer's specialist, a couple of months back. If he was taking care of his sick mother, was he really such a bad guy?

Winston knew it wasn't his place to have an opinion of any sort when it came to his boss, so he pushed it aside.

"Mmm… Kit Kat is my favourite." He practically inhaled the chocolate finger and True let out a high-pitched giggle.

"It's my favourite, too," she said with a tiny hand covering her chocolaty mouth.

She tried to copy Winston by forcing the whole treat in her mouth but began to cough. Winston reached for a nearby bottle of water as he gently but firmly slapped her back and Rosie scolded her for playing with her food. Once she'd finished her mouthful, True snickered with Winston, making them look like a pair of mischievous school children. Rosie chuckled to herself. It was adorable to see him sitting cross legged in such 'deep' conversation with a three-year-old. It reminded her of a meme she had seen. No matter how masculine you are, if a toddler hands you a toy phone, you answer it. She felt strangely at ease with him and considering the circumstances, she thanked her lucky stars that he was in there with them.

"So, ladies, what are your plans for the rest of today?" he jokingly asked.

Rosie smiled tiredly but played along. "Maybe go to a restaurant, catch a movie or go for a long walk…"

"A long walk sounds good," he humoured. Then to True, he said, "We could go exploring. There are lots of hidden rooms in this club. I bet we could find some treasure."

True clapped her hands together, jumping up and down. Rosie laughed at her niece's abundant excitement. "Yay! Let's go exploring, Aunty Rosie."

"Maybe later, poppet. We need to wait for Mummy to wake up." She shot Winston a look of required support as True stuck out her bottom lip and folded her arms in a huff. "Hey, I just want to make sure that Mummy is okay. We can go tomorrow, okay?"

Rosie was clearly trying her best to keep it together and Winston could see the toll it was taking on her.

"Okay," the little girl eventually conceded.

"There you go!" Winston gave her a friendly nudge, attempting to make light of the situation. "Tomorrow. It's a date. But for now, I figure since this is going to be your bedroom for the next few days, how about we build a den?"

True's face was once again beaming. "Yes, yes. Let's build a den."

He exited the room only to return moments later with an armful of items, from umbrellas to torches, coats to cushions. "This should do the trick."

They set about building the den and it was a happy distraction for the best part of an hour. Eventually, they relaxed and carried on eating the last two Kit Kat fingers when True seemed to be deep in thought.

"Winston?" Her voice had lost some of the previous enthusiasm.

"Yes, True."

True looked down and started fiddling with her shoe. "Can that little boy come exploring with us tomorrow?"

Winston looked puzzled.

"What little boy, sweetheart?"

"That little boy with the orange hair."

Winston flashed a glance at Rosie hoping for an explanation. Rosie just sighed and tutted.

"She's been going on about this little boy with orange hair since we got here."

"There's another kid in the building? I haven't seen him." He was genuinely shocked.

"Nobody has." She held her hand up to the side of her face, shielding it from True's line of sight, and whispered, "She's made him up. She does this all the time."

Winston's eyes widened, in understanding.

"Oh, I see."

Winston's mind immediately flashed back to a memory he had from childhood. He too had had an imaginary friend called Toby. He lived in the river and would follow him everywhere with his imaginary dog, Buster. Unfortunately, Winston was only five and when Toby called out to Buster, Winston thought he was saying Bastard and his mum hit him across the backside with her slipper for cursing. He smiled at the memory.

"Well, of course he can come with us tomorrow," he said happily. "The more, the merrier."

True grinned like the Cheshire cat.

"Good!" she exclaimed. "I don't want to leave him out. I don't think he knows anyone here."

"Except you?" Winston whispered, playing along. He could understand why True had made up a friend. Anything to distract from the drama that was going on around her.

"Yes. I haven't spoken to him though. Where is he going to sleep? What if he's scared of the dark?"

"Hmm you're right." Winston looked upset and then his face brightened as he had an idea. "I tell you what, I will make sure that that little boy is not scared at all. And I promise to keep some lights on all night long, okay?"

"Thank you, Winston." She was elated.

Winston got up to leave. "I better get going if I'm going to find this little boy with the orange hair before bedtime. I'll catch you ladies later."

He winked at Rosie and paused momentarily as True wrapped her arms around his tree trunk of a leg in a tight embrace. Her smile was the vison of his granddaughter's, full of innocence and kindness, not yet tainted by the cruel workings of the world. She gleamed up at him and said goodbye. He patted her on the head and walked out of the room. At the door, he turned back to them with a serious look on his face.

"I forgot to ask," he said. His voice was so deep it almost vibrated through the tiny office. "Does this little boy have a name?"

True scratched her head, messing up her perfectly styled bunches. "Well, I don't know his name really, but he looks like he could be called Henry." She thought about it briefly, then nodded with certainty. "Yes, his name is probably Henry."

Winston fought to keep the serious expression on his face.

"Well, all right, then. I'm off to find Henry."

He closed the door gently behind him leaving the little girl and her aunt smiling. As he turned around, he almost walked straight into Kathryn, who seemed to have been right outside the door the whole time.

Kathryn didn't try to hide the fact that she had been listening. "Are they okay in there?"

Winston shrugged, "They're okay for now. The mum's still not woken up yet." He lowered his voice. "I don't think she's going to last very long. She needs to get to a hospital."

"That bad, huh?" Kathryn's mind was working overtime and Winston couldn't help but feel that Vickey's health wasn't Kathryn's concern, at least not in the way he expected.

"I'm going to have a chat with the sister, see how they're doing."

Winston blocked the doorway without even thinking. He felt an overwhelming urge to protect the little family he had adopted and he didn't like the way Kathryn had spoken to Rosie during the meeting. "Her name is Rosie and they're doing fine."

"Okay." Kathryn stared at him; her curiosity spiked. What was he hiding? "Winston, I just want to talk to her." Kathryn's tone started off soothing but rapidly regressed to commanding. "Please move." She stood up straight in front of him, not at all intimidated. "Winston, I just want to make sure they're okay."

The security guard dismissed his normal dislike for the woman and moved away from the door, releasing the handle. There was a sincerity in her tone that he hadn't heard before. She turned the knob and pushed through the door without hesitation. Winston stared after her, worried and trying to work out her possible intentions.

1:35 pm

Charlie and Serhan sat with their backs pressed against the vending machine at the far left-hand side of the hall. The walls were slightly more vibrant in this area, but the rest of the hall was duller, smoke damaged and seemed to create the perfect setting to depict their dire situation. The atmosphere in the hall was suffocating and Craig was making everyone feel uncomfortable. He just sat there staring at people. They questioned whether he even knew he was doing it. His eyes just seemed to glaze over and he would be so deep in thought that staring back at him did absolutely nothing. The further away from him they could get the better.

They'd not even been locked in the building for a day but for the two young lads, it was quite exciting, like a video game turned into reality. But then, they also weren't fully convinced that this could be a worldwide epidemic. It didn't seem real enough. They had seen the panic outside, they had been there, up close and personal but now they were trapped inside, away from it all. It resembled a nightmare more than actual reality, there was no beginning and no end.

They understood why tensions were running high. Everyone had families and no way of knowing if they were safe or not. It was the not knowing that had people losing their minds with worry.

Charlie watched in a trance as Kristie made her way over to where they were sitting. She was so elegant; it was like she was floating across the carpeted ground. Her pencil skirt highlighted her voluptuous curves and her legs moved like she was walking through a dream. A strand of hair had come loose and framed the side of her perfect cheekbone, but she flicked it aside as she neared the two men. As she walked, she played with her plastered finger, and even that looked magical to Charlie.

"Pick up your jaw, dude. You're embarrassing." Serhan pelted him in the arm to bring him back down to Earth as Kristie occupied the empty space opposite the two guys.

"Hey guys. Do you mind if I join you?"

"Go for it." Charlie played it cool but felt his smile threatening to spread from ear to ear. "We're just tossing around theories of what might have caused all this."

"Oh okay." She seemed genuinely interested. "What have you come up with so far?"

"Well, if it's definitely rabies," Serhan intervened. "Then the infected people will basically be all Cujo-like."

"What's that?"

Serhan stared at her, unimpressed. Charlie swooped in with an explanation before his friend could respond with an answer tainted with sarcasm that would undoubtedly offend her. Serhan wasn't the best people person. He identified who he could relate to on an intellectual level based on first impressions. This didn't bode well for him when it came to making friends as he came off as judgemental and narcissistic. Charlie had met him in preschool and they had been friends ever since. He understood Serhan's way of thinking but he didn't necessarily agree with it. Since he himself was a social butterfly, it was hard work introducing Serhan to new people. It was always accompanied with explanations as to both why he was the way he was and why Charlie was even friends with him in the first place, which was always followed with a plea that Serhan wouldn't be invited to their next gathering.

"Cujo is a book by Stephen King about a dog that has rabies."

Kristie placed a hand to her chin. "I think I've seen the film."

"Makes sense." Serhan was still unimpressed at her apparent lack of intellect. Before he could continue, Kristie interrupted.

"But these are people, not dogs."

Serhan put his head in his hands. He had never been the most patient person and he had even less tolerance for people he deemed stupid. Charlie could sense his friend's frustration. He knew it well. Serhan was incredibly arrogant at times and didn't appear to care who he offended. So, again, Charlie intervened.

"Yes. But normally, humans can catch it by being bitten by a dog or a bat who has rabies and then a human can display the same aggressive behaviour. They can start attacking people, foaming at the mouth and if they were to bite anyone, they'd pass it on."

Kristie stared at him, blank faced. Charlie noticed Serhan's clenched jaw and the protruding vein on his forehead. He could see his friend's patience was wearing thin, so he tried to diffuse the situation once more.

"However," Charlie continued as he placed a calming hand on Serhan's shoulder. "This strain of rabies is a lot more aggressive which means it's a lot more dangerous if it were to spread. That means more infected people, more violence, more deaths, and complete pandemonium." He knew as soon as he'd said it, that he shouldn't have used such an advanced word. "Chaos," he rephrased with an apologetic tone.

Her eyes widened in understanding at the less sophisticated verb. They could see her brain working overtime as she tried to wrap her head around the entire concept.

An awkward silence then followed. She didn't have anything to contribute and had, in fact, journeyed away from the topic at hand and had begun thinking about whether or not she had turned her straighteners off that morning before leaving the house.

After a while, the boys continued their speculation theories despite her being there. There was a lot more that Serhan wanted to delve into.

"Viruses evolve all the time. All it takes is someone's body to react differently to it and it can alter its structure and everything else about it." Serhan pulled himself up onto his knees as he spoke with more and more enthusiasm. "For instance, the people who are only paralysed. That's not a new development but why does it only happen to some people? There have been links to people who have had certain vaccinations or have taken part in clinical trials." It was like a light lit up inside his head. "I bet somewhere there is a group of people who are completely immune to this strain altogether because of something in their DNA."

"Dude, I completely agree with you but that's why this is so messed up. If a virus reacts a certain way to a certain body, won't a cure do the same thing?"

"No, it's the body that reacts differently, not the virus. Otherwise, there would have to be several anti-viruses designed to battle the different versions." Charlie scratched his head as he contemplated Serhan's point. When he finally conceded, Serhan posed another question. "All right let me ask you this. If dogs and bats can pass on rabies, can other animals, too?"

"Yeah, I'm pretty sure of it. Probably just mammals though. I read somewhere that cats are the most commonly affected nowadays."

"So, you're telling me if a wasp stung an infected person and then stung you, it wouldn't have an effect?"

Kristie's muscles all tensed as he spoke, holding her attention. Charlie caught sight of Serhan's smirk and realised what he was trying to do. He decided not to play along since these things never seemed to end well.

"I don't think so, man."

"Well, I think it's definitely possible. You could get stung by a wasp and then BAM!" He clapped his hands so loudly that Kristie almost jumped out of her skin.

"What do you mean bam? Bam, what…?" Kristie looked terrified.

"You're infected!" Serhan said the words with such conviction that Kristie's face dropped. He knew he was scaring her so he continued. "You might not even feel it at first but it's there, inside you, just waiting. One day, you'll get a fever and start throwing up. Then you'll lose patience with people over the most stupid of reasons. Eventually, you'll lose all control and you will lash out at one of them, maybe even kill them," he teased, motioning to the other residents of the hall.

Kristie fought back the tears, but she knew she couldn't do it for long, so she stood up, brushing down her skirt and walked away from the two lads and back towards the crowd of people. Serhan turned to Charlie wearing a proud grin.

"You're such an arsehole." Charlie shook his head and pushed past his friend to run after Kristie as Serhan threw his arms up in a gesture of innocence.

"Come on. It was a joke." Some people just couldn't handle his banter. Just like his Year 8 chemistry teacher. He had joked with her about being incapable of teaching teenagers and kidded with her about her incompetence as an educational provider which led to her handing in her resignation in floods of tears. Some people could be so dramatic, he thought.

Charlie grabbed Kristie by the hand and pulled her back towards him. He held her stare with a look of sincerity.

"Hey. Don't listen to Serhan. He's being an idiot."

Kristie shook his hand off of hers. She had already given into the tears at this point. "So, you know that what he said definitely won't happen?"

Charlie took her hand in his again. "He's just winding you up. He heard you talking to the old lady earlier and you said you were stung by a wasp so now he's being a dick."

"Are you sure this isn't going to happen to me? I mean, one-hundred per cent sure?"

Charlie smoothly pulled her closer to him. "The rabies virus is only passed on or carried by mammals. I'm sure of it." Kristie began to ask another question, but Charlie interrupted her before she could. "Wasps aren't mammals."

"I know." She looked offended but placed a hand on his face and said, "Thank you."

As they moved in closer, the moment was thwarted.

"Did you guys just see that?" Craig stood between the two of them and grabbed hold of their arms, squeezing them a little too tightly. His breath was rank and it hit them like a tidal wave causing both of them to draw back in disgust. Kristie struggled out of his grip as Charlie slapped his hand away from his arm.

"Get off me, man."

Craig's eyes were bloodshot and his pupils were two black pools. He looked crazy as he leaned in towards Charlie.

"No, tell me the truth. I need to know that you saw it." His voice was pleading but intimidating at the same time and his unpleasant odour consumed Charlie's nostrils. Charlie wasn't sure what was going to happen next. He softened his tone when he asked the next question.

"Saw what, man?"

Kristie intervened. "Don't talk to him, Charlie. Let's just go." She had been watching Craig since they'd entered the building. She was aware of every movement he made around Sophie and was more informed than anyone else about Craig's nasty habits behind closed doors.

Charlie could see Craig's agitation growing by the second and flinched when Craig shouted.

"You stupid bitch, I'm trying to tell you about the fucking fox!"

Charlie threw his hands up in a diffusing manner. "Hey, hey, hey. I think you need to calm down."

With that, Kristie turned and ran to the toilets. Craig had gained everyone's attention at this point, and Sophie made her way quickly to his side, pulling gently at his arm, trying to lead him away from the onlookers. Everyone's attention was now solely on the scene that was about to unfold.

She whispered, "Come on, baby. Let's go and sit down. I'll make you a cup of tea."

She flashed Charlie an apologetic expression and Charlie used that as a hint to excuse himself from the spiralling situation and go after Kristie. It was clear that something was wrong with Craig and he thought it best to let Sophie calm him down. However, as soon as he turned his back, Craig turned nasty.

"I don't want your fucking tea!" The back of his hand caught Sophie across the jaw and the entire hall erupted. The next few minutes went by in slow motion, a daze to Sophie. Charlie was back and was pinning Craig against the wall. She could hear muffled sounds coming at her from every angle, but they were distorted and drowned out by the ringing in her ears. She was being pulled away by Grace, but it was as if she had forgotten how to walk unaccompanied as her knees buckled. Her face was being carefully examined by a blurry face with dark hair as she fought to regain focus.

Winston had joined Charlie and was restraining Craig who was screaming and sobbing hysterically, about the fox that no one could see. His strength seemed to be magnified. It looked as though he was giving the two men a run for their money when, out of nowhere, Darius punched him full force in the face.

Sophie could hear the commotion and on hearing Craig's cries of pain, found her feet and focused her vision as she stumbled towards her bleeding man. She could hear herself shouting before she made any sense of the words in her head, but she could sense everyone's eyes fixated on her.

"Stop it! Leave him alone. It was an accident. Stop it! All of you just let him go!" She practically threw herself in front of him and everyone stopped in their tracks and stared at this small, frail woman whose cheek was already burning red. She turned to face Craig and held his head in her arms, cradling it and stroking his hair. "My poor baby," she whispered into his hair.

The whole hall was in shock and stared in disbelief as Craig fell to the floor, crying out in pain and cupping his nose, clawing at Sophie for help. She knelt beside him, then aided him to his feet and led him away, all the while maintaining eye contact with Darius, warning him to stay away.

Darius couldn't believe it. "He just fucking hit you, Soph!" He had no idea what had just happened. He did the right thing, didn't he? He was protecting someone he cared about. Why was he the bad guy? He was really riled up as he addressed everyone in the hall. "I'm not going to apologise. You all saw what he did."

Winston tapped him on the shoulder and spoke calmly to him trying to drown out the whispers. "You can't help a woman like that, buddy. You did the right thing. Everyone knows it, come on."

"Show's over, folks!" Charlie motioned to the room and the crowd departed. Some were muttering their opinions amongst themselves, but others were still in shock. Some were even crying. Charlie looked around the hall for Kristie, but she was nowhere to be seen. At least she hadn't been involved.

Darius was ushered away to one side of the hall and Sophie led Craig in the opposite direction. She hated that everyone now knew just how weak she was. She'd managed to avoid the reality of her domestic abuse for two years working with these people and now they were aware of her dirty laundry. She had no idea how she was going to face them now. She had never been so humiliated and mortified in her life. She settled Craig down and tended to his wound as she ignored her own and, for the first time, she felt a sense of worth as she thought about Darius defending her.

3:04 pm

The group of men gathered around the vending machine away from the rest of the crowd. Darius needed a place to vent and Matt had located the keys to the assortment of goodies, laying unattended, in Michael's office so they helped themselves to some snacks. Winston, Matt, Charlie and Serhan all sat quietly eating their chocolate bar of choice as Darius paced up and down the carpeted floor, shaking his hands and flexing his fingers. He would occasionally shake his head, as if in answer to the voices occupying it. No one dared to speak. He needed to let out his anger, so they let him go through the motions at his own pace. Eventually it was Darius, himself who broke the silence.

"I don't fucking get it." The latter two words were spoken through gritted teeth. The men could see from the anguish in his eyes that he was actually torturing himself and questioning his actions. "I mean what the fuck?"

Winston could see that he was going to lose it. "You need to calm down, man."

But Darius shot him down. "Are you fucking serious right now, Winston? I could've killed that prick!" He pointed at his chest aggressively and stared hard at Winston, his eyes wide and erratic. "If Sophie hadn't gotten in the way…"

It didn't take a genius to see he was second guessing his claimed act of heroism. Maybe he had taken it too far, but hitting a man in retaliation for hitting a woman? That deranged psycho needed to be punished for doing it in the first place, right?

Darius was in such a state that no one was sure how to approach him. The tattooed man carried on pacing and rubbing his hands through his hair. He had no idea he was capable of that. Hitting the guy was one thing but the anger he felt was alien to him. He wanted to carry on hitting Craig and, in his head, it was justified. Did that make him a monster?

"Who the fuck hits a woman? I mean what kind of man does that? Look at the size of her!" He looked to the circle of men for reassurance. "She wouldn't say 'boo' to a goose, yet he thinks he has the right to lay a hand on her."

The group nodded in agreeance, still hesitant to give any actual input. He was so highly strung about what had happened that the wrong words could tip him over the edge. He'd already snapped at Winston. Every man present could hold their hands up and swear that they'd never hit a woman in their life and never had any intention to. That wasn't the issue, he knew his actions were right. His behaviour had scared him more than anything else.

"And then she stood up for him. She fucking defended him. Can you believe that?"

And there it was. That was what had him so riled up. Darius didn't doubt his decision to lay into Craig but was shocked at Sophie's reaction to it all. The way she had looked at him tore him apart. He could feel her hatred, and the look of disgust in her eyes was as if he had kicked a harmless puppy to death. He couldn't get that look out of his head.

Their corner of the hall fell silent once more as Darius dropped to his knees and held his head in his hands. Matt, who was now beside him, placed a hand on his back.

"Listen, mate. I know you don't want to hear this, but Sophie loves him. She's so in love with him that she's blinded by any nice moment they've ever had together. It doesn't outweigh the bad stuff on the whole, but she clings onto it for dear life because she doesn't feel like she deserves any better."

"No offence Matt, but that's fucking ridiculous. She's beautiful and the sweetest, most caring person I've ever met. Why on Earth would she think she can't get better than an abusive druggy?"

"Trust me, mate. My dad used to beat the shit out of my mum when he'd had one too many bevvies."

Another silence ensued but Matt wasn't looking for sympathy. He wanted Darius to understand.

"You know one night he came home when we were all tucked up in bed and he starts f***ing and blinding through the house." Matt sniffed, bracing himself for the memories he was about to evoke. "He walks straight up to my mum in bed, grabs her by the hair and pulls her out into the hallway.

"He stops right outside my bedroom door. I shared a room with my two younger brothers who were like six and ten at the time and we can hear her screaming in pain and begging him to let her go." He took a moment to carry on.

"My brothers were in my bed, crying their eyes out. I'd had to listen to those sounds my whole life, but that night was different." He laughed under his breath. "It was my fifteenth birthday and I felt like Billy big bollocks, so I opened my door and he's got her on the floor, kicking her in the belly."

"What did you do?" Charlie was completely engaged in Matt's story.

"I just saw red. I head butted him, knocked him on his arse and threw him down the stairs. He went down like a sack of potatoes. I ran down after him and just started punching him. It felt like all the anger I had pent up over the years was racing out of me.

"I only stopped when the neighbours pulled me off of him and I went mental. It took three of them to pin me down. They knew what he was like, what he'd put her through. They heard the screams but not one of them came to my mum's rescue. It was only then I heard the sirens and saw the flashing lights." He paused to blink away the emasculating tears. "She had me arrested: my own mother. I was finally manning up and doing something about the piece of shit she called a husband and she turned her back on me. I never saw her after that. She's probably still making excuses for him 'til this day. So, yeah mate…" He turned to Darius with a look of sadness and sincerity. "…women like that do exist. They get beaten black and blue and they still love the bastard they're with. No one can make them see otherwise."

The men stared at anything other than Matt or Darius who maintained each other's eye contact in a look of mutual respect. It was Charlie, this time, who broke the silence.

"Man, that's shit. I've never seen anything like that before today. I didn't know how I'd react until it happened." He peered down at his shoes. "I wish I'd had the balls to do what you guys did."

Serhan sighed and thought it was about time he offered his opinion. "Some women just love the drama. They're not happy unless they're in a shitty relationship."

All heads turned toward him. He spoke with an air of arrogant confidence about a topic he knew absolutely nothing about and this infuriated the majority of the group. Winston spoke up before anyone else did. "Use some tact, man."

Serhan realised from the circle of unimpressed faces that he had said something out of turn so attempted to back track. "It's like that Rihanna song," he panicked. "The one she sings with Eminem: Love the way you lie? She's in an abusive relationship but she loves it."

He looked to Charlie for approval and support.

"I know what you mean Ser. You just have a really shitty way of phrasing things," he explained, stifling a smirk. "You're going to have to work on that, buddy."

The rest of the guys let out an uneasy laugh. It alleviated the tension slightly but not fully. Everyone was still trying to process how this was going to affect the rest of their time inside the building and they sat in silence again.

"I just lost it," Darius admitted apologetically. "I didn't mean to upset her. I was trying to protect her. We've all seen the bruises, made the assumptions. She never admitted it and there was no hard evidence to do anything about it sooner. But then he hit her. I couldn't just let it go." It was his turn to lower his head. "I care about her too much."

Winston patted him gently on the back. "You did good, man, even if she doesn't see it that way. People are going to look to you for protection especially if this world does end up going south. You're going to be the one they want to save them."

"Thanks." The reassurance was gratefully accepted. "I just hope she's all right."

Grace had been standing next to the vending machine awkwardly for a good few minutes before she made herself known. She didn't want to encroach on such a heated conversation. At that moment, she decided to join the group, squeezing in between Winston and Charlie.

"Sorry to interrupt your guy talk," she joked half-heartedly, then spoke directly to Darius. "I just checked on Sophie while Craig was in the toilets. She's okay, bruised but okay."

Darius flinched at the word 'bruised' as if it had struck him.

"Nobody thinks you were in the wrong, Darius, not even Sophie. She wants you to know that she's going to be okay."

Grace hoped she had relayed the message with the correct intention. Her conversation with Sophie had been vague and rushed. Neither of the women wanted to be caught talking to each other by Craig in case it sparked another incident. Winston caught her drift and drove it home.

"Listen, it's going to be hard enough staying in here for three days with people that we don't know. You just need to stay away from him. He's on some sort of come down by the looks of things."

"Tell me about it," Charlie waded in. "Going on about a bloody fox, psycho."

"A fox?" Winston didn't think he'd heard right but when Charlie nodded, he could only mutter, "Crazy."

Grace knew she could shed some light on the events leading up to Sophie and Craig's situation but felt unsure about relaying it to strangers. After deliberation, she deemed any effort to diffuse the hatred they felt towards Craig worthy of repeating so she tried.

"Listen, I'm not making excuses for him but there is a reason why he's like this. Two years ago, Sophie and Craig were happy. They had a beautiful baby girl called Isabelle. Craig doted on her; they both did." She tried to talk through the tears. "When the baby was about six weeks old, she died of cot death." The men shared her emotions. "Craig blamed himself because he was the one looking after her. That's why he gets off of his face on LSD every day. He lost his job, they lost their house, and they lost everything, but Sophie still stuck by him. I can't imagine what either of them went through and are still going through but there is a reason he is the way he is."

"Bloody hell." Serhan could only muster a whisper.

"It's not something she would want advertised but I think you need to know the reason why Craig acts like this before you make any judgements about him. I'm not excusing what he does to Sophie but I'm just giving you the whole story."

"Shit. That's really fucked up." Charlie was almost in tears.

The silence was horrible so Serhan attempted to break it with a light-hearted comment.

"Charlie's just pissed because Craig ruined his moment with the bimbo," he teased, unsure of how the other men would respond.

"Shut up, Ser." Charlie became defensive rather quickly but the guys all shared a mocking laugh and began chanting playground songs about holding hands and hearing wedding bells, thankful for the jovial change of conversation. "She was upset because of you; I was trying to…"

"Yeah, we know what you were trying to do," Matt joined in.

"It's not like that. She has a boyfriend. That's the last thing I need on top of a zombie apocalypse," Charlie joked.

"You never know," Darius perked up. "He might be dead already. It could be down to the two of you to repopulate the Earth."

"Hey. That would be a beautiful population," Charlie quipped and leaned back onto his elbow, admitting defeat. "Look, whatever, guys." He smiled with the group but across the hall, he could see Kristie sitting with the old lady and his smile faltered a little.

5:12 pm

In the centre of the hall, everyone was trying to busy themselves with sleeping arrangements. Luckily, the temperature in the hall was quite comfortable so blankets weren't a necessity. It was more about finding a space close enough to everyone so that they still felt safe but far away enough so that they didn't have to engage in constant conversations with strangers.

Rosie and True took up residence in the office where Vickey lay sleeping. Kathryn had volunteered her company and since Rosie was aware that she couldn't watch Vickey all night and then look after True throughout the day, she was happy to accept Kathryn's offer on the understanding that they would work in shifts to watch over her sister. Kathryn's intentions seemed honourable and, although, she did have a hidden agenda, she genuinely wanted to help out. Rosie wasn't the worst person to spend time with and True was a pretty good kid. Winston sat outside the office door maintaining his protective duties and Grace was joined by Kristie and Jean just in front of the stage, in the aisle between the two rows of seats. The two younger women had gone to great lengths to gather as many cushions as they could find in order to make Jean as comfortable as possible. She was already fretting because most of her medication was not to hand. She had the essentials, but this didn't stop her from panicking about all of the effects she expected if she missed her prescribed dosages. Kristie was very comforting and couldn't do enough for Jean to keep her that tiny bit more settled.

A few feet back, the guys laid out their belongings. Darius, Matt, Charlie and Serhan sat around talking about football and anything else that resembled what they considered normal in an attempt to temporarily distract from the surrealism that had plagued their world.

Michael had naturally decided to distance himself from all of the groups. He sat on the step not far from the double doors through which the crowd had gained entry to their new prison. He kept a close eye on his office but kept a safety net of people between him and the potential threat that was residing inside it. If things did go badly, as he anticipated they would, there were a good few bodies Vickey would have to get through before she could reach him. He figured he would have more than enough warning to exit the hall.

The thought had occurred to him that he could very well spend the next few days upstairs, away from everyone but he needed to be aware of what was going on and excluding himself completely would put him out of the loop.

Lorraine and Lewie were over towards the diner with the brand-new cushions they had purchased from the shop next door. Before the insanity had ensued, they were buying items in a hope to put the finishing touches to the remodelling project of their house. They'd spent a solid hour deciding on the décor and had finally settled on a burnt orange flourish to give the otherwise plain magnolia room some character. Lewie had disliked the cushions at first glance and was against making a decision there and then. He rolled his eyes at the thought of her impending smugness but secretly, was glad she was so stubborn and had insisted on their purchase. At least he would have something to lay his head on that hadn't been sat on by multiple people over a disturbingly uncertain amount of time.

Craig had persuaded Sophie that it was in their best interest to stay as far away from the rest of the group as possible, so they'd opted to sleep next to the bar over to the far right-hand side of the hall. That way, Craig was out of the way and hopefully people would feel more comfortable.

Close by were Claire and her cronies, talking amongst themselves about the imminent doom of the world as they knew it. Mark and Danny discussed their choice of weapons whilst Kim just nodded and agreed with everything Claire had to say. She was currently spouting her advanced knowledge of 'zombie' cases from around the world. Her research was extensive according to her and she had looked at every angle, and had questioned every case only to come back to the same conclusion: the end was inevitable and if it was, indeed nigh, she wasn't going to let her unfortunate isolation from the occurrences that would bring the world to its knees, get in the way of her planned methods of survival. It was merely another obstacle in her path.

Claire was raised by a normal couple in Kensington, London. They had normal jobs and appeared to live a mundane existence until one day they both mysteriously disappeared when Claire was ten. She was at school and when no one came to pick her up, alarm bells rang. When her parents had been missing for a few hours, Claire went to stay with her grandmother in Enfield and had stayed with her until a couple of years ago when her grandmother too had disappeared. She'd wandered out of the house one night and was found days later having suffered a heart attack in a park twelve miles from their house.

Needless to say, if Claire's suspicions weren't heightened before, they sure as hell were now. She took to the internet, researching mysterious disappearances which began with alien abductions but somehow led to government conspiracies. One article she pulled up mentioned people with a certain blood type were being experimented on around the time her parents went missing but the government had covered it up. She could only assume her parents blood types, but the coincidences were enough for Claire. Her grandmother, however, was a match and, therefore, a conspiracy theorist of great magnitude was born.

With her grandmother's inheritance in her bank account, Claire quit her job and delved further into her investigations developing an interest in the paranormal activities from around the world. She created a chatroom where she met Kim, Mark and Danny and had progressed in her obsession ever since. Her paranoia had manifested over the years with the more followers she gained, and she'd taken to blogging events happening currently across the globe, giving her opinions and offering solace with her attained knowledge.

All in all, Claire had become a very dangerous person to be trapped inside a building with at a time like this. If the general aim was to keep everyone calm until the doors opened, she would do exactly the opposite.

As dinnertime approached, some of the groups merged just to indulge in a little light-hearted conversation. Gossip always seemed to be the atmosphere inside the bingo hall, just one big playground of whispers and rumours, changing and evolving as each story passed from one person to the next.

The menu wasn't the greatest but, thankfully there was something for everyone and the fridges and freezers were stocked adequately thanks to an error in the delivery the previous day. Grace advised that they all eat dinner at the same time, so that everything was controlled: electricity, cleaning and so on. There were enough staff members to help with the instructions on how everything was cooked but everyone set about making their own meals. The food would easily last them three days, as long as the power held out. That was the main concern.

6:36 pm

The hall filled with a combination of different smells. The chicken curry was a huge hit but some preferred a less exotic beef burger or just plain and simple chips. The desserts were off limits and reserved as a last resort since they were frozen.

When everyone had finished eating, Kristie began collecting crockery and cutlery whilst Grace and Darius filled the two industrial sized sinks with hot water and a splash of washing up liquid. She and Darius scrubbed away side by side, mostly in silence just enjoying the quiet comfort and chilled atmosphere of the empty kitchen. They worked in unison and after forty-five minutes of cleaning, they re-entered the hall, to find its inhabitants all contemplating the inevitable. To Grace's dismay, Claire was heading the discussion.

"Trust me," she promised. "I've done the research. I know what's to be expected and I know how to survive this outbreak."

"Go on then." Matt played along, spurred on by faint curiosity. "Enlighten us."

"First of all, this isn't the first time there's been an outbreak like this. All over the world there have been similar viruses with different names all having the same effect."

"And what effect is that?" Charlie was not swallowing any of her explanations.

"The zombie effect," Claire answered. Murmurs filled their corner of the hall. "And before you all get the wrong end of the stick, I'm not talking about people dying, coming back to life and wanting to eat your brains. I use the term 'zombie' purely because those infected are no longer in control of their own bodies or thoughts. All they want to do is attack whoever is in sight. They want to cause people harm; they want to be destructive and their morals and ethics are no longer present." She paused, as everyone considered her words. "These people aren't dead. They can be killed without shooting them in the head. I just wouldn't advise getting close enough to do it."

"Hold on a minute, you're that blogger." Darius was sure of himself. "Yes. I know who you are now. You're the one with all the crazy scenarios and theories."

"You might call them crazy, but I assure you they are essential. You never know, one day something I write might just save your life."

"So, what do you suggest we do then?" Charlie seemed agitated but Serhan got it.

"We wait it out." The words passed through his lips with a quiet certainty and all eyes turned to him.

"Exactly," Claire smiled. "The infected will eventually die of dehydration. Unfortunately, three days isn't long enough to eradicate the entire infected population but, I plan to haul up somewhere, stock up on food and water and stay out of sight for at least two months."

"You've clearly put a lot of thought into this." Winston sat back in wonder.

Claire looked him dead in the eyes. "It's foolish that you haven't. Zombie outbreaks are everywhere. In films, TV shows, comics, books. For Christ's sake, they even do Zombie Experience excursions now. There is evidence of this happening on a smaller scale where the government have contained it in other countries."

Serhan jumped on the band wagon. "You know, Americans have 'disaster rooms' set up in hidden rooms in their homes where they've got tonnes of tinned food, bottled water and medical supplies."

Claire agreed, "Americans have an advantage over us purely because of their easy access to guns and other weaponry."

Mark got excited then. "I got myself an awesome crossbow. It's a bugger to load though and it's bloody heavy."

"Then it's not practical, is it, mate?" Danny enjoyed this conversation, but Claire had heard it one too many times and cut him short.

"You'd die before you could aim it. This isn't fantasy. It's happening outside. And we all need to be prepared for what's waiting for us beyond those doors."

"Maybe it's not as bad as the news says it is." Kristie hoped to comfort herself rather than anyone else.

Claire just laughed nastily. "Wake up, love. You weren't out there. You didn't see what we saw." Her stare and tone were ice cold. "Take my advice and stick with someone who has more than two brain cells. Then you might stand a chance."

Grace intervened, "Hey. That's really uncalled for." As she finished her sentence, Kristie stood up and retreated back to her sleeping space.

Claire locked eyes with Grace. "Someone had to tell her. People like that don't survive in a post-apocalyptic world." She looked around her at the cluster of misguided captives. "In all honesty, the majority of the people in this room wouldn't survive. If you're not willing to fight for your life, to kill so that you can stay alive, you're too weak. And, no offence," she moved her stony stare to Jean who was clambering to her feet. "But *you* can forget it."

"That's enough." Charlie gave Jean a hand. "You have no idea who would survive in a world like that. You don't even know what the world is going to be like. Reading articles and watching programmes doesn't make you an expert."

"A world like *this*. It's already here, you naïve boy. And, I'm sorry to be the one to tell you, but anyone with children won't stand a chance in hell." She aimed her closing statement in Matt's direction. "You're better off ending their misery before the infected do."

Out of nowhere, Jean reached out and slapped her across the face. The noise resounded through the hall and the sting was immediately apparent on Claire's shiny face.

"You should be ashamed of yourself. People are already scared without nasty little girls like you making it worse." Jean spat the words at her but all Claire could do was dispense the most sinister laugh they had ever heard. It sent chills down Grace's spine and caused the hairs on the back of her neck to stand up on end. As Charlie led Jean away, the rest of the group dispersed and followed their lead.

Claire remained where she was as Mark and Danny slithered away to their corner. Kim sat beside her idol, fussing over the fresh handprint conquering Claire's face. She slapped her hand away. "Just wait," she seethed. "They'll see. They're all going to die."

7:39 pm

Kathryn had had no intention of eating with the rest of the group. She waited until everyone had finished cooking before preparing her own meal. As she passed the dispersing crowd, she carried with her a plate containing two cheeseburgers for Rosie and True. It filled her with an unexpected sense of fulfilment looking after the two of them. She never realised her ability to care was so strong. She gave a gentle knock before entering the office and awaited the soft-spoken invitation before entering the dimly lit room.

True was huddled on the floor with a cushion under her head and a merchandise towel draped over her.

"She's out for the count." Rosie smiled at her niece who looked even tinier when she was asleep.

Rosie's smile triggered her own as Kathryn handed Rosie the food. She took it thankfully.

"You look exhausted. Why don't you let me take over?" Kathryn offered as Rosie stifled a yawn.

"I'm okay for now. I just wish she'd wake up." Her voice broke towards the end of her sentence.

"We all do," said Kathryn taking Rosie's hand. Normally, Kathryn was the last person anyone would choose to comfort them. Her reputation as a heartless bitch preceded her but, on this occasion, she identified with Rosie's suffering.

A year earlier, Kathryn had lost her sister in a car accident but not before she had sat by her side for three weeks while she lay in a coma. Her sister had been hit by a drunk driver. He had drifted into oncoming traffic at 70 miles per hour and it resulted in a head on collision killing him instantly. Kathryn had spent every waking moment with her sister just hoping for a miracle. She would've given anything for her sister to open her eyes.

Seeing Vickey like this brought memories back but she saw this as an opportunity to be there for Rosie and be a shoulder to cry on. Kathryn and her sister had estranged from their parents years before and had no other relatives to speak of. It was just them against the world. They also moved around a lot, jumping from place to place, so it made it difficult for them to make friends, but Grace had stuck by her in her hour of need. She never wanted to see anyone go through that ordeal alone.

"She's older than me but I was always the one looking out for her." Rosie smiled to herself at the memory. "When she was getting bullied, I stood up for her. Whenever she got in trouble, I bailed her out. I was always stronger physically and more outspoken but emotionally, she beat me every time. She'd know how to handle this if it were me lying there. She'd be strong. I'm barely keeping it together and if True wasn't here, I'd be a wreck." Her voice broke. "I just want her to wake up and tell me what to do."

"You're doing great," Kathryn assured her. "There is no other way to handle this than the way you're doing it right now. You're so brave. She'd be proud of you."

Rosie wiped the tears away with embarrassment and tried to compose herself. She didn't want True or Kathryn to see her like that. Kathryn handed her a tissue and pulled her in for a cuddle. She stroked Rosie's hair and whispered that everything would be all right, kissing her discreetly on the head. As she did so, she subtly inspected the mark on Vickey's upper thigh. She couldn't get a good enough look at it in the current light, but it was there, and it didn't look promising. She broke the embrace and brushed Rosie's hair off of her face, maintaining eye contact and holding her face in her hands.

"I need to ask you something."

Rosie tilted her head to one side sleepily. "Sure."

"And I don't want you to get offended," Kathryn pleaded.

"I promise you I won't." Rosie leaned forward and braced herself.

Kathryn took a deep breath and asked her question. "I need to know how Vickey got that mark on her leg."

She prepared herself for any response Rosie was going to hit her with but all she received was a puzzled look.

"What?" Rosie genuinely looked confused. She shook her head slightly. "What mark?"

Kathryn let out the breath she had been holding since asking and began to relax slightly. At least Rosie wasn't trying to hide it, she actually had no idea what Kathryn was talking about. She wasn't sure whether this was a positive thing or not. On one hand, she wasn't denying that it was a bite, endangering everyone but on the other hand, that meant that nobody except Vickey knew if it was a bite which was still potentially dangerous.

Kathryn attempted to explain. "She has a mark on her leg. It looks like it could be a bite…"

"On her leg? Okay. I don't know. I mean, why were you looking at her leg?" Rosie seemed to be getting defensive, but it wasn't in a way Kathryn had expected. She thought Rosie would be fighting her sister's case and trying to convince her that she wasn't infected but instead she seemed offended that Kathryn had even been looking at her sister's leg. The whole reaction was confusing to Kathryn. She fumbled for the words in order to fabricate an explanation.

"Her skirt had been moved when I came in and I noticed it, but I wanted to ask you about it before I jumped to any conclusions." Kathryn thought her reason sounded plausible.

Rosie laughed briefly in disbelief. "I can't believe I was so stupid. Is that why you've been in here? Are you keeping an eye on her?"

"No!" Kathryn lied and then instantly back tracked, hating the way the bitter words tasted in her mouth. "Okay. At first, yes, Michael asked me to keep an eye on you guys in case…"

"In case what? In case she woke up and started attacking everyone? What did you plan to do if that did happen?"

"I didn't think it through. I thought you might need someone to support you, while you waited for Vickey to wake up. That was before Michael told me about the mark."

"Well, who else has he told? That man is such a snake. Is that why everyone is staying away from us? Do they think she's dangerous?"

"They don't know anything. Michael has only told me and Grace. He didn't want to create a panic especially when we've got a looney tunes like that green haired psycho out there. She'd jump straight on this."

Rosie stood in silence, contemplating. Kathryn moved towards her and reached out to touch her arm to which she sidestepped and avoided any further contact.

"Wait a minute," Kathryn paused momentarily. "What are you angry about?"

"What?" Rosie looked offended.

"Well, are you angry because I lied to you about your sister or is it something else?"

"What do you think?" Rosie snapped.

"I feel like it's something else. What are you not telling me? Whatever it is, I'm sorry."

Rosie knelt beside her sister and pulled her skirt to one side revealing the wound. She didn't trust her eyes in the light but that didn't stop her from thinking the worst. She put her hand to her mouth and the tears gushed. Kathryn came down to her level, but Rosie stopped her. "Don't. Please, don't."

They sat in silence for a little while as Rosie's quiet sobs slowly transformed into a gentle laugh.

"Are you laughing?" Kathryn asked, smiling with her.

Rosie wiped her eyes and chuckled sadly. "I thought you were coming on to me," she finally admitted, prior to laughing hysterically through glassy eyes.

Kathryn looked half relieved and half surprised. The thought honestly hadn't crossed her mind, but she was glad that Rosie didn't begrudge her false pretences as much as she'd thought.

"Oh!" she started. "No, I mean, not that there's anything wrong with you…or that…I just…didn't think…"

"It's all right." It was Rosie's turn to assure Kathryn. "I can't say I'm not a little disappointed though," she half-heartedly joked.

Kathryn smiled back at her and took her hand once more.

"We need to talk about this."

"Well," Rosie chuckled. "It's not the most romantic setting but I'm not going to say no."

Kathryn giggled. "You know what I mean," she said motioning to Vickey.

Rosie's smile faded. "I know."

Kathryn squeezed her hand. "I'm going to go and get Grace. She'll help us figure out what to do."

9:03 pm

Outside of the office, Grace was tending to Jean, making sure she'd taken all of the correct medication required and that she had everything she needed before settling down for the night.

"Thank you, dear. You are a good girl." Jean was always so grateful for any voluntary aid offered to her. She hated asking for help but had accepted that her limits were ever multiplying, and it wasn't worth the risk of creating more when you could just ask for a helping hand. Her hands shook as she sipped at her water and Grace could see the web of lines decorating her face. They told a story. The deep creases of her brow told the tale of her constant worry for loved ones and the people around her. The thin sparks at the corner of her eyes sang a song of the many moments she had spent laughing until her sides hurt, and the defined crevices along her cheeks were a poem of the loves she'd lost and the pain she'd endured over the years. Each furrow was a journey, a regret or a memory of its own. Her eyes still twinkled although probably not as often as they had in her youth but on a rare occasion, twinkle they did.

She took Grace's hand and squeezed it tightly, and Grace couldn't help but notice that the old lady's hands felt remarkably like crepe paper and that even though she was squeezing with all her might, Grace still felt that it was more uncomfortable for Jean than it was reassuring for her.

"Don't listen to anything that horrible excuse for a woman says. She doesn't know what she's going on about and she definitely isn't going to scare me."

Grace smiled. "I can't imagine there's much that would scare you nowadays, Jean." She had so much respect for the woman sitting in front of her. Her eighty-five years boasted hardships that Grace couldn't even come close to understanding.

"If I can make it through a war, I can bloody well make it through this. I'm not easy to kill, you know."

Grace laughed. "I believe you."

The serious look on Jean's face suggested she was about to launch into one of her famous stories of the 'old days' causing Grace to disguise her urge to giggle. When she realised Kristie was also in earshot, it only made her self-control worse.

"You laugh, dear but I've come close to death on more than one occasion. But God knew it just wasn't my time to go. I had to grow in the face of my battles and persist no matter what life threw at me. *That* is what it means to survive, my dear girl." She caught Grace's eye. "Not supplies, not weapons, but what's inside you. That is what gives you the strength and courage to carry on. If you lose that, you're dead already. Remember that, Gracey."

"I will, Jean. Try to get some sleep. I'm right over here if you need me and so is Kristie."

"Goodnight my darlings." Jean lay down and shuffled into a semi comfortable position, closing her eyes.

It was then that Kathryn approached quietly.

"I need your help," Kathryn whispered glancing discreetly towards the office.

Grace sighed. Her time to rest was clearly not now.

"Can you watch over her while I'm gone?" Grace motioned to Jean. "I won't be long."

"Of course," Kristie nodded.

Grace followed Kathryn towards the office and almost collided with Craig on his way to the toilets for the fourth time since his outburst. She nearly lost her balance trying to avoid walking into him, but he carried on unaware. She considered saying something but quickly thought against it considering the previous events, not to mention the more pressing matter that loomed behind the office door. She took a deep breath, exhaled and pulled down the handle.

9:30 pm

As Grace entered the room, Rosie straightened up and put her finger to her lips, signalling that True was asleep. To Grace's quiet relief, Vickey was also still asleep. Her breathing was heavier and had a raspy rattle to it, suggesting that fluid had made its way into her lungs. Grace had no idea how much time she had left or whether she could actually wake up which unfortunately created a different concern. If she had been bitten, Grace was still unsure as to what that meant? The harsh truth was that if the wound on Vickey's leg was a bite from one of the infected, she was a danger to them all and the best possible result would be that she never woke up.

"How is she doing?" Grace asked, examining the still body.

"Still unconscious," Rosie answered. "Which, I guess is apparently good, right?" She aimed an accusing look to accompany her tear stained face. It didn't go unnoticed.

"Hey. We don't know what we're dealing with yet. I don't have a clue what will happen if your sister opens her eyes." Grace genuinely was bewildered. "She could be absolutely fine although she is probably in a lot of pain…"

"She could kill us all while we slept." Rosie said the words, but they sounded alien to her, like she was reading from a script and they weren't her own.

Grace pulled a small torch from her jacket pocket. "Let me see it."

Rosie moved Vickey's skirt carefully, trying to avoid making physical contact with the affected area. Grace shone the light directly onto it and the three women leaned in to get a closer look.

The wound was a bloody rash in the centre, decorated with five more defined marks, surrounded by purple bruising. There didn't seem to be any sign of an infection and there was nothing concrete to decide whether or not it was a bite.

"The patterns of the marks don't look like teeth marks. What do you guys think?" Grace looked up to them for an attempt at confirmation.

Rosie just shook her head. "I don't know what else it could be. We live together so if she'd hurt herself like that, she would've said something for the sympathy alone."

Kathryn feebly attempted to reinforce her Queen bee stature by pointing out that the wound looked pretty new. "Is it possible that she could've been bitten when the rioting started?"

Rosie tried to recall the situation in its entirety, but it all had happened so fast. "I don't think so, but I can't be 100% sure. Everyone was panicking, we were all rushing to get away from those things. I remember hearing her shouting at me to run so I grabbed True and I ran." She hung her head, ashamed. "We got caught up in the crowd, then I realised she wasn't with us anymore, so I went back for her. She was already on the floor, but the infected people weren't anywhere near her. They were still smashing up shops."

"Oh my God!" Kathryn couldn't believe she hadn't noticed it before. "They're football studs! Those marks were made when someone wearing football boots must have stepped on her."

As soon as Kathryn had made the connection, it was easy to see and everyone in the room breathed a sigh of relief. It took all of their collective strength to not jump in rejoice.

The joy was short lived, however, when Grace realised something else that was completely off topic. Her brow furrowed and she became increasingly worried.

"Kat, you've been watching the news. How long does it take for these things to turn once they've been bitten?"

Kathryn answered instantly, unravelling her knowledge, "It's a slow process. The wound infects their system and then their temperament changes and they begin to have outbursts of animosity and aggressive behaviour. Eventually, they lose all humanity and attack everything and everyone that's moving. From the moment they're bitten, it seems to take a day or so for them to turn."

Grace contemplated, "So, in the early stages, a person could act normal most of the time except for the violent outbursts?"

Kathryn realised what Grace was hinting at and her eyes grew wide with worry. "Yes."

"What if someone who wasn't rioting had already been infected, and was in here with us?"

Grace stood up, gripping the torch firmly in her hands. Kathryn shot a look of curiosity towards Grace.

"Craig?"

9:48 pm

My face is throbbing. That bastard, who the fuck does he think he is? Fuck, it hurts. Look at the state of me. Come on my lovelies, work your magic. I don't want to deal with these people anymore. Oh, this wall is so cold. Ah, that's nice. I'm going to sit down here for a bit.

The light keeps flickering; tapping above my head. Apart from that, it's quiet in here; peaceful. I need a bit of time to myself; away from that pathetic bunch of cretins. I'm all alone except for that prick over there. He keeps staring at me. What the fuck is his problem? I try to look away but he's just staring at me with these big, black eyes; smiling, freaky bastard. I want to say something to him, but I can't move. Why can't I move? Oh yeah, that's why. Everything's so heavy.

That fucking tapping's getting on my nerves. What is that fucking noise? Where is it coming from? Jesus Christ! I need to get up. The floor's wet. I can hear something dripping. Drip, drip, drip. Fucking hell! I'm going to drown in here. I've got to get up. Everything's moving slowly. Tap. Tap. Tap. That fucking light! Who's this bitch? What are you wearing? Tap shoes? Stop making that bloody noise. I know you. I recognise your red hair. Fuck off! Tap. Tap. I said fuck off!

Sophie? Sophie, where are ya? Oi! Answer me. I can see you. Come here. Bloody orange. Bloody orange. Who paints a bathroom orange? Ha Ha! Foxes, that's who. Dirty, little foxes. I need a drink. It's not working. I'm going to drown in here if I don't start drinking.

I'm going to try. I can still hear you tap, tap, tapping. I hope you drown, you nasty bitch. Tell that prick to turn the light off.

Ha Ha Ha Ha Ha! You silly bastards. What have you done? Jesus fucking Christ! What the fuck is that? Get away! Fuck off, stay away from me! Don't touch me! Please don't touch me. I can't see her anymore.

I'm not... Everything is... Why though? Get off me! Don't touch me. Moving... Around... Shit! The water. Shut up!

76

I see you. I see you. I see you. Help me please, somebody. Ha Ha Ha! You're all looking but you can't see. You can't see it. Open your eyes, little one. Open your eyes!

I've got it. I've got you now, you little shit. I'm going to get you. Where are my hands? Sophie! Sophie, wake up. Wake up please! I need my hands. Where are they, Sophie?

I want to go home now. Get up, you arsehole. Get up. Ha Ha Ha! I'm coming for you. I'll save them. I'll save them all. No time. I'm moving now, little fox. I'm coming for you.

9:52 pm

Grace quickly left the office, her eyes moving wildly trying to locate Craig, but he was nowhere to be seen. At the far end of the hall, she could just about make out Sophie. *Where the hell is he?*

She looked tense by the time she found Winston and tried to compose herself as she got closer to him, but she felt flustered and could feel that her eyes were lousy at disguising worry. Winston saw her approaching and stood as she walked towards him. By the time she got to him, he already knew something was wrong and feared the worst.

"What's happened? Are they okay?"

Grace was confused momentarily before she realised what Winston was worried about. "They're fine. Vickey's still unconscious."

The words sounded insensitive and nonchalant, but Winston was forced to look beyond her abrupt words when he read Grace's eyes instead. He asked again, "What's wrong?"

"I think Craig might be infected." Grace had lowered her voice so much so that Winston had to stoop his posture to hear her better.

"Why would you think that?" Winston's eyes joined Grace's in the manic search for Craig's whereabouts. He was just as unsuccessful.

"Kathryn says that the virus affects you in stages and if he was bitten outside, that could be why he's lashing out so openly in front of people."

Winston's expression calmed slightly. "I don't normally listen to rumours but isn't it common knowledge that he beats on Sophie quite a lot? Why would you think these are different circumstances?"

"He's never hit her in public before."

"But he's also always had access to gear before. I don't think he has any on him and what we're seeing are signs of withdrawal."

Grace had already considered that option. "I just have this feeling that I can't seem to shake. He's dangerous."

"Look, I don't think we're in danger here, not from Craig, anyway. He's the same as all the other cowards who beat up their partners. There's nothing more to it."

Grace didn't look convinced, so Winston offered some solace.

"Listen, tensions are running high right now. I get why you're worried and if it'll make you feel better, I'll keep an eye on Craig. I'll give Matt a heads-up too, but I think you should keep this under your hat."

"Of course, we don't want people panicking."

Winston nodded and gestured at Darius. "We don't want people attacking either."

Saturday, 20th April 2019

3:13 am

"What the fuck was that noise?"

Craig awoke from his disturbed slumber, drenched in sweat. He was already irritable and the trip had just made his condition worse as it so often did when he was trying to quit cold turkey.

"Soph, wake up." He roughly nudged Sophie. "Did you hear that?"

"What?" she replied sleepily.

"That noise, for fuck's sake."

She strained to listen but there was nothing.

"I can't hear anything."

Craig got up abruptly and stormed off as Sophie lay her head back down onto her folded apron.

He walked slowly and unsteadily towards the bar and stopped suddenly in his tracks as he heard the noise again. He turned cautiously and caught sight of something out of the corner of his eye. It was small but it was moving fast. He crouched lower and focused his attention through blurred vision. His head kept twitching. He wasn't sure what time it was or how long he'd been sleeping. In actual fact, he didn't even know if he was still tripping.

Another rustle followed by a distant shuffling. It was moving swiftly along the floor.

He caught another glimpse over by the cleaning cupboard. This time he could positively identify the colour of the thing. Its ginger fur was unmistakeable. He knew he wasn't seeing things. Somehow a fox had made its way into their sanctuary to torment him. How the fuck had that happened? He didn't care how. He was going to sort it out and prove he wasn't crazy.

"Crafty little fucker," he muttered under his breath. He began to crawl himself towards the intrusive creature. Under the protection of the shadows, it made a dart out of the double doors and headed toward the cellar.

The sudden wave of light from the hallway caught him off guard but Craig sprinted after it grabbing a kettle, from the cleaning cupboard, on his way. He pushed through the cellar door and followed the sound of rustling.

Entering the cold room, he noticed the filthy thing had gotten into a box of crisps.

"I've got you now, you bastard."

Foxes were dangerous. They'd become even more vicious in the past few years and far less scared of humans. Foxes ruined lives. Craig knew them as his personal enemies and he was going to put an end to this one's exceeding confidence.

He crept up behind the obviously hungry animal, raised the kettle above his head and with all his might, brought it down across the beast's back. It yelped in pain as it was instantly crippled and forced to the floor. Its tiny paws began to twitch and Craig struck the cub again and again with one final time to the head, finishing the job.

Craig felt an overwhelming surge of pride flood through him. He had protected this blissfully ignorant cluster of desperate souls and they didn't even know it. They were completely unaware of the danger they were in, too busy worrying about the imaginary monsters outside the building, pathetic. He had gotten his revenge.

He bent down to revel in his victory and as he turned the still warm corpse over, its tiny hand hit the ground by his foot. He leaned in closer and pulled back the ginger fur, matted in blood, to reveal the face of a child.

He threw himself away from the bloody mess, scampered across the floor until his back was pressed against the cold steel of a beer keg. The sweat from his forehead seeped into his eyes, blinding him momentarily. This wasn't real. His eyes started to itch, unbearably. He clawed at his face, desperately trying to scratch away the sight before him.

As the itching quickly turned to burning, Craig started to see red. He pulled at his hair in a last-ditch attempt to wake himself up from this hellish nightmare. He'd had bad trips before. They always felt real but eventually, he would wake up and the horrific illusions became unpleasant memories. The itching intensified and he was burning up. He slapped himself hard in the face, knocking his throbbing nose. He groaned in pain. Why wasn't he waking up?

He was yanked back to reality by voices. At first, he wasn't sure if the voices were in his head. If they weren't, he had to think fast. These arseholes already thought he was a loose cannon. And no one even knew this kid was in the hall. Hell, it could still be him hallucinating.

He knew he had to move the little guy's body. He edged forward, cautious. As he pushed his arms underneath the boy, the weight seemed to separate above his hands. Now was no time to be squeamish. He held his breath and lifted the boy along with the tarpaulin he was laying on. He placed the child gently behind the wall of empty kegs and rushed towards the door. The voices were closer now and louder. He peered down at his hands, realising they were covered in blood.

"Shit!" He looked around for a cloth but there was nothing so in a last act of desperation, he smothered the fresh blood over the lower half of his face, underneath his nose. He reached the door just as it was opened from the other side by Matt. Winston was standing close behind him.

"What are you doing in here?" Matt straightened up.

"Looking for food, mate." Craig held his hands up in surrender.

Matt shot a suspicious look at Winston. "The foods got to be shared equally."

"Yea sorry, mate, just couldn't sleep." Craig was twitching even more now.

"What happened to your face?" Winston questioned him.

Craig rubbed at the borrowed blood on his face, accidentally touching an open wound under his eye. The itching started again.

"I had a nosebleed."

Winston stared at him, taking note of his agitated demeanour.

"Okay." Matt moved aside to let Craig pass, but Winston blocked his path.

"Be careful. It's dark in there." It was more of a threat than a helpful warning. Winston stepped out of the way staring him down the whole time.

Craig pulled open the door and unwillingly left Matt and Winston to inspect the room. They had followed him in there, certain he was looking for food to compensate his lack of drugs but when everything seemed to be in its place, they decided to let it go and return to the hall.

Craig spent the rest of the night cuddled up considerably close to Sophie, just waiting for an angry mob to drag him away from her. It was only a matter of time before they found out what he'd done. Would they bother waking him up or would they just beat him to death while he slept? He didn't blame them either way. Anything would be better than this fucking itching.

8:11 am

Kathryn awoke unexpectedly. Her eyes flitted around the room in a frantic effort to identify her surroundings. The room was familiar enough but lacked the comfort you would hope to wake up to, especially after a bad night's sleep. She could hear the gentle, somewhat comforting breathing of other people in the room and she allowed herself a quick moment of reflection. She focused on the cracked ceiling tiles above her and worked to steady her own breathing as she remembered where she was. Her fleeting moment of amnesia was blissful, but the reality cruelly seeped in as she sat up gradually, fighting through the new aches and pains that sleeping on a thinly carpeted concrete floor had gifted her.

She glanced over at Rosie who had dozed off with her head perched on the arm of the couch which was holding her still unconscious sister. Kathryn knew the purpose of her being there was to take it in turns to monitor Vickey's condition and although it could have been potentially dangerous, the air of serenity that surrounded Rosie at that moment seemed to eradicate the danger, she was the image of a guardian angel.

Kathryn questioned the growing attraction toward her new friend and decided against making any decisions at that very moment. Instead, she quickly diverted her thoughts to True as she realised she had no idea of the time and even less of an idea as to what time True would normally wake up. She peered over the desk towards the little girl's sleeping place to find her stirring, as if Kathryn's thoughts had summoned her out of her slumber. She stretched in the most adorable way, which initiated Kathryn to retreat to her original position as she waited quietly to see what the child would do next. She sank back into the shadows of the room and watched, mesmerised at the nonchalant behaviour of a three-year-old.

True rolled over, away from the desk and sleepily rubbed her eyes. She stood up clumsily as if using her legs for the first time and pottered towards the couch, her first instinct being to locate her mother. In her tired state, she attempted to

84

climb on to the couch where her mother laid. Kathryn abruptly jerked into action as she realised what once would've been considered a magical, peaceful moment between mother and child was unfortunately now an unpredictable hazard. Kathryn hurriedly crawled across the floor, scraping her knees on the unkind carpet.

"No, no, sweetheart. Mummy's still poorly." Her unsuccessful effort to whisper caused Rosie to jolt awake. True clambered into her aunt's arms and resumed the protected position that had seemed like a permanent stance since they'd entered the club that previous morning. Only briefly had she strayed from Rosie's side, and even then, she was never far away. Rosie yawned and smiled her apologetic 'good mornings' as she stretched and straightened her back, embarrassed that she'd fallen asleep on her designated shift.

Kathryn also apologised. "I didn't mean to startle you. I just didn't want the little one to get hurt."

Rosie's look unintentionally saddened.

"By falling, I mean." Kathryn quickly corrected her statement, smothering it with some sugary coating hoping it wouldn't cause too much upset.

Rosie smiled. "It's okay. I know what you meant."

Kathryn apologised again and excused herself from the suddenly suffocating office. She needed to stretch her legs and freshen up, her mouth tasted like a sewer.

As she passed through the hall, people were beginning to wake up; some were already sitting around and talking quietly. It was a strange sight for Kathryn to comprehend. She pushed the toilet door open and walked over to the sinks, catching a glimpse of herself in the mirror. The mascara that clung to her lashes from the day before had left her with dark rings around her eyes and her freshly dyed blonde hair was a tangled mess. She grimaced as she turned the cold faucet and cupped the flowing water, splashing it over her face. She felt her rosy cheeks beginning to cool, the chill offering a welcome shock. She grabbed for a paper towel and blotted the remaining droplets haphazardly from her forehead and cheeks. She held the stare of her reflection for a short while, and secretly scolded herself for lying to Rosie again. It may have been a harmless one, but it was still another lie. She had feared for True's safety, of course, but only because she could never forgive herself if Vickey had woken up and hurt that little girl. Kathryn hated them staying in the same room as Vickey but knew there would be no convincing Rosie to do otherwise.

As she stifled a yawn, Grace walked through the door.

"You're up early." Her tone was far too pleasant for the current situation and Kathryn found herself wondering how on Earth Grace had managed to look her normal pristine self after having what could only be described as the most horrendous night's sleep. Her hair was as kempt as when Kathryn had last spoken to her.

"It wasn't the best night's sleep." Kathryn brushed the nest on her head with her fingers as she spoke. "Every time Rosie or True moved, I was awake."

"Look at you, you're like a mother hen," Grace joked as Kathryn tried to disguise the pride in her smile. "No movement from Vickey though?"

The look on Grace's face said it all. She worried for the poor woman's health but was obviously conflicted by her worry about the safety of everyone else in the building. Kathryn took a deep breath, her proud smile evaporating. "No. Her breathing's getting worse; raspy but still no movement, whatsoever."

At that point, she gave up trying to sort out her hair and settled for making the rest of herself look presentable.

"Well, I'm just outside if you need me. I have no idea what our plan of action is if she does wake up, but you shouldn't have to deal with it on your own." Grace headed for the door, then stopped. "You're going to have your hands full with Rosie and True if anything should happen to Vickey. They're going to need someone and it looks like you've already volunteered yourself for that position."

Kathryn kept her focus on her own reflection, refusing to make eye contact with her friend. "It should be me."

Grace smiled at the woman before her. She had come a long way since the death of her sister and it seemed that being there for Rosie and her niece would give her a sense of much-needed and well-deserved closure, "It should definitely be you."

She pulled the door open and walked through it leaving Kathryn alone with her thoughts. However, those thoughts were disrupted when a flush came from inside the cubicle to her right. She hadn't been aware there was someone else in the bathroom and as the cubicle door swung open, Claire emerged bringing with her the poisonous cloud that seemed to engulf her very presence. Kathryn finished up what she was doing and headed for the door before she could get sucked into an unnecessary need to converse. She could feel Claire's stare burning a hole into her back, yet she persisted in avoiding any form of interaction. Unfortunately, Claire had other plans.

"She's not dead yet, then?"

Kathryn halted. She was too far away from the door handle to pretend she hadn't heard Claire's venomous words. She turned slowly, keeping her cool and instantly cursed herself for not carrying on out of the door. "What?" she managed through gritted teeth.

"The mother," Claire clarified, aware that Kathryn knew who she was talking about. "She's not dead yet?"

Kathryn's jaw clenched as her mind sieved through all the defensive threats and violent words that were coursing through it. She'd never felt the need for a filter before. She exhaled slowly, then answered, "No. She isn't."

Claire slithered towards the basins as she spoke in a sarcastic tone. "Such a shame, isn't it?"

Kathryn didn't want to encourage her, but her stubbornness had always gotten the best of her. "Yes, it is," she snapped.

Claire expelled a laugh which made every hair on Kathryn's body stand on end. The sound bounced around the tiled walls and danced mockingly around Kathryn's head. "No, I mean it's a shame because the one person who has a maternal instinct to protect that kid is out of the picture." Claire's malicious grin remained permanently fixed on her face. "It doesn't bode well for her survival, does it?"

Kathryn foolishly took the bait and seethed through her words. "What the hell are you talking about?"

"Well," Claire squared up to Kathryn even though the woman she had chosen to antagonise towered over her. "She stood little chance of survival *with* her mother's protection. Without it…" she paused to let the penny drop. "Well, she's fucked."

"She has an aunty who hasn't let her out of her sight since they've been in here. I'm fairly confident she is just as safe with her," Kathryn snapped, more angry at herself for having had engaged in conversation in the first place.

Claire then displayed a smile that made Kathryn want to slap it right off her face. "Nothing can compare to a mother's love. No matter how much that woman loves her niece, it doesn't come close to what a mother would be willing to do to keep her child safe."

Kathryn had heard enough and began moving towards the door again. "I strongly disagree."

Claire rushed over, slamming her hand firmly onto the door, forcing it shut. "I hope you're right for that little girl's sake. I'd hate to be around when something bad happens to her." Claire wanted a reaction. She was getting a kick out of winding Kathryn up. In a heartbeat, Kathryn had Claire by the throat up against the wall. Her grip was tight and her face was so close to Claire's that her breath ricocheted back onto her.

"Stay the fuck away from them." Kathryn took every ounce of strength she had and focused it on opening the door. Claire's evil laugh escaped into the hall as Kathryn walked away, refusing to give her the satisfaction of any further reactions. Every word the woman spoke was dripping with malice yet was said with such nonchalance. Kathryn entered the hall and walked with a determination fuelled by fury alone.

8:40 am

Grace watched with concern as Kathryn exited the toilets. She could see that something was wrong and considered going to check on her when Claire slithered out of the bathroom a moment later. The smug look on Claire's face corresponded perfectly with the murderous look on Kathryn's, and, with that in mind, Grace decided to leave Kathryn to calm down before approaching her. Instead, she focused on rationing the breakfast orders. After announcing that the kitchen was ready, Grace and Kristie set about putting meals together for Jean, Kathryn, Rosie and True. They decorated the plates with a couple of options from bacon rolls to fruit, just enough for the six of them.

The kitchen fell quiet all of a sudden and Grace turned around to inspect what had caused the rapid change in dynamic. The tension could have been cut with a knife, but it wasn't long before the whispers began as Sophie walked through the sea of sideways glances. She ignored the judgemental stares and the indiscreet comments and headed straight towards Grace who opted for a more casual response to Sophie's courageous appearance. Her face had swollen slightly from the impact of Craig's fist and her cheek was bruised.

"Sophie, how are you feeling?"

Sophie appreciated Grace's efforts at subtleness and attempted to smile through the pain that was so obviously stamped onto her face, which made Kristie and Grace both cringe and then apologise for their knee-jerk response.

"Is it okay to eat with you guys? Craig's out for the count and I don't want to sit alone." She looked embarrassed to even be asking.

"Of course, it is. Don't be silly." Kristie wouldn't have had it any other way.

"Jean wants to make sure you're okay. She's been really worried about you. I mean, we all have." Grace wanted to prepare Sophie for the onslaught of questions that could potentially be thrown at her. Sophie nodded, aware of the overly caring surrogate grandmother that was Jean Saunders. "We were also going to take breakfast to Kathryn, Rosie and True but if it's too many people for you, we'll sit and eat with you instead."

Sophie was adamant. "No, it's fine. I wanted to see how that woman was doing anyway. Plus, it'll be nice to talk to other people. He'll be asleep for a while."

Sophie felt her eyes welling up but before the tears could flow, she grabbed one of the trays the girls had prepared and led the way through the hall of impending awkward silences.

The three women laid out the plates delicately onto a Heaven Bingo branded picnic blanket in front of the stage and Kristie helped Jean to sit down before Grace knocked on the closed door. Kathryn opened it wearily.

"Breakfast anyone?" Grace poked her head around the door and smiled sweetly at True. "We've got lots of goodies and they're all just outside, so you won't have to leave Mummy all alone."

Rosie wore a look of relief. She didn't want to leave her sister but feared she might get cabin fever if she stayed in the office much longer. She got to her feet and took True by the hand leading her to the feast that lay in wait.

The atmosphere in the hall, that morning was subdued compared to the drama caused by the events of the previous day. The women enjoyed their meal in peace for the first five minutes before the silence was ended by Jean who believed she had bitten her tongue for long enough.

"So, how long has this been going on, Sophie?"

The tension caught everyone off guard even though they knew it was an inevitable question.

"It's not all the time, honest," Sophie insisted. "He took Isabelle's death terribly. He blamed himself, fell into old habits, and lost his job."

She allowed herself a brief reminisce of how good things used to be, but it was short lived, and she continued. "When he's using, it's hard work but it's worse when he's trying to stop. Once the withdrawal kicks in, he turns violent."

"How often does he try to quit?" This came from Grace. Her tone was deliberately soft.

"Not often," Sophie assured them. "Maybe once every few months. I know he needs to get help. I know it's going to end up killing him but it's the only time he isn't plagued with what happened."

"But you need to deal with it too, Sophie." Kathryn tried to hide her anger but was still riled up from her earlier encounter with Claire.

90

"It's been eighteen months. I've come to terms with it, in my own way. The thing is, I never blamed him. And this obsession with foxes…"

"Yeah. What is all that about?" Kristie chimed in relieved that someone had finally acknowledged it.

Sophie took a deep breath in preparation for telling them the secret that had haunted her for the last eighteen months. "That's what happened. It wasn't cot death that killed our baby girl. It was a fox.

"I came home from work about four in the afternoon. Craig was sleeping on the sofa and the house was quiet, so I assumed the baby was asleep too." She began fiddling with her shoelace and remained focused on a specific spot on the carpet as she told her story.

"I started preparing dinner and doing the washing up like it was just any other day. When it got to five o clock, I thought it was weird that the baby hadn't woken up for a feed, so I went to check on her."

Sophie had to stop momentarily to concentrate on steadying her breathing before the next part. "I started going up the stairs and as I reached the top, I saw red everywhere. Red stains all along the landing. Patches and paw prints soaked into the carpet.

"I followed them to the baby's room and everything that happened after that was a blur. I remember screaming, then hearing Craig come up the stairs behind me. I'd never seen so much blood."

The group of women couldn't believe what they were being told. It sounded like something straight out of a horror story. They listened intently as Sophie relived that awful day. She couldn't remember actually discussing this with anyone before, but it felt as if a weight was being lifted from her chest as the words poured out of her. The circle of women sat stunned, struggling to process the information given to them.

"I spent the next two weeks in hospital. Apparently, I went into some sort of catatonic state and when I finally came out of it, my dad and my sister were there, telling me they were going to help me through it and take care of me, that I should leave Craig and go and stay with them which didn't make sense to me because Craig and I had both lost her. Both of us had. I couldn't leave him.

"I didn't realise that during those two weeks, Craig had gone back to his old ways. He had overdosed twice and my family couldn't get through to him. I just saw it as a reason to stay, to take care of him, watch over him. We were both grieving and had our own ways of coping, his was drugs.

"My focus became getting him better. He was my distraction, my purpose, I guess."

She laughed half-heartedly as she played with her fingers. Jean took Sophie's hand and squeezed it. "No one should have to go through that. I'm so sorry my dear girl."

"Especially not alone, Sophie. Craig may have found his way of dealing with it, but you should be supporting each other. You both experienced it, you both lost Isabelle." Grace's words rang true. It was unfortunate that situations as horrific as losing a child could not only make or break you as a couple but as a person, too. The heart-breaking fact was that Sophie hadn't been able to grieve, not really. She had been somewhat blissfully ignorant and distracted by Craig's revisited addiction. She needed to take care of him and without him Sophie would have to deal with the truth of what happened to her baby girl. She wanted this distraction and, on some level, who could blame her?

Kristie tilted her head to one side and spoke gently. "Sophie, why didn't you tell us any of this before? We're your friends. We could've helped you."

Sophie smiled more to herself than for their benefit. "We're not friends, Kristie, not really. We're work colleagues. We never see each other outside work. It's easy to just smile and make conversation when we're here but you don't even have my phone number."

Her words made Kristie recoil. "I would've listened and I would've been there for you. We all felt sorry for you when we heard you'd lost Isabelle."

"Yes, you felt sorry for me, just like you would feel sorry for someone who you were reading about in a magazine. It might have felt worse because you actually know me but, at the end of the day, nobody turned up on my doorstep and nobody phoned to check I was doing okay except for Grace and, at the time, I was convinced that she only did that because it was her duty."

"We all worried about you, Sophie. We had no idea how to approach the subject or how to act around you." Kristie was clearly hurt by the bitter truthfulness of Sophie's words and she hated herself for not doing more.

"I don't blame any of you. That's just the way it is. We've all gotten closer since then, but even so it's not something I wanted to talk about with anyone really."

They all hung their heads unable to face making eye contact with the frail woman before them.

Rosie looked a little awkward at having been a part of this emotionally charged secret that Sophie hadn't even told the people already in her life. She squeezed True tightly and left the little girl tense beside her. "Are you okay, poppet?"

"She doesn't look okay. She's gone really pale." The question was answered by Kristie and as she spoke, she got up to grab a bucket from the cleaner's cupboard.

"True? Speak to me, angel." But True didn't answer. Her eyes were glazed over and her head was bobbing all over the place. Rosie put a hand to her forehead and moved quickly. "Oh my God, she's burning up."

She hoisted the child into the air as Kathryn followed her to the bathroom. The two women undressed the little girl until she was only wearing her knickers and patted her with a damp paper towel in an attempt to bring her temperature down. True shuddered and began sobbing uncontrollably. Kristie pushed through the door with the bucket just as True vomited all over Kathryn. True's body collapsed with exhaustion into the arms of her aunt who apologised repeatedly to Kathryn.

"Don't be silly," Kathryn said, keeping her cool. "Maybe that will make her feel better. Take her back to the office, let her get some rest and I'll clean up in here."

"Thank you so much. I'm really sorry." Rosie lifted the feather weight that was her niece and left the bathroom.

Kristie and Kathryn stood in silence for a moment, assessing the new state of the women's bathroom.

"I'll get the floor. You sort yourself out," Kristie said, offering her assistance.

"Thanks," Kathryn managed. "I think I have a spare top in my locker. I'm not sure what I'm going to do about my trousers, though."

"There's always the storeroom," Kristie teased. It was common knowledge that the uniform left in the storeroom wasn't in the greatest of conditions and Kathryn had enjoyed supplying items to staff members whose blouse buttons had popped or whose trouser seams had ripped. Kristie wore a satisfied smile as she remembered an incident when she had been coming down off of the stage and an almighty ripping sound stretched up the rear of her trousers. Her only way to keep her dignity intact was to venture into the storeroom and seek out a pair of trousers that either drowned or hugged her figure. Based on the event that had just occurred, she'd opted for a bigger pair of trousers and had spent the entire evening shift looking like a reject from the gothic seventies' era.

She revelled at the fact that the storeroom was now Kathryn's only option. Karma was a bitch and Kathryn had needed to be taken down a peg or two ever since she became a supervisor. Although, watching her with Rosie and True, Kristie couldn't help but notice a well-hidden gentle nature surfacing.

"You like her, don't you?" Kristie asked as she scrubbed at the floor.

Kathryn removed her shirt, scrubbing at any residue that had seeped through to her vest top and finished wiping down her trousers before side glancing at Kristie. "Mind your own business."

She left the room in the direction of the storeroom and Kristie indulged in another smug smile.

9:22 am

The hall had gradually come to life, group by group but the noise level stayed at the same minimal effect. Everyone had merged into their slightly larger cliques and most topics of conversation revolved around the expected.

Matt tried his hardest to not think about Ashley and the kids. He needed to avoid the frustration of being completely helpless to them.

Jean and Kristie worried for Sophie, the awful situation that had just been shoved into their faces within the last hour, and that Sophie herself had been living with for the last eighteen months.

Most people just sat quietly, still coming to terms with what they had witnessed the day before, how terrified they had been. They worried whether the building really was as safe as Grace had claimed. Most of all, they feared for what the world would be like once the doors finally opened. Questions plagued everyone. What would they need to survive? Where would they go? Should they try to locate their families? The questions were endless and insoluble. Only a minority had already considered, in depth, their survival strategies.

Claire's group sat huddled in the chairs to the left-hand side of the diner and Kim's eyes were fixated on the commotion caused by the three-year-old being whisked away into the bathroom. The girl's aunt and the blonde woman that followed them around were frantically trying to play down the situation to the curious onlookers, but Kim smiled to herself as she watched the panic unfold.

She listened with half an ear to the meaningless conversation that was forever dominating their group. Sometimes she wondered why Claire even bothered keeping the boys around. Their talks of weapons and macho survival plans would probably turn to dust the moment they came face to face with the infected. Kim believed that Claire must have a solid reason for recruiting them but if *she* was in charge, they would've been ditched a long time ago. Maybe they would come in handy. You never know when you'll be in need of bait. She snickered to herself as she pushed the Neanderthals from her mind and focused on the

95

bathroom door, half tempted to intrude and see the scene unfold for herself but before her thought process was complete, Rosie emerged holding the little girl in her arms, close to her chest. The aunt looked worried and the child looked deathly.

Kim smirked again. She had seen something that Claire hadn't. She'd seen it with her own eyes. When Kathryn exited the bathroom doors trying to conceal her overly damp attire, Kim's suspicions were confirmed. Her vindictive grin conquered her face. Now they would see first-hand how these morons would fare in an apocalypse.

She grabbed Claire's arm and whispered, pointing towards Kathryn, "Look."

"What?" Claire demanded, clearly irritated by being touched.

"It's the kid." Kim turned to face Claire. "She's infected."

10:06 am

Kathryn knocked lightly on the office door, then entered attempting weakly to distract from her new outfit. The trousers were tight and did not zip up fully and the shirt was massive, not to mention a hideous royal blue.

"How is she?" Kathryn asked as she tiptoed into the room.

"She just can't seem to get comfortable." Rosie could barely speak through floods of tears. She looked defeated. "What's wrong with her, Kathryn? Has she got this virus?"

"I can't lie to you, darling. I just don't know."

"But you do know the symptoms, right? High temperature, vomiting, chills… They are all connected to that fucking virus and she has all of them."

She was getting irate and Kathryn had no idea how to comfort her. She was helpless.

At that moment, Grace approached the outer door. "Can I come in?"

Kathryn looked to Rosie for approval, but she was too distraught to even acknowledge the request. Kathryn opened the door and let Grace in. She didn't even bother with formalities but knelt to the floor and took Rosie's hand, motioning for Kathryn to come down to their level. Kathryn closed the door, scared that someone would overhear and alert the rest of the hall. Kathryn didn't have a clue as to what she was going to say but already knew that Grace could put Rosie at ease more than she could right now. Grace had a way with people and, most of the time, it aggravated Kathryn to high heaven. She didn't possess the patience or the tolerance to deal with people and she'd often been told that she shouldn't work in customer services. Normally, Kathryn would mock Grace, telling her that she was too soft but right now, it was what everyone needed.

"I think it's best that you guys keep a low profile for the next couple of days."

Rosie looked to Kathryn for a rebuttal, but Kathryn knew it was the right move. Whether True was bitten or not, she was showing symptoms which meant that the virus could actually be airborne, but Grace needed to understand the severity of it all.

"If this disease is airborne, everyone else has already been exposed to it, you and Winston especially."

Grace regarded Kathryn's words with an honest response. She shrugged her shoulders nonchalantly as if there was nothing in their power they could do if the damage was already done.

"If that is the case, then it's too late to worry about it but I'm not asking you to stay in here because of the virus. I just don't want certain people blowing this out of proportion."

"You mean that fruit loop out there and her band of merry miscreants?"

Grace looked obviously worried. "I mean it. She's dangerous. I get this horrible feeling whenever she starts talking. If she got a whiff of this, I dread to think what she'd do. The woman is poison."

Rosie became very aware of Grace's clenched fists at this point. "What is her problem?"

"She has some sort of God complex when it comes to all this apocalyptic crap. She thinks she knows it all. I wouldn't want her to think we have a weakness."

"Me neither," agreed Kathryn. "She already knows we're vulnerable because of Vickey, she's mentioned it before in her little group chats. We can't give her any more ammo."

She smiled at Rosie reassuringly. "We'll keep our heads down. Just don't forget about us, okay?" She turned her attention back to Grace.

Grace nodded. "I promise I won't."

"So, the kid's infected." Claire struggled to keep the conceited smirk from her lips. "Isn't that interesting?"

"What are we going to do about it?" Danny leaned over her shoulder, completely void of boundaries.

Claire grimaced and shuddered away from him in noticeable repulsion. "Well, it's going to be impossible to get her away from her aunt and that woman now."

"It wouldn't matter anyway," Kim stated. "She's probably already infected people."

Claire let her devious mind take over. "I bet half the morons in here don't know the actual facts about this virus."

Mark pulled a confused expression which reminded Kim of a chimp attempting to work out a puzzle. "So, you're saying we should kill her?"

Claire smiled at him as if rewarding a child for good behaviour. "No, what I'm saying is that we merely need to make people aware that they were never safe inside this prison as long as the infected were already among us."

As she spoke, her voice got louder so that people sitting close by could hear every word she was saying.

"We need a plan of action for when those doors open, this is true but how are we going to protect ourselves whilst we're in here in this vulnerable position?"

Claire had a knack of gaining attention and drawing in her audience.

"For the next day and a half, we are safe from the terrors that await us beyond these walls. Nothing can get in…" She paused to let her words sink in. "…but until then, no one can get out either."

"Why would we need to get out?" Lorraine asked, concerned by the sudden surge in dramatics. "Did you see those things out there? We're definitely safer in here…right?"

"Let's be honest," Claire spun on her heel to ensure she had gained the crowd's undivided attention. "We don't know a thing about one another. We don't know where we've come from, or how we ended up in here. We don't know what happened to any of us before we got trapped in here."

Lorraine and Lewie shared a concerned glance. The thought hadn't even crossed their minds. Being 'trapped' was merely an inconvenience to their lives. They hadn't even taken the news reports too seriously. "Well, we were just doing our weekly shop, nothing out of the ordinary there," Lorraine chimed in.

Lewie backed her up with, "We were just going about our normal routine. It was actually annoying that so many other people chose to do their 'end of the world' shopping at the same time. People always overreact."

Michael then emerged from whatever dark corner he had been recoiling in and chose to ignore the couples' mundane attempt at a back story. "Claire has a point. We don't know anything about each other, not even the people we work with. We could all be hiding things and keeping secrets."

"What sort of things are you referring to, man?" Winston didn't take kindly to what Michael was insinuating. "Is there something you're hiding from us?"

"Not me, per say…" Michael's voice failed to hide its nervous quiver. "But there are secrets being kept. Why do you think I chose to keep away from everyone? No one can be trusted in here."

"I thought it was because you're a gutless coward." Grace wasn't going to entertain his accusations either.

"That's rich coming from the girl who's claiming we're all safe. You know all about secrets, don't you, Grace?"

Grace clenched her fists as they hung by her sides. She knew he couldn't be trusted with the knowledge of Vickey's wound, and she'd be damned if she was going to let him give Claire the well-sought-after ammunition she so desperately craved to take control of the hall. She stepped towards him but was stopped by Charlie. Michael's flinch only gave her slight enjoyment.

"Don't let him get to you," Charlie pleaded. "He wants a reaction. Then she'll have more to rant about." He nodded towards Claire who was enjoying watching her puppet show come to life. "See, she's practically frothing at the mouth."

"I don't need a reaction, dear. The people in this hall are well aware of what's happening around them. I'm merely trying to offer consolation for the shit she's put us in."

"Wait a minute. Grace didn't lock us in here. None of this is her fault," Charlie argued.

"No," Claire sneered. "But she's the one who's not being completely honest with us. Isn't that right, Grace?"

The whole hall turned to face Grace. Even her colleagues unwillingly looked to her for an explanation. Grace refused to tell them about Vickey's mysterious wound, but she knew Michael could spill the beans at any given moment and sink them all. "I really don't know what you're talking about, Claire. I don't know what you've been told but there is nothing to report."

"Oh, that's the way you want to play it? Okay, if you won't tell them, then I will." Claire turned her back to Grace and stood eye to eye with the other occupants. "The child is infected."

Some people gasped, in confusion as to what this new information meant, others sighed in reluctance as they were aware of the situation.

Kristie laughed. "Are you kidding me? You demented freak, True was sick this morning. There could be any number of reasons for that."

"What about the main reason?" Kim chimed in. "The one that could be a danger to everyone in here?"

"I don't recall any of the infected victims on the news having vomiting as a symptom." Charlie had watched the news religiously since the first patient was announced.

"No," Claire hushed Kim again by placing a demeaning hand on her shoulder. "But they have a fever, don't they? Vomiting could just be her body's way of reacting to a sudden rise in temperature."

"That is so far-fetched. I suspected you might try to pull this shit with anyone who so much as coughed but pointing fingers at a child who's had no contact with the infected…" Charlie's voice trailed off, he couldn't believe the way her mind was working.

"Now, that's not strictly true either, is it, Grace?" He had done it. Michael had stooped to a new low as he ignored Grace's silent pleas.

"Oh, this sounds good," Claire loomed. "Do, go on."

Michael felt as if this woman was giving him the respect that no one in the club before this day had ever given him so, damn right he was going to tell her what she wanted to hear. He didn't owe Grace anything. "Well, it's almost certain that she's been in contact with an infected person. In fact, a couple of people in here have."

"Are you talking about that woman they carried in? I knew it. I knew something wasn't right with her." Lorraine shoved Lewie in an 'I told you so' manner.

"Oh, pipe down. She was trampled, you twit." Jean was still standing up for the downtrodden even in her frail state.

"The big, old bite on her leg says otherwise, Jean," remarked Michael, looking as condescending as ever.

At that point, the bystanders exploded into a chaotic sea of outrage and incredulity.

"Are you serious?" Serhan shook his head in disbelief, aware that he was one of the few who had been in close contact with Vickey since he had helped to bring her into the hall in the first place.

"And nobody said anything?" This came from a bewildered Tom who had seemed to be keeping himself to himself before this point.

"How do you know? Did you see it?" Lorraine demanded answers from Michael.

"I saw it and so did she." He pointed his bony little finger straight at Grace, who stood there, completely blind-sided.

"Grace, you never said anything." Kristie looked at her with her doe eyes.

"Okay, you all need to calm down," Grace demanded. "Vickey has a wound on her leg from where somebody trod on her. However, some people love to jump to conclusions and assume it is a bite. It was obviously made by someone wearing football boots which is why we didn't feel the need to inform you all."

"And you're sure of that, are you? Did you ask her?" Claire pressed mockingly. "Are you actually willing to risk everyone's life because you don't want to admit that you could be wrong? That's not very 'leader like' of you."

"I'm not anyone's leader," Grace argued. "I made a judgement call. The woman has a mark. She is also unconscious and getting weaker by the minute. She is not dangerous."

"*She* might not be but what's inside her could be." Kim overstepped once more causing Claire to physically push her aside to ensure the spotlight remained on her.

"Like it or not, that child is sick and if nothing is done about it soon, we will all pay the consequences," Claire hissed.

"So, what's your plan? Are you going to murder a three-year-old?" Charlie spat the words at her vehemently. "Is that how you're going to 'ensure' our safety, by killing a kid who has an upset tummy?"

"Over my dead body." Winston stood beside Charlie.

"Who here is willing to help this psycho kill an innocent child?" Charlie continued to address the members of the hall who were lapping up every word that Claire spoke.

Lorraine and Lewie actually seemed to be debating the idea whilst Tom hung his head in shame of even entertaining such horror. Scared people are forced to contemplate obscene measures in order to survive. Grace studied the faces of the people Claire had already reached and despite Charlie's reality check, the fact that they'd considered True's murder an option made her realise that the virus being inside the building was never the danger.

12:21 pm

Darius had taken leave of the conversation before Claire's evil spewing had gotten to its core. He approached the manager's office wearily so as not to draw any attention to his whereabouts. He'd knocked on the door with a false confidence and waited for almost a minute before, to his disappointment, Kathryn answered wearing an expression that could warn off even the most evil spirits.

"What's up?" she'd eventually asked, looking less than impressed.

Darius bypassed her ever-welcoming tone. "I wondered if I could just ask you guys some things?"

"About what?" Kathryn's defensive tone almost deterred him, but he decided to persist.

"About the virus…?" Kathryn's eyes said it all but before she could slam the door in his face, he added, "Kathryn, I'm scared. Please let me in."

Kathryn's expression softened and she considered his request before opening the door and stepping aside to let him in. Rosie, who had overheard the conversation, asked the first question. "What are you scared about?"

Darius looked ashamed. "I heard that True was sick."

He noticed Kathryn and Rosie exchange looks of worry, so was quick to put their minds at ease. "Winston asked after her and Kristie told us not to tell anyone, but I had to come and see you guys."

"Why?" Kathryn knew this visit wasn't out of consideration. She could sense an ulterior motive a mile off, but Rosie had already figured it out.

"Are you sick, too?" She could tell he was struggling to broach the subject. He caught her gaze and she identified with the fear in his eyes. "Are you?"

His lip twitched as he nodded his head. "I think so."

Kathryn stood immediately, outraged. "Then why the fuck have you come in here?"

Darius stood to meet her, annoyed at her whiter than white attitude. "I came here because that little girl is infected. You know it and I know it, and if she is, then so are you two. I can't pose a threat to anyone in this room if you're all infected anyway."

Rosie shot a look at Kathryn for her to remain calm. He had a point. He was no danger to them if he was showing the same symptoms as True. And, in hindsight, none of them really had any idea of what they were dealing with. To say Darius was scared was an understatement. There were so many words to describe that emotion: petrified, frightened, afraid. And yet, none of them quite captured the entirety of his inner battles.

Rosie reached for Darius' hand and pulled him with gentle encouragement to his former seated position. "Start from the beginning," Rosie urged supportively.

Darius placed his hand on top of hers, appreciating her comfort. This led Kathryn to experience a slight pang of jealousy as he began the story of his current turmoil.

"I suppose it all started this morning. I woke up all groggy. My eyes were sore and my nose was blocked. I just put it down to hay fever, to be honest. I took some antihistamines and got ready for work." He shook his head in minor agitation.

"People started pissing me off straight away, really. Someone pushed past me to get on the bus, then someone stopped right in front of me while I was walking to work. These are all little things that I would normally just shrug off. I'm a laid-back guy."

"Yes, too laid back, some might say," Kathryn noted.

Darius ignored her and continued. "Today, these little things really frustrated me but, again, I blamed the hay fever. You know, you get irritated easily. It's not uncommon.

"Then, I guess, when I got into work, I started to get this headache. It was quiet at first but with all the chaos, it changed to a fire inside my head. I've never felt anything like it. It died down when I took some tablets, but I could feel it was still lingering."

"That could've been caused by the stress of everything, though." Rosie offered reassuring words.

"Exactly what I thought," Darius agreed. "But then, Craig happened. You must've heard what I did. Kathryn, have you ever known me to lose my temper like that?"

Kathryn didn't need to think about her answer. She was a cold-hearted bitch at times, but she knew her staff members inside and out. "No."

Rosie wasn't satisfied, though. "But, hold on, you'd just seen a guy hit your workmate, who is also a woman and a tiny one at that. Lots of men would've reacted the way you did."

"But they didn't!" Darius appreciated her trying to diffuse his melodrama, but the bottom line was that he was the only one who had reacted in that way. Rosie and Kathryn sat in silence waiting for him to carry on.

"I felt like I could've killed him right there. If the others hadn't pulled me off, I would've beaten him to death and not even given it a second thought. That's not me. I don't lose my temper. I'm the calm, collected one here but yesterday, I felt like some kind of animal." He hung his head and held back the tears that were threatening his masculinity.

After a while, Rosie reached out to him again. "Darius, can I ask you something personal?"

He sniffed and nodded.

"Are you in love with Sophie?"

He held her gaze for a few moments before dropping it and focusing on his hands, fiddling in front of him. "I care about her, sure."

Rosie had cracked it. "I think you're being too hard on yourself, Darius. We all do drastic things to protect the people we care about. I'd move heaven and Earth for this little one."

She patted True's sleeping head, but her loving look quickly turned into one of sincerity. "And I would kill anyone who even tried to hurt her."

Darius grinned respectfully. "I believe that you would."

"Honestly, I don't think you're infected." Rosie's look evaporated and she was back to her caring, worried self. "I think your mind can make you believe things especially when you don't quite admit the truth to yourself."

Kathryn placed her hand on his shoulder in an act that instantly made both of them feel uncomfortable. "Stay away from Craig. Grace is keeping an eye on Sophie. Anything you do in here is under a magnifying glass and I promise you, that lynch mob out there will jump to the same conclusions that you did."

Darius, although taken aback by Kathryn's sudden empathy, recognised her words of warning and planned to adhere to them. He stretched his legs and stood. "I'm sorry to burden you with all this. You've got enough on your plates. I'll leave you to it but if you need anything, just give me a shout."

Darius pulled the office door open to expose the loud debate taking place in the hall. He only heard a few words, but they were enough. He closed the door to and looked at the women in the small room. "Guys, I don't think the lynch mob is after me. You might want to get out there, Kat."

Kathryn and Rosie felt the dread fill their entire beings. They could hear Claire's poison taking hold and Grace's defence holding strong, but Rosie was terrified for her niece's life. Kathryn grabbed her hand. "I'll go."

But Rosie wasn't going to stand aside. "No. This needs to stop. She's a poorly little girl for fuck's sake."

Darius shut the door completely. "Go. I'll watch over your sister and True. I've been in here too long as it is. If I'm going to get infected, it's probably happened already."

Rosie nodded gratefully. "If True wakes up, tell her I'll only be a minute but whatever you do, do not bring her out here."

"You have my word."

She stopped before she reached the door. "If Vickey wakes up…"

"Don't worry, I'll be here." Darius smiled, whole heartedly as the two women left their forced room of solitude and entered into the fray.

As Rosie and Kathryn made their appearance, the hall fell silent as they studied the accused's every move. Claire wasn't deterred for even a second. "Well, look who's decided to grace us with their presence. Is the child not joining you? Or is she far too sick for all this excitement?"

Murmurs began to circle the hall as Rosie fought the urge to throttle Claire. "What is your problem? My niece is sick. She has a run of the mill bug, not this bloody virus. Why are you making this worse than it is?"

"Because we were herded into this place like cattle, we had no choice and we were led to believe that we would be protected from the evils of the outside world for at least seventy-two hours. So far, we've had to deal with a druggy, a guy who can't control his temper and now a sick little girl, not to mention your 'injured' sister."

"What does that mean? 'Injured'?"

"It means she is paralysed. She's been bitten and, therefore, she is infected and she might not be able to attack anyone but she can still infect them."

"How the hell did you figure that one out?" Kathryn stood proudly by Rosie's side. "The virus isn't airborne. Where are you getting this information from?"

"And it isn't a bite," Rosie argued.

"And we're supposed to believe that? Just because you say it's a boot print, doesn't mean that's what it is." Kim stood behind Claire like one of those extras you try not to pay too much attention to in films because they are merely there to make up the numbers.

"Go and look at it. You can't base your witch hunt for an innocent child and a harmless woman on an assumption of what they might have wrong with them. We're in no danger, True's just sick. Can't you just leave her alone?"

Grace stepped between Kathryn and Kim in an attempt to diffuse the situation. "I think we all need to calm down and focus on the facts."

She waited until she had everyone's attention before continuing. "True is sick. We don't know what she has but in case she is contagious, it's best that she stays in the office. The harsh truth is that we don't know if the virus is airborne, but we have to assume it would've been made public if it was and True wasn't bitten.

"And where Vickey is concerned, we still have no idea about the damage she's suffered. It's easy to jump to conclusions but at the end of all this, don't you want to be able to say you held on to your humanity as long as you possibly could? I mean, we're right at the beginning of things and you're already considering murder. Not self-defence, murder."

As if she hadn't even heard the latter part of Grace's speech, Claire rolled her eyes. "Of course, we wouldn't know if it's airborne. Don't be so naïve."

Grace carried on. "We also don't know when the incubation period is. Chickenpox is contagious through air and contact days before the rash even shows. This could be the same. In which case, we've all already been exposed."

A few hushed words were muttered, and confused, scared looks circled the hall. Grace felt how everyone else did: clueless, lost, and helpless. It was a shit situation and the company didn't make things any easier. In times like these, you're supposed to be able to trust the people you're with but unfortunately, that was far from the truth. Never mind what was going on outside, there was a darkness inside the building that loomed over each and every one of them and it wasn't because of a sick child and her unconscious mother.

Grace decided to round off her intervention with a closing statement. "Look, I know this is going to sound cheesy, but we really do need to stick together. At least until we get out. We have another day and a half to go and then we will be out of each other's hair. There's no point in waging war while we're stuck inside this building. We have food and we have security. We need to focus on what we're going to do once the doors open."

She seemed to have reached the majority, which was all she could've hoped for, so she opted to break the tension if only momentarily. "So, if you don't mind, I'm hungry. Anyone else?"

At that moment, as if by some twisted form of irony, the lights went out and the incessant humming that belonged to the air conditioning unit droned to a halt. The hall went dark coercing its occupants into an unpredictable frenzy.

*****

Darius sat quietly in the dimly lit room trying to make out the monotonous voices he could hear through the closed doors. A lot of people seemed to be voicing their opinions by the sound of things, but he had faith that Rosie could handle things with Kathryn and Grace by her side. He peered over at True to make sure she was still sleeping soundly and was satisfied to hear her angelic snore. Her cheeks weren't as rosy as before and she had tiny beads of sweat above her brow. He sighed to himself suddenly wondering if he, himself would ever father a child. He'd never really given it much thought and if the world really was in this state of rack and ruin, he didn't really see the point of contemplating it any further, but for a brief moment, he allowed himself to imagine just what it would be like to have a smaller version of himself running around, calling him 'Daddy'. It was a temporary moment of bliss amidst the terrifying truth and as he glanced over at the unconscious woman, he froze as she stared back at him with glassy, green eyes.

12:38 pm

"Oh my God!" Darius stumbled backwards staring at the woman lying statuesque on the couch. "You're awake."

He approached with caution as the woman's eyes searched the room in a panic. It wasn't until she spoke that Darius snapped into action.

"Where's my...baby?" It was no more than a whisper, but Darius knew what she had said.

"She's okay. She's fine. She's just over there. Are you okay?" Darius grabbed her icy hand but as she looked over to her child on the floor, she became hysterical.

"What have...you done to...her...? Where's my sister? Who...are...?" She gasped for breath and began coughing erratically, blood splattering over her face.

Darius feared that these could be her final moments. "It's okay. She's sleeping. Everything's okay. I'm going to get you some water, then I'll get Rosie, okay? Just hold on."

He released his hand from her failed attempt at a strong grip and rushed to the bathroom behind the desk, side stepping True on the way. He grabbed a pint glass from the desk and ran the cold water, filling the glass halfway.

He could hear her still struggling to breathe over the sound of the running water and called out to her, "I'm right here. Hold on."

As he turned the faucet, he hurried towards Vickey's bedside but just as he passed the toilet door, everything went dark.

His vision had gone but his body continued forward. He tripped over what he could only assume was the child on the floor and braced himself for the impact of the hard floor. As he hit his head on the side of the desk, he heard a smash and pieces of glass entered his hand and wrist. He lay on the floor, dazed, as a warm liquid spread over his arm. His hearing started to fade but as he lost consciousness, he could just make out a child's cry.

12:40 pm

Screams erupted throughout the darkness as Grace began shouting at people not to move. She knew the emergency lights would fire up at some point in the event of a power outage but that could not be said for the freezers, or their ability to cook any of the frozen products. As if by a divine intervention, the dim lights flickered and partially illuminated areas of the hall. As the scared group breathed a sigh of relief, their eyes adjusted to the new appearance of their surroundings. Grace launched into action, dishing out responsibilities to her former colleagues. "Kristie, make sure Jean's okay. Winston, we need to move the refrigerated food down to the cellar. It'll keep for a while down there. Everyone else, stay here. It's just the power. The emergency lights will hold out until we get out of here. We need to keep the refrigerated food cold."

Charlie volunteered to help whilst Serhan begrudgingly conformed and the rest of the hall tended to their own weakening nerves as Grace's group headed towards the diner.

It was then that Rosie heard the child's scream. She looked straight at Kathryn in a panic and bolted towards the office, with Kathryn close at her heels.

As Grace and the guys reached the doors leading to the cellar's corridor, they were met by a panicked Sophie who instantly offered to help.

"We need to get all of the refrigerated food into the cellar. If we bring it to you, could you take it in for us?" Winston asked politely, all the time looking out for her problematic boyfriend.

"He's asleep," Sophie said, putting their minds at ease. "Just bring me the stuff. I'll put it away."

They hurried along the corridor leading from the cellar to the diner, gathering as much food as they could carry. There was less than they'd thought. They would have to resort to defrosting the desserts just in case they began to run low on food.

The plan was to order as little as possible leading up to the closure of the club but, as always, their less than competent manager had intervened and placed the final order twice which obviously boded well for them now. If they could keep it all cool, it might just be able to last them until they got out.

"Are you going to be okay with all this, Soph?" Grace was anxious to return to the hall but was equally as worried about leaving Sophie with a responsibility that could potentially cause her hassle with Craig.

Sophie was relatively sure she could unpack the food without antagonising Craig. "Yes, of course. Go ahead."

Just as the last of the food had been brought over, Sophie began organising the items around the cellar. She wasn't in there long before she was stopped in her tracks.

"What are you doing in here?" Craig's voice was husky and made Sophie jump out of her skin. Maybe she was wrong about her previous thought process.

"While you were asleep, the electricity went out, so we have to store the food in here because it's the only place that's cool enough." She hated that she always sounded so scared whenever she responded to his questions, but she was so terrified of answering wrong that the more information she could fit into any explanation, the better.

"I don't want you coming down here. Do you understand?" He stared at her with black eyes that seemed to look straight through her.

Sophie knew she shouldn't ask but forced herself to, anyway. "Why not?"

He looked at her with a look that could only be described as irritation. "It's not safe," he barked.

Sophie didn't understand but was convinced that her questions should stop there. "Okay," she said nervously.

Craig stepped to one side in an effort to urge her out of the room and she obeyed instantly. As she reached the door, he stopped her. Leaning in close, he whispered, "That goes for everyone, Sophie. Do you hear me? No one is allowed in here."

Sophie looked at him. "But the food…"

He slammed his palm against the open door making her jump yet again. "No one."

She nodded keenly. If the others wanted their food, they could take it up with Craig themselves. This was not a battle she was willing to fight. She walked past him and took a seat on the floor in the corridor, relieved that she had avoided another harmful situation. She watched him close the door behind him, then lay back down on the ground beside her. Her body was shaking like a leaf.

12:42 pm

Darius could hear the panicked sound of women's voices all around him, but he couldn't make out what they were saying or what was happening. There was a child crying and he vaguely remembered tripping over something. The little girl! He hoped he hadn't hurt her, but he was rushing to help Vickey and then the lights went out. His hand was on fire. He tried to move it, but nothing was working properly. He could feel the wet sensation covering his hand and arm and the ruthless shards of glass that had penetrated them.

The room was still dark, but he could make out a faint light coming from outside the open office door. Rosie ran straight past Darius, moving furniture out of her way like a woman possessed to get to her niece. She could barely see through the darkness but could just about make out a figure lying on the floor. She quickly pieced together what had happened and as Kathryn entered the room behind Rosie, she stopped in her tracks as the tension fuelled air was invaded by a raspy, disturbing sound. They all froze and strained their eyes in the direction of the wounded woman. Rosie's heart sank as she held True's head close to her chest in a desperate attempt to shelter the child from anymore trauma.

As the noise resounded once more, the emergency lights sparked to life in the dingy office room, shedding light on the horrific situation at hand. Kathryn saw it all: the injured woman with blood around her mouth and Darius lying on the floor dazed with a bloody hand. She shouted to Rosie, "Get out! She's infected."

She looked behind her and reached for the fire extinguisher on the wall. She'd never had any experience in killing anything, but Kathryn was going to protect those girls at all costs. She lifted the heavy, metal container high above her head and breathed rapidly.

12:44 pm

Kathryn could hear her own breath noisily echoing in her ears. She could no longer hear the commotion around her, her self-induced silence calmed her.

She lifted the weapon high above her head and exhaled at the height of her ability. As she summoned all of her strength, she brought the hammer down with all her might until it collided with the sturdy base. As it made its heavy contact, the bell rang three times in quick succession as the crowd came to life applauding and whistling. The Strong Man ball hit the jackpot bell at the top, then came shooting back down to its original resting place.

She smiled cockily as her gathered fans cheered and clapped, marvelling at her strength.

As she turned back to face her large, colourful opponent, she lifted the hammer again and brought it down just as hard as she had the last time, sending the ball up towards the bell once more.

She continued bashing the hammer down onto the small podium ignoring the water that was now shooting out at her from the buckling stand, a mere distraction by the stall holder in a pathetic attempt to put her off of her swing.

She pounded down on the podium again and again, each time propelling the ball upwards to its tryst with the resounding bell. The crowd got louder and louder and their cheers began to morph in her head. Mid hit she distinguished a single scream that filled the carnival air, followed by a familiar voice. She didn't let it put her off. She carried on through the shouts and screams until arms surrounded her, pinning her own arms to her side.

She snapped back into the room, taking in the scene before her. The extinguisher dropped to the floor. She became suspicious of the water on her face. She struggled free, wiping ferociously at her eyes and cheeks only to reveal the deep red stains on her sleeves.

She glanced over at Rosie, then looked back at what was left of Vickey. Her stomach lurched and she lost her footing as Darius tried to hold her up. She couldn't feel her body, her limbs weren't working. She followed Darius' arms with her eyes up to his face and looked at him with utter confusion.

"Kat, what have you done?"

Rosie was crying loudly behind him and they could just make out the muffled sounds coming from the child she was cradling.

"She was infected," were the only words Kathryn could muster.

"No, she wasn't. Vickey woke up but she was choking so I went to get her some water, then when the lights went off, I tripped over and the glass broke in my hand." Darius paused and began shaking the woman he could see breaking in front of him. "Kathryn! Are you listening to me?"

She stared back at the bloodied mess on the couch and then wandered out of the room revealing her crimson drenched attire to everyone in the hall. Darius followed her into a wave of horrified gasps. Everyone backed away from Kathryn unsure of what had gone on in the office, but Darius was stopped from going after her by a panicked Kristie.

"What the hell happened in there? We heard screams."

Darius looked through her in Kathryn's direction worried about his colleague's current frame of reference but Kristie was fussing over his fresh wound. "Darius! Look at me. What happened?"

"Kathryn killed Vickey." He tried to speak quietly but all eyes and ears were on him. "She thought Vickey was infected so she…"

"I bloody knew it," Claire announced. "What have I been saying all along?"

"Change the record, Claire. You don't understand."

Claire ignored Darius and focused on the panicked faces of the impressionable group. "Understand? What do I need to understand? Why is your hand bleeding?"

"I cut it on glass…"

"Are you sure she didn't take a nice juicy chunk out of you before the blonde managed to save your arse?" Kim snidely remarked as the rest of the hall continued to make false accusations in their own heads.

"I fell onto a glass. She didn't bite me. She wasn't infected."

Kristie took him by the arm. "Let's get you bandaged up. You're bleeding a lot."

"You need to stop covering for them!" Claire called after him in a failed attempt to get a reaction from him. When that didn't work, she addressed the others instead. "Of course, he'd want to cover his own back. He was bitten by that woman but if she wasn't infected, then neither is he. Unfortunately for him, we're not fools. I think you all know the truth."

Claire's allegations hung in the air and everyone was jumping to the same conclusion. The evidence was too compelling and was piling up fast in her favour. What they heard was terrifying enough and their imaginations could do nothing but run away with them.

12:48 pm

At that moment, Grace and her helpers emerged from the diner. Claire walked towards them, clapping a slow and dramatic applaud as she called out to them from across the hall ready to put on a show.

"All hail our protector!" Her voice lathered in sarcasm as the crowd turned with her to face the team who were completely unaware of the events that had taken place just moments ago. Grace responded to Claire's malice by throwing her the same tired, bored expression that she had come to use frequently when it involved listening to Claire. She went to walk past but Claire stopped her aggressively.

Her words were spoken with volume and blame. "She who said we were safe. Your friend trusted you just as the rest of us did and now he's paying the price."

Grace's heart somersaulted in her chest. Her mind leapt to all kinds of scenarios involving her handful of friends as her agitation melted into genuine worry. "What the fuck are you talking about?"

"You made us all believe that that woman was not infected. You were very convincing…" Claire was so close to Grace's face that her breath made her eye's sting. "…but you lied to us and what happens? She wakes up and takes a chunk out of your friend!"

"What? Who?" Grace tried to push past her, but Claire grabbed her arm.

"Big guy with the piercings and tattoos and, guess what? He's not dead which means he's been infected and is going to turn at some point. The virus is going to make its way through his blood stream turning him into one of those monsters that we all ran in here to get away from."

"Let go of me!" Grace had heard enough. She needed to see this for herself. Winston and Charlie were too shocked to intervene, but Grace managed to pry away the bony fingers that were gripping her arm.

"Just look at the size of him," she shouted after Grace. "None of us would stand a chance. We need to take him out before he kills all of us."

Grace sprinted towards the office while Charlie and Winston took a while in contemplation before warily making their way after her. Serhan hung back and looked Claire in the eye.

"Is this really happening?" He asked more for confirmation than out of denial and Claire could smell his faltering loyalty.

"I saw it with my own eyes. That man is infected and so is the little girl. If we don't take matters into our own hands, none of us will get out of here alive."

She turned her back to him leaving him with the little slither of doom and gloom as she quietly congratulated herself on another soldier recruited for her growing army.

12:50 pm

"You've really made a mess here, hun." Kristie worked hard to remove all the shards of glass with her trusty tweezers. The look of concentration on her face would normally have prompted Darius to smirk in between winces. "I think I got it all. Now, just hold still. This might sting a little, but I have to clean the wounds."

Darius waited for the wipe to touch his skin, then let out a horrendous screech causing Kristie to jump and apologise profusely. Darius snickered half-heartedly and said, "Don't worry. It doesn't really hurt. They're alcohol free."

Kristie thumped him too hard to be considered playful. She wasn't impressed by his attempt to lighten the mood and continued bandaging him up. "How can you joke around after what just happened? Don't you have any feelings? Kathryn just killed someone in front of you and you're messing about."

Once she'd finished, she tossed Darius a glare and openly stated that next time he could find someone else to patch him up as she strutted away leaving Matt with her former patient.

"What's the matter, mate? You don't look too good."

Darius wiped his beaded forehead once more and smeared it down his trousers.

"I don't feel good either, mate." He rubbed at his agitated face, then winced when he brushed his temple. "My head is killing me. Literally, it's pounding. Have you got any painkillers?"

Matt stared at his friend, unable to ignore the recent events and their detrimental meaning. He shook his head. "Sorry, man. Grace probably does though. I'll grab some for you."

Before Matt could stand, Darius grabbed his arm with an unintentional force which caught Matt off guard. He was even more concerned by the look of panic on his friend's face. Darius shrugged it off, realising he had drawn the attention of his colleague. "No, it's all right. She has other things to worry about."

Matt was worried. "Darius, the woman's like Mary Poppins. She'll have something in her bag. I can just ask her."

"No!"

His voice was much louder than he'd anticipated and both men were quietly shocked by his abruptness. Matt sat silently, debating whether or not to press for an explanation but Darius beat him to it.

"Sorry, dude. I'm just not feeling right. And before you say anything, I've had this headache since yesterday morning and I feel like shit. I don't want to worry anyone."

Matt's expression said it all. "You mean, you don't want to draw any attention to it."

"It's got nothing to do with that…"

"Were you bitten?"

"No. No, I wasn't. It was all a massive misunderstanding. Vickey wasn't infected."

"Then why did Kathryn kill her?" Matt looked at Darius for what felt like an eternity and Darius couldn't determine Matt's stance on his story so to ease the tension, he softened his tone and confided in his friend.

"Look, I swear to you, Vickey was not infected and I was not bitten. Look at the amount of glass Kristie just pulled out of my hand. I do feel like shit though. My eyes are red raw and I can't stop sweating but I'm freezing. It could just be a cold and I don't want to scare anyone."

Matt intervened. "The little girl's sick, too. She threw up over Kathryn this morning. Something isn't right in here. What if we're all infected?"

"Then, to be honest, mate, we're all fucked. We can't get away from it if it's already inside, can we? There's no point in raising the alarm if no one can do anything about it?"

Darius sensed his friend's devastation at the harsh prospect of the situation and instantly felt bad.

"Honestly, Matt, I think this could be anything: a cold, a common bug or even some sort of psychological effect. Don't stress about it. I've been feeling like this for the last couple of days. Funnily enough, I was considering phoning in sick this morning, but I need the money. I'm not worried. You shouldn't be either."

Matt half smiled and nodded. "If your symptoms get any worse, you'll tell me, right?"

Darius chuckled. "Of course, I will, man. You'll be the first to know."

2:11 pm

Kathryn sat in the upstairs staff room staring at the wall contemplating what had just happened, the look on Rosie's face as she held that fire extinguisher in her hands.

Grace knocked lightly on the barely open door and entered cautiously.

"Hey," she spoke in a quiet voice.

"Hey," Kathryn replied, not breaking her focus with the wall.

Grace took a seat a couple of chairs away from her friend as she struggled to find words that weren't generic or were specifically sensitive to the current situation. Eventually she opted for a more direct question. "What happened down there?"

Kathryn didn't know where to start. She was battling to organise her thoughts but if she couldn't be honest with Grace, who could she confide in?

"I thought she was infected, Grace. When the lights came back on, I saw Darius lying on the ground bleeding. I heard a noise behind me and Vickey's face was covered in blood. I just saw blood."

She could see it all in her head as clear as day and she knew that that image was never going to go away. "I grabbed the nearest thing to me and just kept hitting her."

Grace held her hand to her mouth to suppress a gasp.

"I just wanted to protect them. I didn't even think, Grace. I just did it. And the look she gave me..." Kathryn's sentence ended abruptly as her voice quivered. She deliberately avoided eye contact with Grace and tried to collect herself.

"When Darius started talking, I felt sick." Kathryn could feel the contempt for herself rising up inside her and no matter how much she tried to convince herself that she had acted on pure protective instinct, she could still feel Vickey's blood seeping into her skin. She still felt like a murderer.

"Kat, you were protecting them. Anyone could've made the same mistake. This isn't your fault, Rosie knows that."

"Does she? Because what she saw was me bashing her sister's head in with a fucking fire extinguisher for no apparent reason." The tremble in her voice betrayed her hard exterior every time she spoke.

"Kathryn, you saw what you thought you saw and you acted on it. Everyone is guessing their way through this whole thing. Nobody knows what to expect and no one can blame you for reacting the way you did."

Kathryn refused to believe that. "And what if Darius hadn't woken up when he did? Grace, I was prepared to do the same to him." Her voice finally broke and she gave in to the tears. "I could've killed him as well."

Grace knew her friend was carrying the weight of the world and was at risk of being swallowed into an abyss of guilt and self-torment. Kathryn had acted with courage and valour but then Darius had come to and her act of heroism had been catapulted into a dystopian scene of unanticipated violence.

"Kathryn, you're one of the strongest people I know. I had no doubt in my mind that you would protect anyone you cared about. Please don't punish yourself for doing that."

Kathryn looked disgusted with herself. "This can never be fixed, Grace. How can I ever look that little girl in the face again? How can I ever look Rosie in the face again? She will never forgive me. *This* will never be forgiven."

Her voice broke again and Grace could see the turmoil her friend was putting herself through but nothing was going to prevent that. Kathryn was trembling from head to toe and picking at her nails in frustration. Grace's heart broke for her friend as she remembered the wreck she had been when her own sister had passed away. She edged closer to Kathryn and wiped her tears away with her sleeve. It was then that Kathryn gave in to the emotions she was trying so hard to keep bottled up. She began sobbing into Grace's arms as her friend held her as tight as she possibly could.

4:03 pm

"Help me! Somebody please help me!"

The pain shot through his head like a lightning bolt burning him back to life. He screamed out in agony only for the pain to return, reaping vengeance on his severely dehydrated throat. He winced as it stopped him from doing it again. The room was pitch black and silent. Blinking furiously, he attempted to establish whether the room was actually dark or if he had, in fact, gone blind. He paused for a moment, trying to produce enough saliva to at least lessen the sting in his throat but even that was like swallowing broken glass. Cautiously, he went to reach for his head but couldn't. He struggled, uncertain of what was holding him down, and tried unsuccessfully to free his arms and legs from the shackles that kept him strictly in place. He clenched his fists and screamed at the top of his lungs but was viciously halted when his voice hit the surrounding walls, bellowing back at him.

"What the fuck's going on? Who's doing this?" He began crying out loudly and as he did so, he felt a cold, metal object hovering just above his exposed stomach. He froze. *What the fuck is that?*

He lay still for a moment attempting to calm himself. He tried to call out again, but no sound escaped his mouth. His throat was hoarse and seemed to be gradually swelling up. *What the fuck is happening to me?*

From the right-hand corner of the room, a single beam of light shot through the air and landed on him. It hit his eyes like a bullet, but he knew it was there, so he still had his sight. He tried again to plead for answers, but his voice was still sawing at his vocal cords. He let his muscles collapse from the strain of trying to break through the metal restraints. He breathed deeply and quickly feeling the hanging metal object teasing his skin with every rise of his stomach. It was sharp against his naked abdomen. As his eyes adjusted to the light, it moved slightly to the left of his head as he was able to identify the mysterious looming object. It hung from the ceiling of an exceptionally tall room and was attached to a spiral contraption that he could imagine would act as a torture device. As his eyes followed the length of the metallic rod, he could just about make out the serrated edges at the bottom of it. He didn't need any more information. He knew what was about to happen. He began struggling once more and as he broke through his sound barrier, his screams were deafening, causing him to shock himself once again into silence. He could feel a warm sensation between his legs and moving towards his knees as he urinated, losing control of his bodily functions.

"Please! I'm sorry…" He was begging for his life. He knew his sins. He knew he had to pay the consequences, but he didn't want to die even though he knew he deserved to. "I'm sorry. I didn't know. I didn't know."

As his pleas dissolved into barely audible whimpers, a small silhouette appeared beside him. He stared over at the faceless shadow and begged again.

"I should've protected you. I'm sorry. I didn't know. I'm so sorry. Please forgive me."

The shadow placed its tiny hand over his and squeezed gently. The man deflated, emotionally exhausted as the child comforted him. As he whispered to the shadow, it released its grip and pulled away, gazing up at the ceiling. He followed its gaze and felt the tension course through his entire body.

He began begging once again but as the metal rod came to life and lowered itself onto his skin, his screams ricocheted off the walls, piercing his eardrums. The serrated bottom of the rod continued entering his lower abdomen, slicing through flesh, organs and eventually, bone. He felt his skin tear and his intestines become tangled around the contraption. His breathing became erratic as he began coughing, choking on his own blood. He looked over at the silhouette again and mouthed another apology.

"I'm so sorry."

Craig was sweating profusely as Sophie tried to cool him down. He was muttering words that she didn't understand. These nightmares were terrifying for her so she could only imagine how bad they were for him. She dabbed his head with a damp cloth and hushed him, calmly whispering soothing words and lullabies. She knew better than to try and wake him but if he got any louder, he was going to wake up the others and she didn't want to give them another reason for a man hunt.

The cries lasted a few minutes more, then he finally jerked awake, panting and grabbing at his shirt. He lifted it up to inspect his torso, feeling around to his back. Sophie moved to him, but he lashed out, slapping her hand away. This wasn't a violent action, she knew. Something inside his harrowing mind had scared him into retaliation. He was shaking and it took him a few moments to focus and realise it was Sophie beside him.

Eventually, the soft expression on her face became clearer and Craig broke down. His sobs shook his entire body as Sophie held his head in her lap. His tears and sweat soaked through her shirt, moistening the skin beneath it. She sat in silence, absorbing his pain and trying so desperately to share the burden of it.

Sophie finally managed to get Craig back to sleep without drawing any unwanted attention to their previously quiet little corner of the hallway. It was a lot colder there than it was in the hall, but Sophie saw it as an ideal way to keep Craig's temperature under wraps. He constantly complained about the chills but to touch, he was burning up. The sweating didn't help either. She had already changed his shirt four times just to keep him that fraction more comfortable. Thankfully, she had helped herself to quite a collection of unused arcade uniform once they'd learned they would be in there a while.

Craig seemed settled, for now, as Sophie placed a gentle hand on his sweat-bathed forehead. He was cooling down slightly which made her sigh with relief. She rested her head against the cold stone wall and let the tears roll freely. At first, they were silent but within moments had evolved into heart wrenching sobs. Her shoulders heaved with every breath and the salty streams bled into her healing wounds, adding physical distress to accompany her emotional turmoil. She'd kept it together for so long but having Craig snap at her in front of people was something else. She could always fabricate a story before but when they'd seen it for themselves it made it all real, and she couldn't cope with the pitiful looks they were throwing at her.

As she sunk against the unparalleled comfort of the wall, she began to question her entire existence at this point in time. Would anyone be affected if her life was to end in this supposed apocalyptic new world? Who would miss her? Craig would. He needed her. He was probably the only one who did. Her family had disowned her when Craig had relapsed. They said they wanted to be there to support her but with Craig using all the time, they were fighting a losing battle. They gave her an ultimatum and they didn't get the decision they wanted so they turned their backs on her. She felt a twinge of self-pity as she recalled the harsh words that had been exchanged so long ago.

She secretly scolded herself for wallowing and then braced herself for the questions she needed to concentrate on answering for the sake of both of their survivals. If they were going to beat this, how was she going to contribute to the survival of this group? Would they even want her to stay with them once the doors opened? What if they made her choose between them or Craig? What would she do then? So many questions and nowhere near enough answers. Her eyes were stinging and if she was honest with herself, she couldn't actually remember a time when they hadn't been.

She was always so busy making sure everyone else had what they needed, whether it was Craig at home, customers or even staff at work. She never wanted to be a burden, she was never one to complain or ring in sick. She even worked the morning after Craig had broken one of her ribs. Didn't she owe herself the release of a minor breakdown while no one was watching? The world could be ending and now was the time to let it all out before things got any worse. And, for once, she didn't care. There was no one around to judge her or think less of her and she needed some form of soul cleansing before plastering on a new brave face for the impending new world.

As she allowed the tears to cascade down her damaged face, she felt a hand grip hers. Flustered and embarrassed, she moved to wipe away her pitiful sorrow when she realised that it was Craig who had reached for her. He enveloped his hand around hers and squeezed with his eyes still shut.

"I'm sorry," he muttered, his grip remaining firm as Sophie succumbed to the flood of emotion that proceeded to drown her.

Craig lay still, absorbing the emotions flowing from his girlfriend. After a while, every tear began hitting him like a bullet. He released Sophie's tender hand and jumped up, agitated and fumbling. He rubbed his eyes vigorously and mumbled his apologies as he belted out of the corridor toward the disabled bathroom.

4:26 pm

Once Craig had made his exit, Darius planned his next move. He approached the double doors and hesitated briefly before knocking as if standing at the entrance of a house. He heard Sophie's mousey invitation through the blue, wooden doors and stepped through them gingerly. "Hi."

His voice croaked uncharacteristically and he instantly tried to clear it before having to expand his vocabulary.

Sophie looked shocked to see him but, at the same time, there was a look of joy in her eyes. He wasn't sure how to interpret that look and felt that it was safer not to assume anything considering the amount of courage it had taken to walk up to the doors in the first place.

He realised he had been staring at her for a while without offering an explanation for his visit. When she softly asked how he was, he snapped back to reality and crouched down beside her.

"Sophie, I am so sorry for the way I reacted. I didn't mean to scare you but seeing what he did to you, I couldn't control myself and I've never lashed out like that before."

She placed her fragile hand on his leg. "You don't have to apologise. I'm grateful you did what you did. No one's ever…defended me before. It meant the world to me."

Darius felt like a weight had been lifted and did everything in his power not to become emotional. "I really didn't want you to hate me."

His voice cracked towards the end of his sentence and Sophie took his face in her hands. "I could never hate you. What you did was very heroic. I'll never forget it."

Darius' heart skipped a beat. He couldn't miss this moment. He leaned in and kissed her, taking her face in his hands. For a moment, she kissed him back before the moment came crashing to an abrupt end when she pushed him away, rising to her feet and backing away.

"I'm so sorry," she blurted out.

"Don't be sorry. I've wanted this for so long, Sophie. You have nothing to be sorry about." He stood to embrace her once more, but she turned away from him.

"I'm with Craig!" she cried.

"Are you serious?" He looked at her as if she had just sprouted wings in front of him. "You can't be serious."

"I am. I'm so sorry, Darius. I didn't mean to string you along. What you did for me was amazing and I do appreciate it, but Craig is my boyfriend." Sophie softened her frantic tone. "For all his faults, he's mine and I love him. I don't expect you to understand…"

"Of course, I don't understand, Sophie. The fucking guy hits you. He doesn't love you; he abuses you. That isn't love, it is control. He is using you. You deserve better."

"Please, don't be angry at me. Try to understand. I need him."

"You need to have a black eye every other week, do you? A swollen lip every month, and what was it last month, a broken rib? Do you really need that, Sophie?"

"Please don't shout at me, Darius." She began to look like a scared child which just made him angrier because he knew Craig was to blame for that, too. Any time a man raised his voice to Sophie she would recoil and await the physical attribute that would accompany it.

"I thought I could help you, take you away from it all but you actually want to be with him."

"It's not that simple…"

"It is that simple. I would never hurt you. I'd die before touching you in anger."

He was standing so close to her; she could feel his warm body near hers and she quivered slightly. It took all of her strength to mutter her next few words. "Please, leave."

His face dropped and his heart sank. She could actually pinpoint the moment he had lost all hope of saving her. You can't save someone who doesn't want to be saved. His eyes filled with unwelcome tears and he dropped his gaze before turning and exiting through the doors behind him. He pushed the door so hard that it slammed against the wall behind it, chipping the brick and destroying the handle but he never looked back at her.

The individuals in the hall all turned sharply in the direction of the destructive man and the suffering door he had passed through. It caused a minor stir of concern due to the fact that Craig had only recently emerged from the toilets and was on course to collide with the much bigger man. The hall indiscreetly watched as Craig had to physically jump out of Darius' way. He felt too weak to provoke any sort of confrontation and after what Darius had just done to that door, he knew he wouldn't fare well. His attention, however, then fell to the person standing behind the battered doors from which Darius had stormed. He could feel his fury bubbling beneath his skin as he returned to the restroom. He was filled with rage but breathed through it. If he were to lash out at her now, Darius would surely kill him. Even Craig wasn't that much of an idiot.

*****

Darius had managed to clear a path to the back of the hall as people dodged and side stepped to avoid disturbing his determined strides. They all gazed after him in confusion and, as they did so, Craig had regrouped and snuck back to Sophie.

Darius hardly noticed the room of concerned inhabitants as he marched solidly to the other side of the hall. He was too busy filing his thoughts and inner arguments in unison with his angry movements, but he was forced to slow down when Matt appeared in front of him. Although he was resolute in not stopping, Matt was standing firm and had braced himself for impact. Begrudgingly, Darius stopped himself from walking through his friend, and when Matt didn't offer an explanation as to why he had intervened, Darius began to seethe.

"Get out of my way, Matt."

He attempted to veer around Matt but grew even more frustrated when Matt side stepped to intercept him again.

"Matt," he growled. "Move out of my way."

"What's happened?" Matt asked calmly.

"It's not what you think, Matt."

"Oh, I see. So, this isn't you showing signs of unnecessary anger and aggression?" Matt was scared to his very core, putting himself in potential danger to check on his friend's wellbeing.

"Matt…"

"You almost took that door off of its hinges, Darius. What could Sophie have possibly said or done for you to react like that?"

Darius was getting more and more agitated by the minute. He just wanted to be left alone.

"You don't know what you're talking about, Matt."

"Then explain it to me, mate. You asked me to keep an eye on you and that's what I'm doing. You're storming about, breaking doors, not to mention, Craig's face. If these aren't ringing alarm bells for you, I don't know what will."

Matt had barely finished his sentence when Darius grabbed him by the scruff of his collar and spoke through gritted teeth.

"Matt, I am fine. I just need a minute. Now, please get the fuck out of my way before I move you myself."

He let go with no force and Matt moved to one side maintaining eye contact the entire time. He watched as Darius continued into the arcade and resisted the urge to lock the wooden doors behind him. He didn't want to antagonise him further, but he fought with himself as to whether or not he should tell anyone about his concerns. As he looked around the hall for a friendly face, he stopped at Grace and instantly knew what he had to do.

4:49 pm

Grace's attention had already been drawn to Darius' dramatic outburst and although she was well aware that anyone in that state needed time to cool down, she still wanted to make sure he was okay. Seeing as he was seen leaving the corridor where Sophie and Craig were residing, she knew the two were connected. She hoped Sophie was all right.

Matt made his way over to Grace and having witnessed his altercation with Darius only moments ago, Grace could prematurely identify the topic of conversation.

"Grace, can I have a word?"

"Sure," she replied, following Matt to the storeroom.

"Tell me you saw that." He seemed incredibly agitated.

"With Darius?" She was 99% sure that everyone in the hall had seen it. "What happened?"

"Grace, I don't know what to do. He told me earlier that he'd been feeling rough all day…"

"Rough?" Grace didn't like where this was going.

"He has a temperature; a headache and he's sweating a lot."

"Okay."

Matt looked confused as to why this wasn't worrying her as much as it was him. "Grace, I'm losing my mind here. What if whatever virus was out there yesterday is now in here with us? First the little girl now Darius… We still don't know what actually happened with the kid's mum. What if it's in here? How are we supposed to protect ourselves?"

"Okay, Matt. Two people are feeling ill. It's not a conspiracy but I don't think it's anything to worry about either. Vickey is dead so we don't know if she had any symptoms, but the bottom line is that she is dead hence no danger. If you want my opinion, I think True has a bug and I think Darius' symptoms are psychological."

"All right. What about his anger? When he attacked Sophie's fella? In the years you've known him, have you ever seen Darius lose his temper like that?" Matt refused to believe Grace's flamboyant stance.

"He's never had a reason to before. And he didn't attack Craig. He was defending Sophie. There's a big difference."

Matt looked unconvinced and Grace could see that she wasn't getting through to him.

"I understand why you're worried, but I think you're focusing on the wrong danger."

"What do you mean?"

"Well, look at Craig. He's aggressive, and not just towards Sophie. He sweats profusely and he looks like death."

"He's a druggy. Of course, he looks like that. He's having withdrawal."

"But he's still a danger." Grace tried to reason with him. "Look, I just think you're jumping to conclusions. I did the same thing with Craig but right now anyone with a cough could be accused of having this virus. We're all being watched."

"I bet that zombie wench out there will agree with me." Matt knew his comment would get a reaction.

"If you're referring to Claire, you are seriously demented. That twisted psycho is the reason we're all suspicious of each other."

As if summoning the devil herself, the door to the storeroom swung open as Claire stood in the doorway. "Now, that's not very nice, is it?"

The moment she started talking, Grace felt cold, as if her very being had iced over.

"What are you even doing in here?" Grace was losing more patience with this woman every time they had an encounter.

"I'm making sure these good people aren't in danger which is more than can be said for you conspirers." Grace tensed at her words as Claire continued. "You make me laugh. You might have been the supervisor here but that doesn't mean you get to make the life or death decisions for the rest of us."

Claire's voice was unsettlingly calm and eerie. Grace could see in her eyes that she truly believed she was built for this type of scenario, that she could actually prosper in one.

"I don't make the decisions for anyone." Grace stood her ground. "There is no danger inside this building except the ones that you are concocting in that disturbed little head of yours. You're the danger in here, no one else."

"You think I'm dangerous?" Claire's laugh was unexpected and startled Grace. The expression that followed it however was far more harrowing. "You have no idea how dangerous I am."

Grace held her disturbing stare. "I think I might."

Claire held the door open. "You're hiding information from us. It's a fact. And, you know what they say, the truth will always out. One way or another, it never stays hidden."

Grace met Claire in the doorway and snarled through gritted teeth, "Do me a favour, Claire. Return to the hole you crawled out of and try to have a bit more faith in humanity. We're not all monsters like you and, believe it or not, I will actually do anything to protect these people, all of them."

Claire's face was ruled by her devious grin as she slowly made her exit back into the hall leaving her parting words of wisdom as she went. "I have every faith in humanity, you stupid bitch. When an animal is cornered, it's forced to attack. Humans are no different."

5:28 pm

Craig had been asleep for a while and Sophie was getting hungry. Now that she didn't have to condone herself to the torment of being sociable whenever she wanted something to eat, she felt a lot more at ease. She was also quite curious as to why Craig had snapped at her about going into the cellar in the first place. Normally, her curiosity could be pushed aside following Craig's threats, but her hunger was overpowering and she needed to eat.

She checked on him once more before venturing into the cold room and entered quickly and quietly still. She grabbed a bread roll, some butter portions and a few slices of ham before turning to make her hasty exit. As she moved towards the door, the corner of her cardigan got caught on a beer bottle top and as she neared the door, the hijacked bottle followed her, smashing to the ground behind her. She jumped at the sudden noise and cursed herself for being so careless. If she didn't clean the mess up, Craig would know she had been in there, for sure, assuming he hadn't been woken up by the noise.

She placed her lunch items on top of a nearby keg and knelt down to gather the pieces of broken glass from the cellar floor. She stared at the brown liquid now marking the concrete like a beacon displaying her treachery. She grabbed a dish cloth and began furiously mopping up the excess beer in a hope that the remains would dry before Craig awoke.

She reached over to the outskirts of the puddle and noticed that the colour was darker over by the empty kegs. The pale brown liquid had mixed with a darker substance and had turned almost black. Sophie continued to soak up the mess with her dish cloth following the darker substance to its point of origin. She crawled towards it on her hands and knees, blotting the liquid as she went. Moments later, she wished she hadn't.

Sophie placed a shaking hand over her mouth as her eyes turned to pools of remorse. Her lip was quivering as she uncovered the body. Her entire body tensed. She dropped to one side as her legs failed to support her.

It was impossible to tell how long she had been staring at the child, but she was awoken from her trance when she remembered she had stopped breathing. Panicking, she lost her balance and hit the concrete floor hard. Once again, she came face to face with the nameless child. The distance between them was barely a metre but she wanted to stroke his hair, take him in her arms and cradle him. Her fear stopped her. His body was broken, in so many ways. He didn't look real. She wanted to convince herself that he wasn't real. He was a child's lost ragdoll: misused and over loved. Sophie crumbled. She found herself whispering to the boy, "Poor baby."

She whispered the words over and over again, as she stroked his fragile little head.

She didn't hear Craig enter the room from behind her.

"I told you not to come down here." His voice sent chills down her spine as she realised his tone conveyed disappointment but there was no guilt. She stood up and turned to face him. The cold air in the cellar acted like an icy blanket, aiding the goose bumps she could feel rising over her entire body, but Sophie didn't flinch. His intimidating stature no longer mattered to her. Her fear had vanished as soon as she had laid eyes on the boy.

"What did you do?" Her voice was quiet but it was laced with resentment. The concrete room was silent except for her strained breathing. A while passed and he hadn't answered so she repeated her question, this time with more intent.

"What did you do, Craig?" she screamed at him. Her words forced her to acknowledge the child's death. She felt a rush of emotions surge through her, viciously led by anger. Without warning, she launched herself full force towards Craig, throwing punches from all angles. He fell backwards against the door frame and quickly attempted to cover her mouth with one hand whilst blocking her attack with the other. Normally, this would've been an easy task, but her strength was fuelled by an inner maternal nature that had been suffocated for so long. Craig struggled to maintain his balance as she tried to force him away from her. His hand cupped her mouth and muffled her frantic screams, but she wasn't tiring.

"Sophie, I'm sorry." He tightened his grip and as he did so, Sophie bit down hard on his hand causing him to push her with all his might into a metal cabinet. She caught her head on the corner and lost her footing momentarily. Her vision blurred and there was an immense ringing inside her head. She tried to focus on the blue door across the room, but the taste of his blood was making her feel nauseous and faint. She put her hand to her now throbbing head and waited for her vision to adjust. Everything seemed to be moving in slow motion now. Craig's face remained a distorted picture and, as he came towards her, she used her last ounce of lingering strength to push past him and slam the door behind her, trying her hardest to maintain her steady course despite her impaired state.

Craig stood frozen staring at the metal cabinet where Sophie had landed. This was it; he couldn't stop her. She was going to tell everyone what he had done, reveal him as the monster he really was. She had never blamed him for their daughter's death, she'd never blamed him for the way he'd chosen to deal with it. She hadn't even blamed him whenever he'd beaten her black and blue, but this was different. He had murdered a child, a small, defenceless human being. He'd never seen her fight back. This had triggered something inside her and he hated himself for it. He struggled against the pitiful tears as he braced himself for what was about to happen. The villagers would soon be wielding their pitchforks, demanding he be burned at the stake and he was ready to accept his punishment. He was ready for them.

Sophie made it to the corridor and lost her footing just beside their belongings. Fumbling for her makeshift bedding, she curled up into the foetal position and held her hand to her head. She could feel the warmth seeping from her wound and as she pulled her hand away to inspect it, her vision ceased along with her strength. Her head felt heavy and just as her head hit the cushion, everything went dark.

7:16 pm

At dinner, Matt was feeling secluded and had lost his appetite so he made his way to the disabled toilet. He splashed his face with cold water and began reasoning with himself. He believed that he had reacted the right way. Darius had confided in him that he wasn't feeling himself and the entire hall had witnessed both his violent outburst with Craig and another one after speaking with Sophie. Both acts were completely out of character for his friend.

Matt had tried to talk to him, tried to calm him down but Darius was raging. There was no getting through to him. Matt was concerned initially when it was just the feverish symptoms but to make matters worse, Darius had now had an 'altercation' with the possibly infected woman who may or may not have bitten him. Matt was at a loss for words or explanations, so he retreated back to the hall where he was stopped abruptly by the witch hunter herself.

Claire pushed him firmly backwards into the shadows. "What's going on, Matt?"

Matt could see her moving awkwardly and assumed it must be her way of using her femininity as a form of coaxing out information.

"Nothing." Matt spoke but the word sounded like a lie to his own ears. He was fooling no one.

Claire moved forward slightly. "You don't even sound like you believe that yourself. You know what I've been saying is true. The infection is in here with us and we need to do everything within our power to survive it."

Matt knew in his heart that that was the only thing that mattered to him right now. He needed to survive until those doors opened so that he could finally get to Ashley and the kids. He hadn't thought about anything else since he'd been in there and Claire could see she was hitting a nerve. To drive it home, she added, "Matt, we've all got loved ones out there who depend on us. If someone in here is a potential threat, don't we all have a right to know about it and make a decision as a group?"

Matt shook his head at the prospect of betraying his friend's trust, but he needed to look at the bigger picture in this situation and he hoped sincerely that Darius would understand. "What kind of decision?"

"Well, he just needs to be quarantined…for our protection. If he is infected, we're out of harm's way. If he's not, then the worst thing that happened was he spent the last couple of days in a separate room to everyone else."

There was a brief guilty pause from Matt before the words stung as they came out of his mouth. "I think Darius is infected… Maybe even from before he got bitten."

Claire let her excitement briefly escape her lips. This was perfect but she needed facts.

Plastering on a sympathetic expression, Claire put a comforting arm around Matt's shoulders and whispered, "Tell me everything."

8:10 pm

Once everyone had finished eating, Kristie decided to go and check on Jean. She'd been asleep for a good few hours and Kristie didn't want her to go without food especially when her medication was due soon. She washed up her plate whilst thinking that it was quite lucky that no one was coming to collect the crockery and cutlery until Tuesday, otherwise they would've been eating off of the back of the bingo boards. The day after a bingo hall closed, the vultures from the company's neighbouring clubs would come and gather up whatever they needed for their own clubs and thanks to Michael's incompetence in over ordering of their food, the staff members were told to take the food home with them and it would have to be recorded as wastage. She chuckled to herself. She guessed that everything really did happen for a reason. She dried her hands on some kitchen roll and made her way out of the diner towards Jean. She deliberately made no eye contact with Queen Freak and her weirdos. She'd already seen Claire corner Matt earlier that evening and didn't want to give them any sort of impression that she was as easily intimidated. She may come across as being ditsy and vulnerable, but Kristie was fiercely loyal and an extremely good judge of character. She had always been wary of Matt and had disliked Claire from the first time she had spoken. It actually worried her that Claire's foursome had now turned into a cluster of eight.

As she approached her trusted work colleagues, she smiled at how old habits die hard. Grace had found a pack of cards from reception and was playing poker with Winston, Darius, Charlie and his rude friend. Winston called to her as she passed them.

"Hey, girl. Come on. Do you want us to deal you in?"

"In a bit. I just want to make sure that Jean eats something."

In the two years she had worked with them, they really had made her feel like a part of their little family. Most of the customers were just as welcoming. Of course, you had the odd few who were never satisfied and always had

142

something to moan about, but the majority were lovely and, if she was honest, Jean was definitely one of her favourites.

She kneeled down next to the old lady she had grown to love and thought of how peaceful she looked whilst asleep. Normally, her face was a tapestry of worry for everyone around her. Kristie rested her hand on top of Jean's and began shaking her gently.

"Jean, would you like some dinner?"

When she didn't respond, Kristie stopped and stared at the woman lying in front of her. She sat completely still as her eyes filled with tears. Her lip trembled as she muttered Jean's name once more. She held her breath as she leaned in towards Jean's unresponsive body, listening desperately for her breath. She strained with her ear pressed against Jean's face for what seemed like hours before sitting back on her heels, hands over her mouth letting a heavyhearted sob escape involuntarily. She began breathing rapidly trying to regain her calm. She would have to tell the others.

As she took a deep breath, she tilted her head to one side. Jean really did look peaceful. Kristie placed a careful hand at the top of Jean's delicate head and stroked her hair ever so slightly.

"Sweet dreams, Jean."

*****

The card game had taken a competitive turn as the players were now staking anything they could get their hands on: straws, milk pots and even some salt and pepper sachets. Grace and Charlie had folded, leaving Winston trying to bluff his way out of two pairs while Serhan was fronting an absurd amount of confidence for his hand, too. The tension was running high and the spectators awaited the final reveal. As the boys showed their cards, Serhan responded with shock followed quickly by an uncharacteristic victory dance.

The celebration was halted immediately upon looking at Kristie's face. She stood in front of the group looking like a china doll with a sullen expression.

"Kristie?" Grace was afraid to speak too loudly in case her spoken words might derail her colleague.

"What's up?" Winston draped his arm across her shoulders in an act of protective, joviality.

She looked Grace straight in the eye and clearly stated.

143

"Jean's dead."

Darius sat up, joining the dreadful conversation.

Grace's hands reached up to her mouth in shock as she gasped. Darius just stared at Kristie, his mind racing to process this unexpected devastation.

Winston turned Kristie around to face him. "Are you serious?"

Kristie nodded and burst into tears as Winston pulled her in to his broad chest.

Charlie rested his head in his hands, dreading the unnecessary uproar this poor woman's death could cause in the hall.

"How?" Grace managed.

"I don't know. She wasn't feeling herself, so she went for a lie down a few hours ago," Kristie blubbered.

Grace rose to her feet with outstretched arms to embrace the crying teen. "Oh my God," she whispered under her breath as she consoled her friend.

Charlie disrupted the moment with the query they all anticipated. "What are we going to tell everyone?"

Kristie broke away from Grace's hold wearing a look of confusion. "What do you mean? What is there to tell them? She's dead. She died. She went to sleep and she flipping died. That's it."

The group exchanged the same worried glances that Charlie had referred to, but Kristie was having none of it. "I don't see how that's so hard to grasp. It wasn't a virus or an infected person, she was an old lady who died in her sleep."

Grace spoke to her in a hushed voice. "We know that, sweetheart. Charlie's just worried about how the others will take it. You've seen them over there."

Darius sided with Grace. "That woman's following is growing larger by the day. She's already put her own spin on what happened with me and Vickey."

"We have nothing to hide. Jean's death was natural and I won't have her disgracing it and making it something it's not. I'll tell them myself," Kristie decided. She marched over to the space between the other groups. Her sights were fixed firmly on Claire who always seemed to be in the centre of any gathering and Kristie was irritated by her very existence.

"I'm really sorry to tell you all this and to add to the drama of everything but Jean is dead. She died in her sleep. Before you turn it into something that it's not, she died of natural causes. There was nothing sinister about it. She just died," she stated, trying her hardest to hold herself together and not lose face in front of

Claire. Her announcement was met with a few gasps mixed in with some low murmurings, but Kim delivered the punch line that tipped Kristie over the edge.

"Who's Jean?"

Kristie saw red as Grace ran over to her, fearing her reaction to the insensitive question. Kristie launched herself at Kim as Winston intercepted. He could feel her body shaking with anger.

"How dare you!" she snarled at Kim. "Winston, let me go!" Her small frame was surprisingly strong when it was fuelled by so much rage and Winston had to re-evaluate his grip.

"Not going to happen, baby girl. Don't stoop to her level. You're better than that."

Despite the hypnotic tone of his voice, Kristie was an animal. "You ugly little bitch, how dare you come in here and disrespect her! She died because of you fucking pricks, making everyone more scared than they needed to be. You make me sick. She was a harmless, old lady and you fucking scared her to death."

Winston lifted the flailing girl and carried her towards the other side of the hall, as Kristie became more and more irate. None of her colleagues had ever seen her like that. She was the quiet, innocent receptionist who offered everyone teas and coffees as they clocked in for work. This was new. Someone she cared about had actually died and not just anyone, a defenceless, caring woman who had thought the world of her. And she hadn't just died. She had been so scared for the safety of the people around her, exemplified by people like Claire.

Grace looked over at the guilty party and felt her own blood boil as Claire displayed that same smile that was present every time a little bit more of her unwitting master plan fell into place.

"You can wipe that smug grin off your face. She died in her sleep, nothing more to it." Grace turned to walk away as Claire delivered yet another sentence Grace never thought she would hear in real life.

"Still, we should burn the bodies, hers and the mothers."

When Claire's words provoked little to no reaction from her newer, larger assembly, Grace realised just how lost they really were. Her eyes filled with stubborn tears as she looked directly at Claire.

"…just to be on the safe side." Claire drove the final nail into the coffin with a sledgehammer and Grace feared that she was beginning to doubt everything she once believed about the sanctity of humanity.

Charlie stepped forward. "We'll *move* the bodies," he said definitively. "…into the arcade. We can barricade the doors."

Claire's eyes seemed to be tearing through him but he stood his ground. "We're not burning anyone."

9:17 pm

Darius and Charlie lifted Jean with surprising ease and carried her through the building under the watchful eyes of the hall's mourners and its vigilantes. Charlie's eyes met Serhan's as he provided no desire whatsoever to help them. They exchanged glances and Charlie could feel his friend slipping away from him. He always knew that Serhan's logical mind would dominate any morals or ethics he might possess. He just never expected it to be put to the test. As he passed Serhan, Charlie thought about all of the times he had come to his friend's defence, all the times he was being bullied for his unique take on the world. Charlie briefly wondered if it had all been worth it.

Kristie and Grace held each other as they cried silently, watching Jean's floating body being guided towards the space outside their solitude. Following closely behind was Winston carrying Vickey's body, carefully wrapped, to the same locale. He cradled her like a child and sniffed away any rogue tears that threatened to escape his eyes. Rosie watched from the doorway of the office as her sister was banished away. Never before had she felt more alone. She allowed herself to reminisce over their many fond memories and felt a remnant of a smile appear temporarily only to be wiped away when she caught sight of Kathryn watching too, from a neighbouring doorway. She held her gaze for no more than a couple of seconds, then turned away.

Matt felt a twinge of remorse watching the fallen being escorted to the arcade. He fleetingly considered whether he had chosen the right side after watching his friends mourn the people they had lost but he knew he must stay the course. He believed in his reasons for following Claire and he had to concentrate on the bigger picture: the greater good.

The atmosphere in the hall was bleak and raw. Claire's group stood by emotionless as the grieving residents said their goodbyes before securing the doors with chairs, couches and tables. All was silent and eery for a long while before the hall's occupants went back to their artificial bunks. Nobody spoke.

Nobody made a sound. Everyone laid their heads down and feared what the following day would bring.

11:19 pm

It was dark again. Dark but this time, he was freezing. Freezing and moving. The surface beneath him was moving, rocking. He was in the middle of the ocean, floating on a raft. He was completely alone and terrified.

"Soph! Sophie!" he kept shouting, calling her name, listening to the waves carrying his voice back to him.

"Sophie, please come back. Where are you?"

He began to cry. It was happening again. When was he going to wake up? He knew he was dreaming, he just needed to wait it out, let it play out. He closed his eyes, but the imagery was still there, glued to his closed eye lids. He was going to have to see it through. He strained his eyes in order to make out any of his surroundings but there was nothing as far as he could see.

He'd been floating for what seemed to be an eternity before he caught a faint glimpse of a solitary light in the distance, amongst the infinite darkness. He began paddling towards it, being drawn to its comfort.

He felt weak as he used his arms as oars to get to this light. After a while, he collapsed onto the raft expelling any excess energy with every breath. As he lay, drifting into the abyss he heard the faintest sound floating in his direction. It was her, calling to him like a haunting memory reaching through the infinite threat to console him, to lead him. He could hear her voice, like a melody amongst the silent, salty air. As the light came into focus, he could see it was attached to a majestic lighthouse. He could make out the sheer size of its silhouette.

Then he heard the voice again. It was his Sophie, calling to him like a siren across the wind. In an act of desperation, he launched his frail body into the black water. He would swim to her. Her voice travelled through the air and drew him towards the lighthouse.

He'd been swimming for hours it seemed but the rocks at the base of the beacon would soon be in reach. He started treading water, trying to catch his breath. When he felt the hand, it closed around his ankle and pulled him under.

He fought against it, attempting to keep his head above water. The hand was clenched firmly around his bony ankle, pulling him towards a deep watery end. He began splashing, calling out for Sophie once more but every time his head surfaced, he could see the lighthouse moving further and further away. With one final kick, he managed to break free of the grip from beneath. He felt his body deflate when the lighthouse was nowhere to be seen. He called her name over and over again but there was no answer. Her voice had vanished along with the guiding light.

He woke up drenched in his own sweat. His fever had finally broken, he was over the worst of it. He breathed deeply, calming his erratic heartbeat. He turned over to raise Sophie, stroking her hair gently, whispering to her.

"Soph, I had another dream. You were slipping further and further away from me. Soph?"

Sophie rolled over to face him and smiled sweetly. "I would never leave you, my darling."

"But it was so real. I was on a raft and I could hear your voice, but you kept drifting away. It was so real."

She sat up, touching his face softly with her hand. "You're being silly. That would never happen."

Craig looked into her loving eyes and took her hand in his. "I'm sorry about the little boy. I promise you I had no idea. I thought he was a fox…"

Sophie hushed him, placing her finger over his chapped, dry lips. "I know, my love. I've always known."

As she spoke, water began trickling from her ears and nose. Craig stared at her in disbelief. "What have you always known, Sophie?"

She smiled enthusiastically at him as though he had asked her a ridiculous question that shouldn't require an answer. "That you would kill that fox, sweetheart. The one that killed our baby, the one that killed our Isabelle."

Craig didn't understand what was happening. He looked around him and nothing was different. Everything was the same. It was the same hallway he had fallen asleep in. He rubbed his eyes initiating the soreness to return. "But it wasn't a fox, Sophie. It was a boy. Remember?"

She stared at him with bright, unfaltering eyes. She didn't blink once. The water continued to pour from her ears.

"Sophie? What's wrong with you? Where's this water coming from?"

She moved her hand to the back of her head and when she brought it back to inspect it, it was covered in blood. "Wow. You finally killed me."

Craig's body jolted awake. His breathing was frantic as his hand combed through Sophie's tangled mess of hair and dried blood. The wound was worse than she'd let on, but it seemed to have stopped bleeding now. He rolled her towards him and moved the hair from her face. She was frozen to touch. Her lips were blue and her skin was a ghostly grey. Her black hair made the bruising on her face even more defined as it draped across her eye, highlighting his ongoing mistakes.

He shook her rigid body, but she didn't stir. His eyes filled with tears as he processed what had happened. How long had she been like this? How long had she been sleeping? He held his head in his hands. Through the waterfall of tears, he never removed his gaze from her. He didn't know what to do. What would he do without her? She was his rock, the one who was always there for him, to put up with his shit. He had done this to her. This was his fault. He had killed the little boy in the cellar and now he had killed Sophie. He was losing it. He rolled her back and covered her cold body with his jacket before drying his eyes and cosying up behind her, holding her body close to his.

Wednesday, 17th April 2019
6:14 pm

Anna Seymour was waiting anxiously to be discharged from her thorough and horribly invasive six day stay at the Harlow General Hospital. She had been patient with all their blood tests, urine and stool samples, and she'd even cooperated when they had quarantined her and confiscated all of her personal belongings. But enough was enough. She had been in there for six long, draining days and neither the doctors nor the specialists had found anything except a slightly high blood pressure and a mild case of eczema. Her patience had well and truly run out.

As she sat on the edge of the bed, she peered out of the curtain at the other two patients who were due to be discharged that day. The man, Adam Warner, was in his mid-thirties and was not happy with the situation at all. In fact, he'd done nothing but complain and moan about it his entire stay which seemed pointless to Anna. It didn't make the situation any less degrading or compulsory.

The other patient was a woman, Nancy Angelus, and was a lot more placid. She just sat back and let the doctors do their thing. She was in her late twenties and Anna didn't recall seeing her make any phone calls to family members explaining her whereabouts. Anna felt a pang of sympathy for the young woman since her own phone had been ringing nonstop from concerned parents, children, siblings and cousins. Everyone wanted to know how she was getting on and if the doctors had found anything yet.

Despite her calm attitude, Anna had been terrified for the majority of her time at the hospital. She had had to deal with the chance that she might never see any of her family again. She feared she would miss the moments that every parent looked forward to, watching her son graduate from university, shedding tears at her daughter's wedding, the birth of her first grandchild. She had never accepted that she might not be around to enjoy those moments. In all honesty, she had been praying to a God that she had neglected for years that she would. She was prepared to do anything if it increased her chances of making it through this, including returning to a religion that had once been forced upon her.

Apparently, her restored faith had rewarded her as it had been two days since the doctors had confirmed that she'd passed all of the required tests, yet she was still in there so now she was getting restless and rightly so.

Breaking her train of thought, the doctor on shift bustled through the dull blue curtain asking for her name and date of birth in a very robotic manner.

So, she replied just as monotonously as he had asked, "Anna Jane Seymour. 17th of November 1970."

The doctor checked his papers without acknowledging her mocking tone and murmured to himself.

"So, we're sending you home today?" He kept his eyes glued to her chart.

"Not a moment too soon." Anna smiled politely.

"Of course, I understand this must've been quite traumatic for you." He reached inside his pocket and pulled out a leaflet as if he had rehearsed this part to no end. "If you need to talk to anyone about your experience, there is a number you can call."

Anna took it from him, unconvinced that he cared, even in the slightest. "Okay, thanks."

"But you do understand why we had to be so thorough, yes?" Only then did he make eye contact.

"Yes, I understand. I'm just happy it's all over and I can go home."

"Of course," the doctor paused and then added, "Take care, Ms Seymour. The nurse will bring you in your things soon and once you've signed a few forms, you'll be free to go."

"Thank you, Doctor Eastwick," she said, as he hastily exited the cubicle.

Anna breathed a sigh of relief and wondered how long it would take for the nurse to make an appearance. She laid back on to the bed resting her head on the pillow as she closed her eyes, momentarily, to the room she had known as home for the past six days.

It had been about five minutes when the curtain was swiftly drawn to one side, forcing Anna's eyes open.

"Right, let's get you on your way, shall we?" The nurse entered the bay ticking things off of her clipboard as she walked.

"Slightly elevated blood pressure and a minor case of eczema?"

"Yes. That's all they found," Anna said, weirdly proud of her newly discovered ailments.

The nurse smiled briskly and continued filling in the discharge form. "There's a prescription here for medication for both of those. If I can just get a signature from you, you'll be free to go."

She handed the clipboard and the pen to Anna who took them keenly, scribbling her autograph on the dotted line. As she handed the pen back to the nurse, she caught sight of a tattoo on the nurse's forearm. It was an unmistakeable symbol: the biohazard sign.

"That's an interesting choice of tattoo," Anna commented.

The nurse smiled as if she had received the same reaction a dozen times before. "Yeah, some people think it's inappropriate in my line of work especially at times like this but I think it's actually rather relevant."

Anna couldn't help but admire the nurse's sordid sense of humour. "I suppose it is."

"Have a safe journey home, Ms Seymour."

"Thank you."

Outside the hospital, Anna was greeted by her brother, Scott. He lifted her off of the floor with a big bear hug and then made a joke about leaving his protective mask in the car to which Anna responded with a playful punch to the arm.

The car ride home was filled with intrusive questions and probing queries but as Anna explained for the fourth time, they hadn't told her anything about the other patients or the state of emergency which was much to her brother's disappointment.

On her arrival, she was welcomed by what appeared to be her entire family tree. She enjoyed being a part of a close-knit family but all she wanted to do right now was have a shower, throw on her pyjamas and rest up in front of the television but she smiled politely none the less.

After enduring hours of the same questions, Anna got ready for bed feeling like some sort of celebrity. She turned off the lights and cosied up in bed after what seemed like the longest day ever. She pulled the clean duvet up under her chin and let her head sink into the duck down pillow. The room was partially lit by the streetlamp outside her window, casting shadows across the silent room.

In the distance, she could hear an ambulance siren further on down the road and she felt strangely at ease with all the background noise.

She closed her eyes and prepared herself for a good night's sleep. It was then that she heard it, a floorboard creak.

By the time she'd opened her eyes, it was too late. A hand covered her mouth and she felt a sharp prick in her neck. In one swift movement, the hand that had been over her mouth worked down to her side. Her arms were then pinned down by her attacker and in spite of her survival instincts, she failed to overpower them. She tried to scream for help but no sound escaped her lips. She struggled for only a moment or so before losing control of her limbs and movement. As the dark room grew blacker around her, she could just about make out her attacker's face. Within a few moments, she had lost consciousness and her struggle for breath became a defeat.

The woman left the house throwing the syringe into a nearby wheelie bin. She removed her surgical gloves and threw them in after the syringe. Across the road were three silhouettes waiting for her. As she drew closer, a female voice asked, "Is it done?"

"Yea, give me something more challenging next time."

"Well, that's the first. Three were released today from Harlow General. The team in Cambridge already got the three released from their local hospital on Monday. Now it's our turn. So, who's up next?"

One of the men stepped forward. "I'll go next. Who have we got?"

"A Mr Warner, five streets away. Let's go."

She pulled her hood over her head revealing the tattoo on her forearm.

"So cool," the man commented.

The woman smirked. "I think it's relevant."

Friday, 19th April 2019
8:22 am

"Mum, can I have this?"

A blonde-haired doll dressed in a glamorous red ball gown was thrust into a mother's face as she fanned herself with a recently acquired magazine on home furnishings. Vickey Gardner sighed loudly and stopped fanning.

"No, True. You've got loads of dolls at home." The heat was starting to get to her. Clearly the shop had forgotten to activate their air conditioning in the urgency to open their doors to all the rushing shoppers.

"But this one's beautiful. Look at her dress."

"True, I said no. Put it back." At that moment, a heavyset man dumped a basket full of energy drinks and snacks onto the conveyor in front of them. Vickey lost her cool. "Excuse me we're standing here for a reason. There's a queue!"

The man shot her a disgruntled look and begrudgingly joined the end of the queue as the child thought she would try her luck once more.

"But, Mum, I've been really good today and…"

Having made her obvious lack of energy well known, Vickey summoned her last ounce of patience and shot True a look that warned her instantly to back off. Sadly, she took the hint and returned the doll to the nearby shelf.

They were shortly joined by Vickey's younger sister, Rosie. "My God, it is mayhem in here today. People are going crazy. I just saw two women fighting over the last pack of tampons." She loaded up the trolley with six big bottles of water as Vickey shot her sister the very same look she had just aimed at her daughter.

"What?" Rosie asked, shrugging.

Vickey was losing the will to argue. "We're supposed to be buying essentials."

"Is water not essential?" Rosie had not lost the will to argue. She thought this whole scare was ridiculous and unnecessary.

"You can get water from a tap..." Vickey's voice trailed off. She was officially done arguing.

True brushed up against her aunt wearing an exaggerated sad expression which her mother chose not to encourage. Rosie, on the other hand, indulged the little girl playfully, "Cheer up, Truie. Don't be sad, little one. We'll be going home soon."

Vickey paid for their items, loaded them into bags and left the store in search of her car. Rosie had True by the hand as she looked both ways before crossing the car park. The parking spaces had filled up significantly since they'd been inside and Vickey shook her head and marvelled at how easily manipulated the public could be. She tightened her grip on the filled carrier bags and followed her sister and daughter across the car park.

She stopped dead in her tracks when she heard a window smash not far behind her. As she turned quickly to inspect the noise, she saw a group of people throwing objects through car windows and at nearby shoppers. She didn't hesitate. She let go of her bags, turned back to Rosie and screamed at the top of her voice.

"RUN!"

Sunday, 21st April 2019
9:18 am

Rosie awoke in a sweaty panic as she gasped for air and tried to focus on her surroundings, remembering the awful events that had occurred not even a day ago. The atmosphere in the hall that morning was no different than when they had gone to sleep the night before. There was a thick cloud lingering over the residents as they milled about in neutral phases, still unable to make sense of the previous days' tragedies. Still, Rosie was thankful that they hadn't had to spend another night in that office. The hall shared her pain, but it felt comforting to know that she wasn't so secluded.

Kristie was one of the first people to awake that morning. She sat staring at the ceiling for so long she actually wondered if she had fallen asleep with her eyes open. She wanted to say she was thinking about everything that had happened but that would've been a lie. In truth, she was just aimlessly staring at the ceiling, not feeling and not thinking. She was just staring.

Out of nowhere, a thought crossed her mind. She hadn't had time to say goodbye to Jean and she was betting that Rosie needed that closure too for her sister's death. This made perfect sense.

She bolted upright and crawled over to where Grace was sleeping and nudged her, like an oddly excited child.

"Grace, wake up," she nudged.

Grace awoke, startled. "Kristie? What is it? Is everyone all right?"

"Yeah, yeah, everyone's fine. But I just had an idea." Kristie's animated state made Grace feel quite uneasy.

"Okay. What is it?" Grace enquired, rubbing her eyes.

"We should have a funeral for Jean and Rosie's sister. It'll give people a chance to say goodbye and it might lift people's spirits a bit."

"You think a funeral is going to lift peoples' spirits?" Grace knew there was logic in her point, and she couldn't bear to break the girls' heart even further. "Sure. We can do that."

"I think that's a great idea." Winston rolled over and faced the two women.

Grace yawned. "Let me know what time you're thinking of doing it and we can let people know."

Kristie smiled half-heartedly and bounced off to spread the news.

Darius sat up and stretched. "Someone should tell Sophie."

"I'll do it," volunteered Grace.

"No, Grace. I appreciate you trying to keep the peace, but I have to apologise for the way I acted yesterday. It'll be all right."

"What if Craig's there?"

"I'm not going to do anything. Sophie's made her decision. I just want to tell her about Jean. I promise that nothing will happen."

"Okay, just don't let him get to you."

"Cross my heart."

Grace kept a watchful eye on him as he made his way across the hall towards the isolated corridor.

Darius hesitated slightly before tapping on the double doors. He waited a few seconds, then tapped again. On the other side of the door, Craig's heart jumped into his throat as he scuttled about trying to cover up any sort of incriminating evidence.

When there was no response, Darius pushed the door open and whispered, "Sophie?"

Before he could get too far, the door was forced to a halt by Craig.

"Can I help you?"

Darius took a palliative breath and released pressure from the door.

"Sorry. I was just looking for Sophie."

Craig looked behind him, then back at Darius.

"She's sleeping."

"Oh okay. It's really important. Something's happened and I think she would want to know about it."

Craig interrupted, "Oh, you know what she'd want, do you?"

Darius could feel his fists clench and Craig noticed his change in demeanour.

"Look, she's not been sleeping at night so just let her sleep it out, ay? I'll let her know you were looking for her when she wakes up."

Darius eased up marginally. "Yeah, thanks."

He left as quickly as he had approached and Grace let out the breath she had been holding since Craig had answered the door. She had no idea of what had been said but no punches had been thrown which she counted as a win.

Her moment of relaxation was swiftly dominated by an overpowering feeling of misery as she endeavoured to plan a double funeral.

2:00 pm

"Thank you everyone for attending. We find ourselves in a horrible time where we are forced to question everything we've heard, everything we've seen and everything we believe. Amongst the confusion and terror that has surrounded us these last two days, there have been moments, albeit fleeting and few, but moments, none the less, where we are reminded of who we were before the attack.

"Jean Saunders was a humanitarian. She loved people. She loved talking to them, listening to their stories, relating to them. She loved company. She never judged or had a narrowminded opinion. She believed in people coming through for each other, defending one another. She believed that humanity would always win.

"It very well may have been Jean's time to go but I, for one, am glad that she was with people who loved her instead of being alone at home.

"We will miss you, Jean. You meant so much to us all and you never failed to put a smile on our faces or make the world a brighter place."

Grace bowed her head along with the other attendees and finished her eulogy.

"Goodbye, Jean."

She motioned to Rosie to stand and say a few words about her sister. To look at, Rosie appeared to be keeping it together exceedingly but as soon as she began to speak, her façade was ruptured.

"None of you knew Vickey but if you had, you would've liked her. She was a lot like you, Grace. She wasn't scared to take charge. She wasn't scared of anything. My big sister was never scared." Rosie wiped the tears aggressively from her cheeks. "She didn't deserve to die the way she did. She didn't deserve any of it…"

The tears made it impossible for Rosie to continue so she sat back down. Wiping at her eyes with a tissue in her hand, she caught sight of Kathryn hovering in a doorway across the hall. She held Kathryn's sorrowful stare for a moment and then looked away. Kathryn felt her heart shatter into a million pieces as she closed the door behind her.

2:34 pm

After the service, Darius seethed at the absence of Sophie. He knew she would've had the decency to make an appearance if she had known. That bastard Craig must not have passed on the message. He was fuming. She would be devastated that she'd been denied the chance to say goodbye to Jean.

He was on his way to give Craig a piece of his mind when he was stopped abruptly by a tiny figure. True was sat in the middle of the aisle playing with a bingo board and talking to herself. He almost went flying over the top of her.

"Little one, what are you doing down there?"

True looked up at the giant with a grief-stricken face. "…just playing."

"Just playing? I almost squashed you, sweetheart." Darius knelt down beside True and ruffled her hair. It was a strange feeling, but this little girl had become so important to them, so many of them were willing to protect her. She was a symbol of innocence in a drastically demonised world.

"What are you playing anyway?"

"…just a game. I wanted Henry to join in, but I can't find him."

Darius looked confused. "Who's Henry, True?"

True looked up at Darius as if she was fed up of having to explain about her orange-haired friend. "He's the little boy. I saw him when we first came here but then he ran away and I lost him. He's all alone and I don't want him to be scared."

"No, of course not," Darius sympathised. "Have you spoken to him?"

"No. I waved at him though, but he didn't wave back. He was hiding from everyone."

"Why was he hiding?"

"He was just scared," True said in a frustrated tone.

Darius sensed that she had had the same conversation before, but he was intrigued none the less. He was well aware that kids had imaginary friends or exaggerated the truth, but what if another child had gotten inside the building and because True was the only one who had seen him, everyone else was fobbing

163

it off as her imagination? It was possible. He could've been separated from his parents in the commotion and he could very well have been too scared to reveal himself when everyone was panicked at the beginning. It wouldn't have gotten any easier with all the arguments that had been going on and now two people had died. The little guy would be terrified. Darius just couldn't get his head around the fact that nobody else had seen him. That was odd. And, what had he been eating?

Darius figured it wouldn't hurt to do a sweep of the building, having a look in all the nooks and crannies. It would give him something productive to do even if it was a wild goose chase. He needed to kill some time and to clear his head.

"I tell you what True, I'm going to have a look for Henry. If I find him, you can help me to look after him, is that okay?"

True nodded enthusiastically.

"Okay, kid. I'll see what I can do."

Her smile melted Darius' heart and he was determined to find this kid…if he did actually exist.

Just as Darius got to his feet, he noticed the doors leading to the cellar opened slightly. Craig stumbled into the hall looking even more dishevelled than normal and made his way to the toilet. Darius felt an undeniable fear that something wasn't right. He hated the way he had left things with Sophie and he hadn't spoken to anyone about it since then. He wanted to speak to Sophie. After all, she was the reason he went to work every morning. That was why he couldn't just watch Craig treat her like shit. He couldn't allow that to happen in front of him or behind closed doors and he needed to let her know that she deserved better than that. No, Darius did not regret his words or his actions. He didn't regret kissing Sophie and he certainly didn't regret hitting Craig. Nevertheless, he needed to fix things with Sophie. It couldn't be left like this between them. Whilst Craig was indisposed, he saw his opportunity.

Darius had prayed for a distraction from his ever-building anger towards Craig and True had given him a justifiable one, but he couldn't stop himself from walking towards the cellar doors.

He just needed to talk to Sophie before Craig got back. She needed to know about Jean and that arsehole had obviously not passed on his message.

He walked cautiously past the disabled toilet and could hear Craig vomiting. He could be in there a while, but he gained speed anyway as he headed for the double doors.

2:44 pm

Darius didn't even bother knocking before entering in fear of losing time before Craig returned. He opened the door cautiously in case Sophie was getting undressed, but he quickly saw that she was still asleep. She must really be ill to be in bed at this time.

He whispered her name and got no response but as he got closer and she didn't budge, Darius felt a wave of dread flood over him. Something didn't feel right. He said her name louder but still there was nothing. He stopped in his tracks, afraid of what he was about to discover. He got onto his knees and placed a shaking hand onto Sophie's shoulder, moving her gently at first, then more aggressively and when she still didn't stir, Darius froze.

He braced himself and reached for the blanket covering Sophie's neck and shoulders. He pulled it away to reveal the dried mask of blood that had soaked into her clothes and matted her beautiful hair. He scampered back away from her as tears ran down his cheeks carelessly. He wanted to see her face one last time, but he couldn't force himself to move her. He imagined her looking peaceful and angelic, like she was just sleeping. But as he sat staring at her lifeless body, he then imagined how this could've happened, how terrified she must have been and how alone she must have felt. How long had she been like this? When was the last time anyone had seen her? It was him. He had seen her last and they had argued. He had shouted at her and probably made her feel like she had no one left to turn to.

He began imagining how Craig had done it. Had he just beaten her to death? Was it quick? Of course, it wasn't quick. No, she had suffered. She had suffered for as long as Darius had known her and everyone knew about it but nobody had done anything to help her. He tried to push the hideous thoughts from his mind but at that moment, the door swung open and Darius saw red.

Craig hadn't even noticed Darius until he was tackled to the floor. Darius was like a wild animal let loose and all he could see was Craig's face. He couldn't stop himself. His fists flew through the air towards the Devil's face with every ounce of strength he possessed. He felt bones shatter and skin split beneath his knuckles as blood stained his hands and clothes. One punch caused Craig's nose to explode again but Darius wasn't deterred. He was driven by anger, guilt and regret and he wanted Craig to feel everything he had ever made Sophie feel.

2:51 pm

Grace had seen Darius making his way over to the corridor and had decided it was best to stay close in case things went south again. Claire would already be fully aware of Darius' whereabouts for the exact same reason.

She made her way slowly towards the double doors and just as she passed the disabled toilets, she was almost knocked over when Craig too was heading towards her destination. Knowing that that could spell trouble, Grace regained her balance and picked up the pace as she watched Craig vanish behind the double doors. She pushed through into the corridor just in time to see Darius launch himself on top of Craig, maiming his face.

"Stop it, Darius! Get off of him!" Grace screamed at her friend and threw herself onto Darius' back hoping to put an end to it all, but Darius didn't budge. In his blind fury, he propelled Grace against the wall behind him.

She crashed to the ground and came face to face with Sophie. She didn't need to question what had happened. She knew then and sat back in shock as someone else entered the corridor.

"You fucking piece of shit!" Darius continued punching the pound up face that used to resemble Craig. He couldn't even feel bone anymore and his fists were covered in blood, a mixture of both of theirs.

Craig's head flopped loosely as Darius pulled him up for yet another punch. He drew his arm back ignoring Grace's sobs behind him. His fist made contact with Craig's face one final time knocking him onto the floor with a hefty thud. As Craig's broken skull hit the floor, Grace screamed, "No!"

Darius turned to face her and was caught off guard by a sharp impact to his throat. He looked Claire in the eyes as he attempted to contemplate what had just happened.

"I knew it." Claire pulled the broken bottle out of Darius' neck, releasing a furious red fountain behind it. Darius held his hand over the wound to contain the charging blood, but it was not enough. He could feel his pulse cascading through his fingers.

He tried to explain as he choked on his words. "He…killed… Sophie."

Darius lost his footing as Grace's cries got louder and the corridor began to blur.

Grace hurled herself at Claire. "What the hell have you done?"

Claire grabbed her by the throat and forced her up against the wall. "I just saved everyone, you ungrateful bitch. I did what you didn't have the balls to do."

Grace's knees buckled beneath her as she was held up by Claire's grip. "He wasn't infected."

Claire released her and made a noise filled with pure frustration. "How are you still denying it? He's dead now. He can't hurt anyone anymore."

"Sophie's dead," Grace screamed.

"He killed her, too? And you're still defending him?"

Grace couldn't make out whether Claire believed what she was saying or whether it was all a part of her plan to convince people she was right. "No, he found her and that's why he was attacking Craig. He wasn't infected."

Claire pulled Grace's face close to her own with her blood-soaked fingers. "And who do you think people will believe?"

Grace stared at the monster before her and muttered words unconvincingly. "They'll believe the truth."

"Will they?" Claire smiled sarcastically at the thought. "You're not so sure anymore, are you?"

Grace really wasn't. She knew Claire would stick to her guns but so would she, and as the rest of the hall began to pour through the doors, Claire began reeling off her story, as Grace sat frozen against the wall, crying over her two lost friends.

"Don't worry everyone. It's okay now. He's not a danger anymore." She feebly attempted to keep the crowd away from the view at the same time as strategically stepping aside for all to see. "He killed twice before I could stop him but at least Grace is safe."

Winston rushed to Grace's aid as he was followed by people who had inadvertently emptied their stomachs at the sight. Ignoring Claire's self-proclaimed heroism, Winston turned to Grace. "Are you all right? What happened?"

"No, she murdered Darius. Sophie was already dead before he got here. It must have been Craig. You have to believe me. He wasn't infected." Grace was difficult to understand through her sobs and Winston feared she was in a state of shock.

"I tried to stop him, but he was too strong and then she came in…"

"Yes, just as he threw you against the wall," Claire stated.

"He didn't mean it." Grace's words sounded weak in her own ears, but she knew the truth.

Claire looked at her peers proudly covered in Darius' blood. "It's clear that Grace cannot accept what actually happened here. She's obviously in shock."

The sea of faces looked on in horror at the massacre in front of them. Those who didn't know Grace had no reason to believe her or what she thought she had walked into. Even some who did know her were still unsure. One by one, the crowd lessened, taking with them a materialised version of events.

"I just want to point out that even though Darius is no longer a threat, there are still threats amongst us. Maybe now you'll start taking me seriously." Claire pushed through the double doors into the hall leaving everyone with the terrorising thoughts she had just created for them.

3:16 pm

Claire's words were a sharp reality check for everyone in the room whichever way they were interpreted. As she marched back into the hall, a crowd of confused and unsatisfied people followed her.

"What do you mean there are other threats? What threats?" Matt didn't know what to think or how to act. He had just seen his friend's blood covering the walls of the corridor and he knew it would be a long time before he would get that image out of his head. He didn't even wait for Claire to answer. He began pacing the floor with his hands on his face questioning whether he had been the cause of this. If he hadn't said anything to Claire, she might not have attacked him. But then if he was infected, isn't it a good thing that she was able to do what Grace couldn't?

Claire drew everyone's attention away from the spiralling Matt. "You all know what I'm talking about. It's not a secret. Darius was sick, the mother was sick and the little girl is sick. Anyone else see a pattern?"

"How do you know Vickey was sick? She was unconscious!" Charlie wasn't standing for her manipulative deceit.

"Forgive me but doesn't the fact that she was unconscious in the first place mean she was sick?" Lorraine had adopted Claire's way of thinking and Charlie's face dropped as more people nodded their sheepish heads in agreement.

"You can't be serious. You do realise that Sophie is dead, right?"

Claire spun around on her heels like some kind of fairy tale witch to face the group with dramatic flair.

"Exactly, how many more would he have killed if I hadn't done what I did? I mean, the druggy had it coming. He was showing signs of infection but his girlfriend... She wouldn't say boo to a goose. Did she deserve to die because we didn't take action sooner?"

Charlie looked at her in utter astonishment. He couldn't believe that mob mentality was this easy to orchestrate.

At that moment, Grace entered the hall. "Darius attacked Craig because he found Sophie's body. He found her; he didn't kill her." Grace fought back the tears and the whimper in her voice. "She was cold. She's been dead for a while."

"Do you really expect us to believe that? We all saw the argument they had," Kim goaded. "Wasn't he the last person to see her alive?"

Indistinct murmurings erupted in her ears as Grace yelled, "No, you fucking moron. Craig was!"

Kim held up her hands in surrender letting her accusations sow their oats.

"Darius wasn't infected," Grace shouted. "Claire murdered him and you're all lapping up every word she says. What is wrong with you all? She wants you to turn on a child, a child, for fuck's sake."

Winston grabbed Grace's waist as she confronted Kim and he was surprised to see how easy it was to lead her away. He figured the fight had just left her at this point. She was weak with devastation and grief.

Charlie, Kristie and Serhan followed Winston as he led Grace back to where Rosie and True were sitting under the radar, but Claire didn't let their departure silence her when she was clearly hitting home with so many.

"I did exactly what your blonde friend did. She saw a threat and she stepped up. You can dress it up any way you want but, when it comes to the crunch, its people like us who will protect the feeble and the ignorant."

Grace let Claire's venom course through her as she read the angst in Rosie's eyes. Claire paused to appreciate the impact of her words and pulled Kim to one side. "She's a problem."

Kim looked around her, confused. "Who? Grace? She's weak. No problem at all."

"Not her, the blonde one."

Kim's face drew a blank and Claire's blood began to boil at her ineptitude.

"She will do anything to protect that woman and the kid. If we're going to go forward with the plan, we need to even the playing field. There are already too many of them that won't let us near that kid."

Kim got the message loud and clear. "What do you want me to do?"

"Nothing," Claire said. "I'll handle this myself."

3:27 pm

Kristie excused herself from the moronic drivel that was pouring out of Claire's mouth. She couldn't take it anymore. She didn't want to listen to the complete lack of respect for the people who had died in the last 48 hours, people that she had known and loved and had partially considered family.

She wasn't feeling right either. Her head was hosting a marching band procession and she couldn't think straight. Her cheeks burned as she walked towards her things. She reached them just as the room began to spin slightly. No, she definitely didn't feel well and her finger was itching incessantly.

As she rubbed it against her clothing, she remembered what Serhan had said about the possibility of a wasp carrying the virus. She was almost certain he had been messing with her and Charlie had tried his best to support that theory, but she couldn't help but wonder if he had maybe been right.

She looked closely at the sting on her finger. It didn't look infected but then she didn't know what it was supposed to look like. She shook her head. Regardless of the state of her finger, she knew she couldn't let the others see her like this. If Claire thought she was ill, she might as well tie a noose for herself.

Kristie was suddenly terrified. On one hand, she could become infected and attack her remaining friends. On the other hand, she could confess to her illness and be attacked herself. She wasn't going to let either of those scenarios play out. She had to do something and she had to act fast.

She gathered up her personal belongings and headed for the double doors beside the stage. She tapped in the access code and pushed the door open. In the general office upstairs, there was a hatch that led to the loft. Few staff members were aware it was even there, but Tyrone had shown it to her a while back. Apparently, it was only him and the handy man who knew about it. She would be safe up there but more importantly; everyone would be safe from her if she locked herself up there.

She bundled into the open office and clambered with the hatch door. It was pretty stiff, but she managed to wriggle it open. She put her handbag strap over her head and pulled down the connected ladder.

As she mounted the first wrung, she caught a glimpse of a shadow in the corridor. She froze, not knowing whether or not she had been seen. She contemplated explaining the situation to whoever it was but decided against it. She suspected it was probably Kathryn who had far too much on her plate right now to even begin concerning herself with Kristie's dramas too.

She climbed the steps and hoisted herself up onto the ledge. She then carefully moved the ladder to its original closed position and shut the hatch, locking it from the inside.

She took a deep breath. Mitch (the handy man) rarely went up there, so the cobwebs were a work of art. Luckily, spiders didn't bother Kristie in the slightest and definitely not in comparison to the hoard downstairs hungry for more blood.

She laid her cardigan on the floor and fanned herself with her magazine. It was going to be a long twenty or so hours. The heat conducted by the metal roof made the loft space similar to a boiler room. At least she might be able to sweat out her fever. Failing that, she could always pray for rain.

3:32 pm

Kathryn heard the door close in the corridor and felt her body tense. She didn't want to speak to or see anyone but when the noise wasn't followed by an unwelcome visit, her curiosity got the better of her.

She wandered along the corridor quietly as she could hear heavy breathing and something metal being moved around. She didn't want to draw any attention to herself, but she was intrigued.

She figured it was probably Michael looking for a dark hole to hide away in but when she saw it was Kristie, she lost interest fast. At the risk of having to engage in a mindless conversation, Kathryn simply turned and walked away, leaving Kristie to her own devices.

As she retreated back into the solitary staff room, she passed a table with a newspaper on it. The headline read, "Angel of Death."

She had nothing more productive to do so she grabbed the paper and sunk onto the couch.

"Three people have been found dead following their earlier discharge from the Harlow General Hospital after being given the all clear to suspected contraction of the rabies virus. Although we do not have the victim's names at present, the local police officials have compared the deaths to those of Herbert Fairbrother (89) Patricia Bellis (64) and Angel Frost (16) who were found dead in their homes on Tuesday morning after being released from a hospital in Cambridge.

"Police are conducting a search for hospital staff member Alice Gunn after discovering patient personnel files had gone missing following her shift on Wednesday Evening. Miss Gunn worked with all three of the victims on the quarantine ward and also aided in their aftercare and eventual discharges.

"Police speculate that she may be involved in the murders of the recently released patients either directly or indirectly."

Kathryn studied the CCTV image printed in black and white on the front cover of the newspaper and her heart felt like it had just run a marathon. There was no mistaking it. The picture was as clear as day. She'd just told them all a fake name. Kathryn had to warn everyone. Claire had been absolutely right all along: there was a danger inside the building.

As she made her way to the corridor, she was stopped in her tracks when she heard the door to the stairway open. When Claire stepped through it, Kathryn couldn't move.

"What are you doing up here?" she asked through gritted teeth.

Claire glided through the corridor as if she owned the place which immediately put Kathryn on edge.

"I just followed your friend up here, young girl, very ditzy. She doesn't look too well." Claire's singsong voice resembled a sound straight out of a horror movie and it mocked Kathryn as she looked around the staff room for Kristie. "She left the door open so I'm guessing she was in a bit of a rush. You don't think she's ill, do you?"

Kathryn didn't take her eyes off of Claire. "I didn't realise how much you cared. It's touching." Kathryn avoided Claire's unsubtle hints that Kristie could be infected.

"I care about the safety of everyone in here. I always have and I'm willing to do whatever it takes to keep everyone alive." She stopped and held Kathryn's loathing gaze. "You know what I mean, don't you?"

Kathryn could feel her blood beginning to boil but there were more pressing matters that needed to be taken care of.

"I did what I had to do." She didn't want to get dragged into a heart to heart with Claire. There wasn't time. She needed to tell people the truth.

"Oh, I know and I've got to say that I was pretty impressed by the way you handled it."

Kathryn attempted to sidestep around the malignant woman standing before her but Claire was quicker.

"I mean, really, the way you showed no mercy whatsoever. You knew she was infected and you didn't hesitate for a moment."

Kathryn tried to calm her tone as she said, "Like I said, I thought they were in danger, so I did what I had to do."

Kathryn went to walk around Claire once more but was stopped again to her frustration as Claire leaned in close to her ear.

"I know. I admire your protective instincts." Claire's breathy whisper made Kathryn shudder. "It's a shame that that is exactly what's going to get you killed."

Before Kathryn could react to Claire's threatening statement, she felt Claire's fist slam into the side of her neck accompanied by a sharp jab. Kathryn was blindsided as the pressure increased momentarily down her throat and through her veins. She winced as the object was withdrawn.

Kathryn held her neck as Claire stood back. "What have you done to me?"

Claire watched as Kathryn's eye contact began to falter.

"I know you'd do anything to protect that woman and her niece. You've already proved it but that's where our priorities differ. You see, I see that child as a threat and the less people there are to protect her, the better. With you and the tattooed idiot out of the picture, we stand more of a chance at eradicating the danger."

Kathryn tried to regain focus but could feel her vision escaping her.

"You killed Darius," she stammered. "Just like those people…from the hospital."

"Oh, you know about that?" Claire was intrigued. "Now I understand why you were trying to leave in such a hurry." She laughed to herself. "And I thought it was just me. Well, I suppose it was."

Claire grabbed Kathryn's head and forced her to the floor. She took a hold of Kathryn's nose and forced her mouth shut. Kathryn struggled but could feel her strength dwindling away with each movement.

"I've only injected you with a sedative, so it won't kill you, but it does make it easier for me to kill you myself. You're bigger than me so I know you'd be able to hold your own if this was a fair fight. I can't have you getting away and you've already got the perfect motive for suicide."

As Kathryn's arms fell limp at her side, Claire placed an empty pill bottle in Kathryn's failing hand as her opponent lost consciousness.

"No one will know anything," Claire whispered as Kathryn's body started having compulsions. "Ssh, ssh, ssh, ssh. Don't worry. It'll all be over soon."

Claire stood in silence for a while just staring at the defeated woman at her feet. She took a deep breath and reached for the newspaper that Kathryn had been reading. She read the article briefly, then pushed it down the back of the fridge.

Wow. That was easier than I thought it would be. I guess killing the kid's mum really took it out of her. She seemed bigger before; stronger.

Oh well. She won't be an issue any longer. That's one less person to worry about converting. I mean, honestly, most of the people in here are just screaming out for a leader, a guide; just someone to tell them what to do next.

Controlling the masses is easy once they have something to be afraid of. They have no idea how that fear can be exploited once it's manifested.

Now that I've proved myself as a fearless champion, they will flock to my side in a desperate attempt to be saved from the horrors of the outside world and I'm ready for whatever it has to throw at me.

Once those doors open, we will step into the harsh light of day and it will be a moment of reckoning. The weak will be consumed, the gutless will be abandoned and the self-righteous will be outnumbered. Yes, we will have our moment in the sun.

This new world has a lot to offer those who are willing to do anything to survive and I am among those chosen few. Once I've vanquished the menaces that protect the threat under this roof, everyone will turn to me for absolution. Once they've been divided, I will conquer.

10:06 pm

Rosie sat stroking her sleeping niece's head. "Claire's right, you know."

Grace faced her interested to know how anyone could come to that conclusion.

Rosie saw the judgement in her eyes and quickly added, "Kathryn thought we were in danger and she acted on it. She didn't know the situation. She just acted on pure instinct."

She lifted True's head gently off of her lap and placed it onto a folded jacket. "I need to see her."

Grace was glad at Rosie's sudden realisation. Kathryn needed her forgiveness and understanding before she could even begin to forgive herself.

"I think that's a great idea, Rosie. Come on. I'll show you where she is."

"Winston, can you watch True for me, please?" Rosie thought it was only polite to ask even though Winston had already moved closer to the tot in case she woke up while her aunt was absent.

"Sure thing," he replied.

As the girls made their way to the staff room, Charlie looked around for his friend.

Serhan had distanced himself from both of the groups and had made his way over to the solace of the vending machine. He had so many thoughts cascading through his mind that being on his own was the only thing that made sense to him. At least, alone he could decipher what he made of everything and exactly what he planned to do about it.

He knew that if it came down to it, he would always join the side that was going to survive. He had always been a coward. He was fully aware of that fact but at least it meant he would be safe. The problem was Charlie. Charlie had always had his back from the day they first met. It was as if Charlie saw there was more to him than some nerdy dweeb who couldn't take care of himself and although his honestly voiced opinions had gotten them into a few sticky situations, Charlie had never turned his back on him. He was Serhan's oldest and dearest friend, his only real friend if he was being brutally honest with himself.

This is something that they definitely wouldn't agree on. Charlie's nature to protect the downtrodden was going to shine through. There was no question about it. That's the kind of person he was: a hero.

Normally, Serhan was the more vulnerable party but against a three-year-old, he didn't stand a chance. Besides, Serhan was willing to bet his life that Charlie didn't have it in him to kill anybody let alone be an accessory to the murder of a child. She could be fully infected and tearing people limb from limb and Serhan still believed that Charlie wouldn't have the heart to kill her.

His musings surely became more apparent when Charlie made his way over to him.

"You okay, mate?" Charlie tilted his head to one side. "You seem…deep in thought."

"Yeah, I can't help it. I'm sorry, man. I'm just…" Serhan lowered his head.

"Scared?" Charlie finished his sentence. "I get it, man. We're all a bit shaken up by all of this."

"Shaken up?" Serhan looked at Charlie in disbelief. "Charlie, I'm not shaken up. I'm fucking terrified, scared out of my wit. I thought my fear and anxiety could be delayed until we actually had to go back out there with those things but apparently not. The scary things are happening in here as well and it's not just one incident. They just keep coming and with every new one, my fear escalates by another ten points and I'm going out of my mind trying to decide how to handle this or who to believe because it's so fucking insane, all of it."

"Ser calm down. It's okay."

"Nothing is okay, man, wake up. How many people have died since we've been in here? It's not okay. We're not safe. People are turning on each other and it all boils down to that little girl."

"Dude, she's not infected. Don't listen to that green haired twat."

"She fucking is, Charlie. And so was her mum."

"No, Darius said that was a misunderstanding."

"…right before he turned into one of those things and killed that druggy and his girlfriend."

"No, man, that's not what happened. You heard what Grace said. You can't let that evil bitch fill your mind with her poison. She's just playing on your fear."

"Well, I'm sorry to tell you but it's working. I've never been more scared in my entire life. I'm not made to handle this shit well."

"I know that but that's why I'm here to help you through it, like always. We always handle shit together."

"Would you kill that little girl to save everyone else in here?"

"I wouldn't need to because she's not a threat."

"But, if you had to, could you do it? Could you do it if it meant saving the life of everyone else in here?"

Charlie stared helplessly at his friend. Serhan had already made a decision. He was just too scared to see that it was the immoral one.

"I know you wouldn't kill her, Chaz."

"And you could?" Charlie asked.

"No…" Serhan admitted. "But I could close my eyes and let someone else do it."

"You could actually live with yourself after that?"

"I would be able to live," Serhan stressed.

"Your moral compass is fucked, mate."

"I'm just trying to stay alive, Charlie." Serhan knew Charlie would find his reasons both lame and cowardly but he couldn't change that, not now.

Charlie's disheartening realisation came to a quick halt when Rosie came barging through a door in floods of tears. He could hear her from halfway across the hall and knew he had to brace himself for the next mind-blowing terror. He turned to Serhan to motion for him to follow and Serhan just stared back at him with eyes that were portraying his emotions. Another reason to be afraid was about to present itself and no amount of preparation was going to make him ready for it.

The two made their way over to the commotion side by side, both of them knowing that there was now a time limit on how long that would remain their stance.

10:08 pm

Rosie followed the staircase leading to the staff room. She entered the six-digit code that Grace had given her and pushed the door following the buzzing noise confirming the code. She wanted to call out but couldn't bring herself to do it. She wanted to get Kathryn's honest reaction to her approach.

She followed Grace's directions and turned right as soon as she entered the top hallway. The flickering secondary lights made for an eerie atmosphere and Rosie felt a cold shiver run along her spine.

She knocked on the blue door and when she didn't get a response, she considered retreating. She turned to unlock the door to the stairs, then stopped and forced herself to knock again.

This time, she made it louder and didn't wait for an answer. She pushed the door open and poked her head through the gap.

"Hello?" she called softly.

Still no reply so Rosie stepped inside the unfamiliar room and noticed that there were locker rooms at the back. If Kathryn was in there, she might not have heard her. She entered the room with a stubborn determination and headed for the locker room to the left.

She'd only gotten halfway when she realised why Kathryn hadn't responded. She didn't give herself time to think about what might have happened.

Kathryn's motionless body was lying on the floor like some sort of child's rag doll that had been strewn onto the ground, unwanted and unloved.

Rosie ran towards her. Her knees gave way as she reached her and it was then that she saw the pills in her friend's hand.

"No, no, no, no, no!" Rosie was becoming irate as she frantically checked Kathryn's pulse and airways and began performing CPR. Her efforts were meaningless and she knew it. Rosie had no idea how long she had been like this, but she carried on relentlessly.

After what seemed like hours, she collapsed on the floor beside the stillness that had been her rock for the last two days. She pulled herself together long enough to find her feet and make it back to the stair well where Grace was waiting restlessly at the bottom.

"Grace!"

Looking at Rosie's tear-soaked face, Grace replied with, "What's wrong? Where's Kathryn?"

"It's my fault," she blubbered. "I should've spoken to her sooner."

Grace felt her heart sink. "Rosie, where's Kathryn?"

Rosie handed her the pills she had removed from Kathryn's clenched fist. "She blamed herself, Grace."

Grace stared at the empty bottle in disbelief.

"No," she shook her head furiously. "No, she wouldn't… She hasn't…"

She threw the bottle to the ground and bolted up the stairs. She struggled with the code lock, pressing buttons by mistake, then cursing herself for making an error. She eventually got through the door and Rosie folded onto the step, completely numb. Her nerves jumped back to life as she heard the anticipated scream from above her.

What had she done? Kathryn had ended her life because of her reaction to an honest mistake. She had wanted to protect them. That was all. If she had just spoken to her and explained that she understood.

Grace sat in shock examining Kathryn's uncharacteristic means to an end. This wasn't her. She wasn't the sort of person to give up even if she was shrouded in guilt for her actions. Grace closed her friend's eyes, making note of their blood shot appearance. Grace also noticed that there was no vomit, she hadn't frothed at the mouth at any point. That was what always happened in the movies, but she dismissed it as a common misconception.

She swept her hair from the side of her face and tucked it behind the heavily pierced ear. It was then that Grace surrendered to the tears. The world around her was being torn down on top of her, burying her alive.

The building was supposed to be a safe place and people were still dying. They were far from safe. As much as Grace didn't want to agree with her, even in the slightest, Claire had been right.

Grace grabbed Kathryn's hand and squeezed it tightly. She just couldn't get her head around the fact that her friend would do something like this. She studied the china doll face that was left to portray her peer. She looked worried, even in death. She had carried that burden with her to the afterlife. The light caught her extensive ear jewellery and Grace cracked a smile thinking about how much Kathryn had bragged about them only to be shot down by an older customer who said she looked like she could join the circus. In response, Kathryn had promised in jest to tattoo her entire body right up to her neck.

Her neck… Grace stared at it, unsure of what she could see. She leaned in closer to examine a tiny red dot, no bigger than a pin prick. She ran her finger over it to make sure her eyes weren't playing tricks on her, but it was there. The area around it was ever so slightly raised and the dot itself was soft as if it had only recently begun to heal.

Was what she was seeing real? Or had she somehow fabricated a more traumatic death for her friend than the atypical choice of suicide? It was so out of character. Something didn't fit the profile. She had spoken to Kathryn. Sure, she was taking Vickey's death badly but not enough to do something like this. Grace considered the possibility of what she was already suspecting. Kathryn wouldn't kill herself. No way. Someone else had been up here. She had been injected with something. The proof was right there on her neck. This was a cold-blooded murder.

10:38 pm

Grace felt like she was being carried down the stairs and towards the hall, like she wasn't in control of her own body. She couldn't feel the ground beneath her feet or the air around her. Her body was profoundly numb.

She pushed through the door that seemed heavier now than ever before and made her way towards the weeping sound coming from Rosie's direction. She was sitting with Winston, Charlie and Serhan but Grace knew she would have to drop the bombshell that Rosie had innocently overlooked.

Winston rose to meet her as she approached their circle. "Grace, are you okay? Rosie told us about Kathryn."

Grace could do nothing but nod. No words wanted to volunteer themselves.

"Is it true?" Winston pressed. "Did she kill herself?"

Grace looked into Winston's gentle, brown eyes and then over at Rosie. "No," she whispered.

Rosie wiped away a tear mid flow. "No? What do you mean? I saw her there with the pill bottle in her hand."

Grace fought to get the words out. "It was staged. Somebody did this to her."

"What?" Charlie's eyes were as wide as saucers as he quickly prepared himself for whatever insanity Grace was about to offload.

"There's a mark on her neck. It looks like an injection mark. I think somebody did this to her and then made it look like suicide."

"You've got to be fucking with me. Are you serious?" Charlie couldn't process the words coming out of her mouth. "This is insane. Do you realise what you're actually saying?"

Grace watched his reaction as it mirrored her own. "I know it sounds crazy, but Kathryn wouldn't have done this. I know her and the mark on her neck proves it."

Charlie and Winston exchanged a worried glance and Charlie decided it was best to let Winston handle this one.

"G, are you sure you're not just…clutching at straws?"

When she shot him a look of betrayal, Winston back tracked.

"I agree that Kat didn't seem like the sort of person to commit suicide but honestly, do you really think someone in here is capable of staging a suicide? What reason would they have?"

"We don't know half the people in here, Winston. Why is this so hard to comprehend?" Her voice sounded defeated like she had no energy left to convince them otherwise.

"I believe you," Rosie whispered. It was loud enough for the three of them to acknowledge it. "She felt guilty, but she knew we still weren't safe. She wouldn't have left us behind like that. I believe you."

Grace smiled in the comfort of knowing she wasn't the only one who was entertaining this crazy concept. "I just wish we knew who had gone up there."

The group fell quiet once more and were slightly alarmed when a voice broke their silence.

"Oh, no." Serhan had been so quiet his peers had almost forgotten he was even there.

"What's up?" Charlie asked, his face a picture of concern.

Serhan looked down at his feet for a moment, then lifted his head to face them.

"I know who went up there."

10:45 pm

Grace gathered a small group at the front of the stage. Rosie cradled her niece as Winston pulled funny faces to make the infant laugh. Charlie sat beside his friend of fifteen years and had never felt more estranged from him. The awkwardness they shared was felt by all present, but they urged themselves to concentrate on the matter at hand.

"I'm telling you guys I think Claire killed Kathryn. Serhan saw her go up there and no one had gone up there since I last spoke to her, that I'm aware of." Grace was convinced that Kathryn's death was no suicide and once Serhan had confirmed who he had seen going upstairs, she knew she was right.

"But, why? I mean, I know she's a pain in the arse and obviously has a few screws loose, but would she really murder Kathryn?" This was pointed out by Winston.

"Why not? She killed Darius in front of my eyes," Grace said defensively.

"Hey, I know and I'm not making excuses for her, but she could've misjudged the situation like she said."

"She didn't misjudge anything," Grace argued.

"Why not? Kathryn did." All eyes turned to Serhan who held up his hands and continued. "I'm just saying that just because you don't like her doesn't mean she doesn't get to use that excuse."

Rosie shifted position uncomfortably very aware that True was listening to everything. "It wasn't an excuse and I don't want to hear any more about that. The fact is that you saw Claire go upstairs and apart from Grace, we haven't seen anyone else go up there.

"Now, either she saw what Kathryn had done and didn't tell anyone about it or she got into something with Kathryn and it ended badly. Either way, she's not an innocent party."

"How do you know that? You weren't there. None of us were. You don't know what happened. She could've gone up there and not even spoken to

Kathryn." Serhan wasn't dropping it and Charlie was getting more and more irritated.

"For fuck's sake, Ser! She threatened a kid! What kind of person does that? If you're going to keep defending her, maybe you should go and join her little cult officially because, honestly, if she can even consider doing something to that little girl, then she is capable of anything."

Charlie got up and walked over to the doors leading to the arcade. Serhan got up to follow him but Winston stopped him.

"Just let him calm down, man."

Serhan shrugged him off. "I'm just doing what he said. Good luck, guys."

Serhan headed towards Claire's group and felt a bitter twang as nobody tried to stop him.

The group fell silent for a while before Rosie spoke. "Let him go. We need to protect each other, no matter what. God knows what she's planning over there."

Winston placed his hand on her shoulder and squeezed it gently. "We only have ten hours left until those doors open. Then we can get the hell away from her and face a whole new lot of trouble."

"Maybe it is a case of 'better the devil you know'. We really have no idea what we could be facing out there." Rosie's face filled with panic.

Grace shook her head. "A lot can happen in ten hours. We need to stick together and keep our wits about us. We're already outnumbered. Maybe we should take it in turns keeping watch tonight."

"Yeah, that's not a bad idea," Winston agreed.

Charlie made his way back over to the group. "Sorry to foil your plans but has anyone seen Kristie?"

Rosie looked around her. "I haven't seen her in a while, since this morning."

Grace looked up at Charlie. "She was really upset. I figured she just needed some time on her own but that was hours ago."

"With everything that's been going on, I didn't even realise she'd gone." Winston looked truly disappointed in himself.

"Do you think we should go and look for her?" Charlie suggested. "I don't feel right leaving her alone right now."

"No, you're right," Grace stood. "We should find her and bring her back here. At least we can look after her then."

"I'll come with you," Charlie offered.

"I'll stay here with Rosie just in case…" Winston was worried about Kristie but there were only so many places she could be and it didn't take three people to search for her especially when trouble could be lurking if he were to leave Rosie and True on their own.

"Shouldn't we all stay together?" Rosie asked, knowing that there is always strength in numbers.

"It's probably for the best," Charlie offered a hand to help Rosie up. "That way, none of us are vulnerable."

With everything that had happened in the last couple of hours, Grace had completely lost sight of her colleague. No one had seen Kristie since Claire had murdered Darius. Grace worried about her. She knew her friend had trouble dealing with loss and had a history of depression at such a young age.

As much as Kristie was naive and seemingly oblivious to the world around her, she cared and loved very deeply so when she got hurt, she took it badly. Grace had even heard rumours that when Kristie and her ex had split up, she'd attempted suicide before someone walked in and stopped her, but Grace didn't like to pay too much attention to idle gossip.

Right now, her main concern was Kristie's whereabouts and how she was coping with all of this. There was no part of her that believed Kathryn had killed herself, but she just couldn't bring herself to assume that Kristie was exempt from that frame of mind. Jean's death had definitely rattled her, but Darius may have pushed her over the edge.

Grace had to be sure. Their group was dwindling by the hour and Claire's was getting larger and more aggressive. She needed to rally her remaining troops and find Kristie before another 'freak suicide' happened.

"Okay, we better get a move on then." Grace led the search party towards the double doors beside the stage in a hope to find their missing friend.

Monday, 22nd April 2019
2:40 am

The night was dragging and everyone had been on edge. Whether it was the haunting memories of the past couple of days or the numbing fear and realisation that in just over six hours they would be freed from their cell and released into whatever the world had turned into.

Lewie wasn't the only one who was restless. He'd been pretty mellow about every situation that had previously arisen but tonight had hit him like a tonne of bricks. He lay on the floor staring up at the ceiling contemplating their next move. He remembered exactly where he had parked the car. They would need to make a run for it. They would drive to their house. It was secluded and they could probably lay low there for at least a week, that was assuming the electricity outage wasn't a nationwide concern.

Lorraine was far too laid back to even think of a survival plan so he would have to prepare for every possible scenario. He was, however, very aware that he lacked the imagination or 'knowledge' that Claire had referred to, in order to battle all plausible predicaments.

What he did know for sure was that he was hungry and that wasn't going to help him get to sleep. He decided to help himself to a late-night snack if only to give himself something to do other than plan the upcoming escape to victory as it were.

Lorraine was fast asleep beside him blissfully unaware in her trouble-free bubble. He'd always joked that that woman could sleep anywhere and amidst any situation. He smiled and kissed her on the forehead before climbing to his feet.

There were still plenty of people awake in the hall. He could hear the hushed conversations and he bet that there were a few people who were quietly dwelling on their own escape plans.

He made his way past the bar and towards the doors. As he entered the corridor, the smell hit him full force. He almost retched and pulled his shirt over his nose in an attempt to eliminate the foul-smelling odour of dead bodies. The blood stains smothered the walls and he hadn't paid too much attention to them when the scene had first unfolded. He was quite content not to analyse the extent of the situation but standing there now, he knew nothing but death. He pushed the cellar door open and let the chill overwhelm him. It didn't smell much better down there but at least it wasn't stuffy.

He rifled through some crisps, then decided against them since the rustle may serve as an added distraction from sleep to the other occupants. He pulled out some bread and slices of cheese and took a bite, grimacing at the dry texture in much need of some butter.

As he turned to leave, he glanced down at the stained floor and wondered what had spilled. It was probably one of the kegs: beer mixed with rust seemed like a reasonable explanation. Still, he took a look just the same.

He got closer to the wall of kegs as the pungent air became stronger. He pulled his shirt over his nose again and peered behind the metal barrels.

Amongst the coagulated puddle, he made out a small feature resembling a hand. He jumped back dropping his poor excuse for a sandwich. He wasn't sure what he had just seen and he had to be certain.

He forced himself to look again and as he did, he could see the outline of the boy's body, draped in a brown mess amongst a tangled web of formerly orange curls. Lewie let out a noise that felt foreign to him, then dropped to his knees, retching. His stomach strained as it expelled its contents onto the floor.

For the first time in Lewie's life, he was terrified. The terrors that had been locked outside became real and the evil that had seeped inside the building was being paraded in front of his very eyes. His eyes filled with tears for the dead child and he couldn't stand to look at him any longer. He needed to get back to Lorraine. The others needed to know. Before he could make sense of it all, he was sprinting back towards the hall. He fell through the doors and began screaming at the top of his lungs.

"There's another one! There's another body!"

2:52 am

Grace felt bile rise in her throat as their undivided attention was drawn once again to the double doors concealing the dreaded corridor. She instantly felt lightheaded and couldn't move as she struggled to acknowledge that she had failed yet another one of her friends.

Kristie had been missing for hours and they'd had no luck in finding her. They'd been so wrapped up in the blood shed that they'd forgotten to keep track of the living.

As both groups made their way over to Lewie, Grace turned her back in need of some time to ready herself for another gruesome discovery.

Lewie began hyperventilating and pointing frantically to the doors. Lorraine rushed over rubbing the sleep from her eyes. "Lew, what's happened?"

"It's a kid, babe. It's a fucking kid!"

Winston stopped in his tracks at the word 'kid' and looked straight at Rosie. She repositioned the child in her arms as True whispered his assigned name, "Henry."

Grace also snapped back to life at Lewie's description and was hit by a rush of emotions. She was thankful that Kristie was still just missing but at the same time, confused beyond belief that there was another child, a dead one.

Claire made it to the cellar first and took in the devastating scene before her. She actually looked saddened by the boy's appearance and her followers all drank in her sudden show of humanity. She spoke under her breath and only those in close proximity heard her. "I knew there was another kid in here."

"You knew?" Kim asked quietly.

"I thought I'd just imagined it. I only saw him the once, on the first day when we all came in."

She became very aware, suddenly, that her voice was the only sound in the otherwise silent cellar and all eyes were fixated on her. She chose to then lay it on thick. "He must have been so frightened. What kind of monster would do this to him?"

"That's one question but what about the obvious ones?" Serhan began shouting hysterically. "Where has he been hiding this whole time? Where are his parents? Who is he?"

Winston stepped forward. "He came in when we all did. He must have been separated from his parents in the commotion. He was too scared to come out of hiding."

Grace stared blankly at the man standing next to her. "How do you know all of this?"

Winston looked down at his feet racked with guilt that he hadn't believed True.

"True saw him," he spoke softly. "And spoke to him when she first got here. She told me and her aunty about him, but we thought she had just made him up, some sort of imaginary friend."

"You were told there was another child in the building and you didn't think to make sure there wasn't?" Kim accused.

Winston felt deflated and deserving of the oncoming criticism. "Nobody else had seen him." His words were barely audible.

"I had." Claire wore her best look of betrayal and she wore it well.

"So, why didn't *you* say anything?" Charlie wasn't going to let her play the innocent party.

"I did say something, but I was quickly reminded by the redhead that her niece was the only child in the building and since he was never seen again, I had no reason to believe otherwise.

"Anyway, if someone else had said something I might have been able to make more sense of it all."

"Who the fuck killed the kid?" Tom's outburst made everyone jump. Besides the fact that he'd hardly said two words to anyone since they'd been in there, he also was showing clear signs of unresolved inner emotional torment. This guy had seen and heard the same things as everyone else, but he hadn't shouted about it or even voiced his opinions mildly. He had taken it all in and had quietly chosen a side without drawing any attention to himself. Even though he'd sat with a certain group, he still remained what he had entered the hall as: a loner.

Everyone stared at him as his large frame shook from head to toe. The sweat glistened from his hairline down to his double chin and his brown eyes were wide with worry. He appeared to be in some state of shock.

Winston refrained from placing a hand on the shuddering giant's shoulder. This guy was a ticking time bomb. Instead, he offered words of comfort. "I don't know, man. I don't think we'll ever know for sure."

"And everyone's okay with that, are they?" Tom couldn't be consoled. This had pushed him over the edge. "A kid who was all alone and scared was murdered and no one gives a shit who did it?"

"That's not what we're saying." Grace wanted to offer him peace of mind but was fully aware of how ill equipped she was. She couldn't offer an explanation any more than anyone else could. All she could do was state facts. "But if nobody knew he was in the building, how are we going to figure out who killed him?"

"Well, it is simple, isn't it?" Claire had moved closer to inspect the little boy's body. "This was a savage attack. This boy was beaten to death. This looks like the work of your tattooed friend."

Grace knew what Claire was going to say before the poisonous words even passed her lips, so by the time she had finished her sentence, Grace was already at the door. She wasn't about to entertain any loose accusation that Claire could get her devious hands on. Darius was not infected and he would never have attacked a child. She refused to even listen to the theory, but Claire wasn't deterred by Grace's abrupt exit. In fact, she used it to her advantage. "There she goes, still defending that maniac. How much more evidence does she need? This is his handy work. He beat this child to death just like he did with the druggy and his girlfriend."

She then pulled on the crowd's heart strings by forcing herself to tear up.

"This is my fault. I knew he was infected and I didn't do enough about it until it was too late. I should've made you all listen to me. If I had, this child may still be alive."

She paused to wipe away a tear dramatically, then turned on Winston and Charlie.

"Do you see what's at stake now? Do you see how dangerous it is to have that little girl in here with us? We only have to survive in here for another ten hours. You think this is a difficult decision? Imagine the ones you're going to have to make out there.

"Who has children of their own? Grand children? Nieces? Nephews?" Claire needed to make them understand that outside these walls their worst nightmares could be realised. It wasn't just the horror of the infected but who they might encounter along the way.

"You don't know that little girl. You had never met her until a couple of days ago and our consciences are hard wired to tell us to protect children at all costs. But what if a child is the threat? What if this child in particular, has the power to wipe us all out because we wouldn't let ourselves hurt her? Is she even a child anymore when she's that dangerous? She is infected and she will end up killing us all if we don't do something about it.

"How many people have lost their lives because she's spread the infection through the air to people who have tried to help her? We need to stop her."

Claire sounded genuinely concerned for the welfare of her people. If it was all an act, she was one hell of a ring master. The scared occupants lapped up every word she had to say and they did so with heavy hearts, knowing that they were ignoring their ethical means but also that she was right. They needed to be prepared for much more sinister scenarios once they were in the outside world.

"We need to control this situation and if there are still people stupid enough to want to 'protect' her, they will need to be taken out of the equation. It's survival of the fittest. If you want to survive, you have to fight for it. Don't be scared. Fight back. Don't let them stop you. Your lives are in your own hands and they are just a handful of people."

Charlie and Winston couldn't believe the lies that Claire was spewing but, looking around the room, they could see that everybody else did. There was no winning this argument. These people weren't going to change their minds no matter what else was said to exonerate True. They were a lost cause and that meant that True would need as many people protecting her as humanly possible.

The two men looked around at the anger and fear in everyone's eyes and edged towards the door, in an attempt to get to the little girl before the rabble did but Claire was too quick.

"Stop them! We need to end this. We need to get to the girl before they do."

The crowd turned into a blood thirsty mob at the click of her fingers. Before Winston and Charlie knew what was happening, they were surrounded by eight hostiles who began hitting them with anything they could get their hands on.

Winston was hit over the head with a bottle from behind. As the glass shattered and the alcohol exploded into his wounds, he received punches from all angles. His face and his ribs were bruising with every impact, then out of nowhere, Tom delivered a nose-breaking head butt as Lewie brought down an empty crate on top of Winston's head. He crumbled to the floor as the room went dark around him.

Charlie watched amongst punches and kicks as his friend was taken down. He'd never been a violent person and if they could knock out Winston, he knew he didn't stand a chance. He got a few kicks in before something penetrated his skin just below his rib cage. He looked into his attacker's eyes and wondered why he would even think that these lunatics wouldn't play dirty.

Danny pulled out the blunt screwdriver and shoved it into Charlie's lower abdomen twice and then a third time in between his ribs. Charlie gasped for air as he looked down at his bloody wounds. He collapsed onto the concrete floor and laid clutching his wounds as Claire rallied up the mob.

"Leave them in here. We need to put an end to this now."

3:18 am

As the group herded back to the hall, Claire hung back and pulled Mark to one side.

"This is your time to shine, Mark." She didn't make eye contact with him but remained focused on the army she had created.

Mark looked at her, confused. "What do you mean?"

"I showed you how to take out a threat with that girl from the hospital. Kim and Danny both got a chance to prove their worth to our cause, but we got trapped in here before you did so now is the perfect opportunity."

"Wait a minute, you want me to kill the kid?"

Claire broke contact with the group and stared directly at him. "That kid is a threat to all of us. You told me when we started talking in the chatroom that you have what it takes to destroy the ignorance that forms our humanity and now, you have a problem with taking out one child? Never mind. I'll do it myself."

Mark grabbed her arm as she went to walk away. "No, no, I'll do it. I can do it but how?"

"With this," Claire smiled. She held up a nail gun. "On an adult, you'd have to fire a few shots before it actually kills them but if you use it on a child, straight through the temple, death will be instantaneous."

"Where did you even get this?"

"Our newest recruit had it on him. I figured it would do the trick since I used up the last of the sedative on that blonde bitch."

"Right..." Mark looked unsure which didn't go unnoticed.

"Look, if you haven't got the balls for this, then I'm sure we can find someone to replace you."

"No, it's fine." Mark hesitated before taking the nail gun. "It's all for the greater good, right?"

"Exactly," Claire grinned. "One little girl or everyone else in here is not a difficult choice, is it Mark?"

She walked into the hall following her flock and left Mark trailing behind her.

3:23 am

Claire made her way to the front of the assembly and locked eyes with Grace who was trying to bundle Rosie and True out of the hall.

"Stop them!" she shouted and as if obediently trained, the group split and seized Grace and Rosie.

"What the hell are you doing?" Rosie screamed.

"Get off of me!" Grace struggled with her captors.

"I'm sorry it's had to come to this, but you leave us no choice." Claire's voice was calm and collected as she sauntered towards the restrained women.

Grace fought helplessly against Michael, Tom and Danny as they pinned her arms behind her back whilst Rosie's hair was grabbed by Lorraine as Lewie and Matt held onto her flailing arms. True clung to her aunt's leg screaming as Kim taunted her like a wolf circling its prey waiting for the opportune moment to pounce.

Serhan was distracted, looking around the entire time for his friend to emerge from the cellar. Claire took note of his actions and was not impressed. She feared that she may have a traitor in her midst so quietly suggested that Mark keep an eye on him at all times.

Diverting her attention back towards the sobbing child, Claire motioned for Kim to take her.

As soon as she felt the grip from her leg release, Rosie launched all of her strength towards her frightened niece. Lewie and Matt struggled to keep a hold of her until Lorraine hit her over the head with a vase from the abandoned office. She didn't completely lose consciousness, but her head was bleeding and her vision and perceptions had been compromised. She tried to focus on True's little sobs, but her limbs were powerless.

Claire took hold of the infant and came down to her level.

"Don't worry, child. No more tears. This is for the best. You don't want to hurt your aunty, do you?"

True stared through tears at the woman before her and uncertainly shook her head. Grace shouted at Claire. "Don't touch her! Get away from her!"

Ignoring Grace's outburst, Claire continued. "I know you don't want to hurt her but you're not well and soon you are going to hurt everyone in here. Now, I know you're not a horrible little girl, but you won't be able to stop yourself. Do you understand? That's why we need to stop you."

The scared little girl nodded.

"No, don't listen to her True!" Tom placed a hand forcibly over Grace's mouth.

Claire took True by the hand and led her closer to the others.

"This has to be done. There's no way around it. I wish there was, but we need to think of the greater good."

She turned to Mark and invited him to come forward. As she handed the little girl over, Claire looked her in the eyes. "Close your eyes, little one. It'll all be over soon and you'll be with your mummy."

Grace was going crazy trying to fight against the monsters that were stopping her. Her muffled screams sounded haunting as she desperately tried to get through to Rosie whose head was still spinning. She could hear every word spoken but her reactions weren't in time. She could just about see the blurred outline of her niece next to a taller figure knelt beside her. She couldn't make sense of the words but put all of her energy into the picture slowly becoming clearer.

Mark held the little girl close to him and raised the nail gun to her tiny temple. He paused in mid-air for what seemed like an eternity. His hand shook and his eyes were tightly closed, mirroring his victim. As he exhaled, he dropped his arm and began to cry.

Claire was enraged. How dare he make her lose face at such a detrimental time? She strode angrily toward him before the crowd lost their bravado too but before she reached him, Kim appeared out of nowhere pushing him to the floor and snatching the nail gun.

As she grabbed True and took her aim, Rosie saw the whole thing unfold and screamed like a woman possessed as Kim pulled the trigger.

3:35 am

The entire hall fell silent. Those who had been watching intensely let go of the distraught women and those who had averted their eyes from the unimaginable turned back in fear and with curiosity.

Grace dropped to the floor with a thud, crying hysterically and refusing to look at the horrific scene in front of her but Rosie flew past her, hurtling her body into Kim, knocking her to the ground.

The two women fought dominantly but Rosie was fuelled by rage and an overwhelming, if temporarily delayed, strength. The trigger had been pulled and the shot had been executed by the woman she was on top of. Her anger was beyond compare to Kim who fought like a wild animal. All Rosie could see was the heathen who had murdered her niece.

Her attacks were fatal and unforgiving as her rings punctured Kim's eyebrow and lip. Blood leapt from her face as she frantically tried to block Rosie's punches, but she was unstoppable. She had no reasoning left inside her so as the punches weren't doing enough justice, she took Kim's head in her hands, placed her thumbs over her eyes and pushed with all her might. She could feel every ounce of vengeance leaving her body through her hands as she pushed harder and deeper. Her rage ran through her giving her the added force to destroy this woman.

Kim's shouts for help turned to screams of undeniable pain as Rosie's thumbs entered relentlessly into her skull. The sound was harrowing as Kim's eyeballs gave way beneath the pressure.

Nobody even tried to stop Rosie. They all stood motionless and terrified.

Grace's loud cries were only disrupted when a small hand touched her shoulder. She jumped with shock and then realised it was a child's touch. She grabbed True's face in both her hands as if to make sure the angel before her was real. As her hopes were confirmed, she turned her attention to the brawl on the floor and held True close to her chest, shielding her young eyes.

Once the screams stopped, Rosie withdrew her hands from inside Kim's head, panting uncontrollably, blood decorating her face, hands and clothes. She stood up clumsily, never taking her eyes off of Kim.

The other occupants feared her every move, backing away slowly. As she turned to face them, she caught sight of True and her heart flew. She took one step towards the child and was stopped immediately.

"She's infected! They all are! Don't just stand there. Get them!"

Claire's reaction was as genuine as the rest of the groups. She had completely underestimated Rosie's reaction, but it couldn't have worked out better. Now she had all the fuel she needed to take out the remaining non-believers. Her followers were terrified and easily convinced that an attack so brutal must be down to the virus.

Michael quickly kicked Grace under her chin sending her upwards only to come crashing to the floor, losing her grip on True. Rosie, soaked in blood, was dragged away from Kim's ruined corpse and slammed against the stage as Matt, Lewie and Lorraine proceeded to hit and kick her.

As Danny apprehended the little girl, he felt a blow to the back of his head, propelling him forwards as he nosedived into the carpet. True was suddenly swept up by a large pair of arms and as she looked up at her rescuer, found warmth in the familiar brown eyes of Winston. She looked behind him at Charlie clutching his side and hobbling towards them. Even in her young, terrified state, she could see he was hurt.

Winston passed her to Charlie and warned them to stay back. True buried her head into Charlie's sweat soaked shoulder as Winston made his way heroically towards her aunt who could barely be seen. He lost control as he grabbed Matt with both hands, turning him to face him. He headbutted him with full force which would have been enough to render Matt unconscious had Winston been at full strength but a follow up right hook was needed as well and did the trick. He let Matt's body crumple as he moved on to Lewie. Once again turning the man and throwing two hard punches to his face before tossing him aside. By this point, his adrenaline was running low so he merely shoved Lorraine out of his way to get to Rosie.

He lifted her dead weight and threw her over his shoulder. She was barely conscious at this stage and flopped against him like a ragdoll knowing she was now safe. He placed her onto a chair leaning her against Charlie whilst he went back in for Grace.

As Winston approached her attackers, he was joined by Serhan who took out Michael with one swift blow to the head with a metal stool. Winston met his gaze fleetingly with a look of gratitude as Serhan kicked Tom in the back of the knee to allow Winston to get him into an easy chokehold. He held his grip as Tom struggled for breath, grabbing frantically at his assailant.

Claire watched the mayhem unfold before her and turning to Mark, who was still hanging his head in shame, demanded that he do something. When he didn't react immediately, she kicked him and screamed, "Get the fucking traitor!"

Mark snapped into action and made a bee line for Serhan. He pulled a Stanley knife from his pocket and aimed for Serhan's jugular. Winston saw Mark making his move with the weapon in his hand and dropped Tom, yelling for Mark to stop.

His warning came too late and Mark buried the knife deep into Serhan's neck as Charlie's screams echoed throughout the hall. He rushed over to his friend as Winston tackled Mark to the ground.

Blood cascaded from Serhan's punctured artery and clung to Charlie as he attempted hopelessly to plug the hole. Serhan didn't panic. He didn't even try to stop the bleeding. He just looked at his friend and his eyes were filled with peace. He wasn't scared anymore. He had chosen a side, the wrong side, admittedly but he had redeemed himself.

"I…made sure…the safety was…on before I…gave them…the nail gun," he choked.

Charlie's vison was distorted by his shameless tears. "Ser…"

"I'm okay," his friend spluttered. "She's okay."

"Yeah…" Charlie managed before his friend's eyes glazed over.

He had redeemed himself. He had saved the little girl. He could finally rest in peace. Charlie broke down as Winston grabbed him under his arms. "Come on, man. We've got to go."

Grace hobbled over to Rosie and True and pulled the aunt to her feet. "Rosie, come on."

The redhead looked sleepy as if she was fighting to regain her vision. She rose to her feet wearily, having to steady herself every few steps. Grace could hear Claire shouting to her troops, "Get up! What are you doing? They're getting away!"

She was losing them. Mark, Danny, Matt and Michael clambered to their feet in a hot pursuit after their former captives as they raced to the back of the hall towards the door marked 'Treasury'.

Winston yelled, "You need to stay in here. No matter what, don't let anybody in and do not come out. There's only a few hours left. You will all be safe."

Grace fumbled with the key as their attackers neared. Winston propped Charlie up against the wall and began charging at the oncomers.

Grace opened the door; her hand uncontrollably shaking and led the others to safety. She supported Charlie under his arm and guided him into the familiar cash office, as she glanced behind her to see Winston violently thrashing at the four men, taking repeated hits himself.

She closed the door, locking it from the inside so that not even Michael's spare key could get to them.

She peered through the peep hole and watched as their protector snapped Michael's neck with his bare hands. His limp body was thrown against Matt, knocking him over some tables due to the weight of the useless manager. Then she lost sight as Winston headed towards the bar, the other two men on his tail.

3:48 am

Winston could feel his body slowly failing him as he sprinted across the hall towards the bar. The adrenalin rode through his veins but with every step he took it dissipated. He knew he had to take them out and they were right behind him, he was running out of options.

He launched himself over the bar smashing through glasses and landing heavily on the floor. He winced in pain but pulled himself towards the bottle room at the back. He had the CO_2 tanks in his sight. He had one hand stretched up to release the valve and with the other, he pulled his lighter from his trouser pocket. He waited for the small room to fill with as much gas as possible before the men bombarded it.

As he met their gaze, he said a silent prayer before igniting the toxic air, setting off an explosion that sent Mark and Danny flying back through the bar.

The fire roared through the bar like a mighty dragon, threatening the integrity of the glass optics containing the last of the alcohol, another gift for the staff from the 'ever generous' higher authorities.

Claire and Lorraine held their hands over their heads as the eruption mercilessly took out the final two of her original group, their burning bodies thrown from behind the bar.

Lewie sprang into action, running full force towards the bar. "Grab the extinguisher! We've got to put it out before it hits the spirits."

His sights were set on the red beacon placed handily beside the bar and he was already closer to it than the others by the time he'd finished his sentence. He tore it from the wall and fiddled with the contraption. In an emergency, you never remember what they taught you in the fire safety courses. All of the tests and refresher exams were useless if you had never operated an actual fire extinguisher. He paused to read the instructions on the canister and was thrown back, winded by the second explosion.

Once the bottles of alcohol had been compromised, the fire spread through the hall like a tidal wave. It thrived along the beer stained carpet and reached from table to table spreading its thick, black smoke in all directions.

Claire, Lorraine, Lewie and Tom all backed away from the threat, heading towards the treasury door. The fire had already reached the front of the hall, denying them access to the cellar, the stairs, the office, the toilets and the corridor, as if it had been summoned to all possible exits.

It then occurred to Claire that this was all part of a plan.

Winston and Charlie had escaped from the cellar after the attack. She could recall seeing a solitary case of six bottles of champagne in the centre of the room. They must have spread the alcohol whilst she was dealing with the others, the crafty bastards.

Both doors to the arcades had been locked on Claire's command in order to keep the dead at bay. The only person who could've unlocked it was the deceased owner of a key which was secured within his blazing office.

Claire began banging violently on the treasury door. "Open this door!"

The others joined in, begging and pleading for their lives but the door was solid. Tom continued to throw his weight against it in a hope to snap the hinges to get inside.

"What are you doing? Stop it!" Lewie cried. "If you break the door, we're all dead from smoke inhalation anyway."

Tom crumbled to the floor, crying. "I don't want to die. I'm only 25."

"Get the fuck up!" Claire shouted at him and then turned her anger towards the door. "Let us in. We're going to die out here."

"Please!" Lorraine began choking as the smoke began to assault her lungs. "Please open the door."

The fire had made its way past the centre of the hall and was hell bent on reaching their location. As it surged forward, Claire watched it until she could feel the heat threatening to melt her eyes.

3:49 am

Charlie was thrown through the open door and landed on a large grey coin counter sitting in the corner of the room. Gripping his wounds, he screamed out in pain. They were bleeding heavily and he was finding it hard to concentrate on anything. He vaguely recalled somebody hoisting him over their shoulder and launching him into a dull room. Maybe it wasn't that dull but he couldn't be sure of anything. Grace pulled him up towards her to move him away from the door but his painful howls deterred her from doing so. She returned him to his previous position quickly, all the time apologising. She ripped open his shirt to inspect the damage hushing him as she did so. His chest was dotted with three neat bloody holes. She began examining them and then realised that one of the holes was not so neat. As her hand hovered over it, Charlie's hand grabbed hers.

"I think it was a screwdriver." Grace stopped. His voice was gravelly, weak. She touched his face, so full of youth and hope. She smiled at him, he reminded her so much of her younger brother.

"I think you're right."

"I hope it was a new one, though." It was taking more effort for him to speak now and his breathing was becoming strained. "I don't want to die from an infection." He could just make out a smile through her sudden burst of tears. She raised his legs and arranged a pile of cloth bags under his head. The entry wound in his stomach was the worst. It wasn't as clean cut as the rest. This one had been contorted. She found an old shirt and wrapped it around his lower torso. She pulled it tight and he winced in his sleepy state. She could see that he was trying to be strong, but he was so young, and it was getting more difficult by the minute. She squeezed his hand softly and looked into his eyes. "Charlie, look at me." He tried to focus on her eyes but had to settle for an area above her brow which still kept moving to the left. "I'm going to see if the others are okay. I'll be back in a few minutes and I want you to tell me all about your plans for when we get out of here, okay? Promise me, you'll stay awake."

He stared directly at her and squeezed her hand back. "I promise."

She left him with a surge of distress and looked around to register who the others in the room were. Rosie was holding her niece tightly. Too tightly, Grace feared. She was worried the little girl might not have escaped the attacks from outside uninjured. She moved towards them and could see the reason for Rosie's desperate efforts to hold True close. The aunt herself was hurt. Blood leaked through her jumper onto the floor beside her. Grace went to help her, but Rosie held up her hand to motion her away and then whispered, "She mustn't know." Grace looked at the fragile infant the woman before her was cradling. True had already lost her mother. Her aunt was all she had left. Rosie would sooner comfort the little girl in her final moments than have her scared and watching her bleed to death. She was stroking True's back and rocking her ever so slightly, hushing her and whispering that everything was going to be okay.

In that moment, Grace sunk to the floor with the realisation that 'okay' was no longer an option. The shouts and pleas from beyond the treasury door were creeping in with the ominous smoke. They couldn't be silenced but the smoke could be slowed. Cloth bags were wedged urgently into the crack under the door. It would delay their fates slightly, Grace thought. She crawled over to Charlie and could see he was drifting in and out of consciousness. He could feel her there. "So, who's left?"

Grace lay down next to him and took his hand in hers. "Rosie and True."

"That little girl is so awesome." Charlie cracked a smile. "You're going to survive a horror film if you have a name as awesome as True."

"This is a horror film now?"

"It is in my head. I just wish I could see the ending."

"You will."

"Not likely."

Grace turned her head towards the huddled pair across from her. True was now sobbing quietly. Rosie was in a bad way. She was breathing softly, stroking the child's hair and, all the time, whispering a lullaby. The words to *Truly Scrumptious* floated eerily across the room. They filled the air with false hope. Pretence created to soothe a single child on the verge of breaking. Everyone in that room had given up. They had no hope left. Why should they? They were locked inside a room of a building that was now on fire with no hope of contacting anyone outside. They couldn't even comprehend the state of the world outside those walls. Was it in apocalyptic disarray? Were there any survivors?

Maybe a lucky few like in the films Charlie studied and lived by. These thoughts swarmed around Grace's head as she felt herself slipping out of consciousness. She knew she wasn't hurt, just physically and emotionally drained. Her body was telling her that she needed to be numb. She needed to be asleep in order to drown out the voices. She needed to forget, if only for a little while. She could erase the images she had seen in the last two days. Pretend the events hadn't taken place. She hadn't had to convince an angry mob not to kill an innocent child. For a fraction of a second, she didn't want to wake up.

5:25 am

Time had gone by, although she was unsure of how much time. There was no more screaming, the singing had stopped and the room was cloudy with fugitive smoke despite the clogged doorframe. There was a noise, though. She rolled over and released Charlie's hand from her own. The room still seemed as bright even with the added fumes. She felt feeble but dragged herself across the floor towards the sound. It was coming from above her, on the ledge, perhaps. Her body weight, as petite as it was, was a struggle to lift to the appropriate level of the familiar ringing noise. She investigated the nearby counter to no avail and collapsed back to the floor. Suddenly, Grace was hit by a flood of realisation. Her body rebooted and she leapt to her feet throwing herself at the glass window dividing the sorting office from the inner office. She forced her arm through the gap at the bottom and reached for the phone by the side of the computer. It was still ringing. She grabbed the handset and focused on the voice. It was Tyrone. It seemed so long ago that she had even seen him. He had made it away from the infected. He was okay.

"Ty?" Her voice rasped at his name. The smoke was thicker than she thought.

"Grace? What's going on in there? What's happened? Where's Kristie?"

"She's gone, Ty. I don't know where. She just went. Where are you?"

"What do you mean she's gone? Where could she have gone? The whole club is on lock down. Where is she?"

"Ty, everybody's dead." The overexertion caused her to start frantically coughing. When she quietened, he was still talking. He was saying something about fire alarms and half an hour. Something about taking half an hour to get to them. "Tyrone, where are you?"

"Grace, I'm right outside. I time locked the doors from outside. There's still time on the clock but the fire brigade can have you out in about an hour…"

"What about the infection? It's not safe for you to be out there."

The line went quiet. Grace feared for the worst. They'd got him. He'd risked his life to save his friends and they'd got him. "Ty...? Ty!"

"Grace... There is no infection."

Grace shook her head. She couldn't have heard him right. She rubbed furiously at her eyes. The smoke was thickening by the minute, it was becoming unbearable.

"Grace? Did you hear me?"

"What do you mean?" she managed. A forced sound disguised as a weak laugh escaped her lips.

"There is no infection, Grace. I was wrong. Everyone was panicking and we all thought the virus had reached us." His positivity was surreal. He seemed relieved, somehow. How had this happened?

"Why didn't anyone know we were in here?" Grace choked through the billowing smoke.

Tyrone let out an exhausted breath. "I had an accident when I was trying to get away from the crazies. I ended up in the hospital. I woke up about two hours ago. I'm so sorry, Grace."

Grace couldn't comprehend what was being said to her. She couldn't make sense of his words let alone form her own in order to respond.

"Grace, the doors will be opened in under an hour. Tell everyone to get ready. Who else is in there with you?"

Grace clutched the phone loosely to her ear. She peered through the smoke around the room. Charlie's hand had been cold when she'd left him. Rosie and the child were lying motionless. She exhaled suddenly and forced herself to answer. "It's just me."

"Grace? What do you mean? Where's everyone else? What's happened? Grace..."

She dropped the phone. She couldn't answer him. She didn't know where to start. They had been trapped inside a building for practically three days and of twenty-three people, she was the last one standing. The smoke was filtering in quicker and quicker. There was no hope. An hour was just too long. She couldn't wait. She closed her eyes and prayed. Prayed to a God she'd never really believed in and found herself wondering if he even listened to the non-believers. She rested her head heavily against the wall behind her and waited for the end. She found herself wondering how it would feel. Would she choke on the impending smoke or would it just send her to sleep? Maybe it wouldn't hurt as much as she thought. She'd never been good with pain.

From out of nowhere, she was snapped back to reality.

"She's not waking up."

Grace sat up straight, as if the voice itself filled her with electricity. The girl was still alive. Little True was still alive. She grabbed the child with both hands and shook her slightly, as if she didn't believe she was real. Her hands moved to True's face and she held them there for what seemed to be an eternity. She then let go really quickly in a fear that she might be hurting her. "You're okay," she whispered. "Oh my God. You're okay."

This changed everything. Grace couldn't give up when there was a child's life in the balance. The same child that she'd fought so hard to protect the past three days. She pulled herself to her feet and searched the room frantically. The inner office held three dead bolt safes. At the moment, they were still filled with all variations of cash. Grace believed one of them could hold a three-year-old for an hour, just long enough for her rescuers to get inside the building and get her out safely. She looked weak already and was finding it hard to breathe as it was. There was no way Grace could get through the separating door without the key but there was a chance she could break through the window. She picked up a chair and threw it with all her might at the glass. It cracked from side to side and with one final blow, the window shattered, exploding into the inner office. True held her hands over her ears and tried to fight off the tears showing her age and innocence. Grace looked at her apologetically and then scooped the child up into her arms. She weighed next to nothing. She sat on the countertop and crawled through the debris, shielding True from any rogue glass edges. She could feel fragments splintering her own body, but it didn't matter. She placed the child down on the floor next to the door and turned her attention to the safe that was going to save the child's life. The middle one was the best option. It was easier to empty and stood taller than the rest. It would seal in more air than the others. Grace turned the keys and unlocked the grey handle. The sticker on the inside of the door read 'Fire resistance 60 minutes'. Grace prayed the firefighters would reach them before the fire did. She would wait until the latest possible moment before shutting the safe.

As she considered all of her options, the room was rocked by a massive explosion. The entire room vibrated and things were jolted from high shelves, falling onto them as if aimed at the two occupants. Grace was struck by a box to the head. The pain shot through her brow and everything went dark. Hitting the floor brought her to but her vision was blurry and the ringing in her ears was deafening. Once again, she dragged herself to her feet and stumbled over to the now open safe. She eyed the trays of coins piled ten high and two wide and began reaching in and grabbing as many as she could, throwing them behind her. Each one was filled with two hundred pound coins which, before today, she had tediously filled over and over again. It now meant nothing. Coins flew through the air stripped of their former statuses. Next, was the removal of the bags. Each one contained five hundred pound coins and the sudden change in weight rapidly took its toll on Grace. She fell to her knees and began coughing once more. Her sight was still blurry, but she didn't need to know what she was grabbing at, just that she was clearing the compartment. The harsh material of the cloth bags scraped at her already weakened skin. She pulled at the shelf above. It didn't move. It didn't matter. She didn't need to be comfortable. It was only for a little while. It was good enough to play host for a small amount of time. She pulled the little girl upright and held her chin steady. She, too, was feeling drowsy. "True, listen to me. You are so brave, the bravest little girl I've ever met, but I need you to be brave just a little bit longer, okay?"

"I'm really tired."

"I know you are, sweetheart. The smoke is making you sleepy. That's why I need you to get into the safe."

"No, I can't. It's going to be dark. I'm scared of the dark."

"It will be dark, but it will only be for a few more minutes. I promise. My friend is on his way in to get you."

"What about you?"

"I'm going to sit outside and make sure nobody tries to hurt you again."

True looked wearily at the safe.

"Can you do that for me, True?"

"Okay...will you sing to me?"

Grace kissed the little girl on her forehead and squeezed with her last remaining energy.

"Of course, I will, my darling."

With that, she sat the girl inside the metal safe and slammed it shut. She twisted the lock and slid down to the ground. Stationery and money covered the floor and Grace reached for the phone one last time. She squinted at the buttons and pressed them hoping she was hitting the right ones. Tyrone's phone went straight to voicemail so in her dreary state, she left a message.

"There's a little girl in the middle safe. You need to get her out." She hung up and let the receiver fall into her lap.

A faint sobbing could be heard from within the safe which served as a soft reminder of her promise. She closed her eyes and began singing *Truly Scrumptious* until her melody turned to a whisper which eventually merged into a broken string of sounds and breath.

1:30 pm

The TV screen came to life to show a young woman with curly brunette hair and pale skin. She wore a grey suit jacket, concealing a salmon pink blouse which highlighted the blue in her eyes through her silver rimmed glasses. She spoke confidently and clearly to the camera in front of her, conveying all the remorseful and informative tones needed in order to report on the devastating scene behind her.

Monday morning had been a relatively slow shift up until the fire response team received a call to a very recently closed bingo hall on the retail park in Enfield. A concerned shopper made the call to the emergency services after an alarm was relentlessly sounding for three hours.

Lola Wray commented, "I heard the alarm going off when I passed in the car on my way home from work but you hear alarms all the time around here. I didn't pay any attention to it until I remembered that the bingo hall had shut down a few days ago. My mum told me about it so I wondered if anyone would be notified if an alarm was going off. I called it in just in case."

However, when the fire fighters arrived at the scene, they were unable to gain access to the building.

Fire Chief Rob Cooper ordered his crew to begin breaking into the building. The metal shutters proved to be a difficulty and required special equipment in order to get through, but after forty minutes, they reached the glass and they were in.

"The smoke had filled the arcade area completely. When we got through the shutters, it started pouring out. The guys followed me inside and to be honest, I've never seen anything like it."

Police are still scouring the building in search of missing shoppers and employees said to have been trapped inside following Friday morning's riot by another employee, Tyrone Lindsey. From what we can tell, Tyrone witnessed the disturbance and, in an attempt, to keep nearby shoppers out of harm's way, locked them inside the building. We are still unsure as to why he placed the building under an emergency lock down for 72 hours as he is currently being questioned by the police, but we will keep you updated.

This has been Jade Thompson for Local News, back to the studio.

1:45 pm

Tyrone moved uncomfortably in the hard metal chair. His palms were clammy and his cheeks were burning but he felt cold all over, more than likely a side effect from leaving hospital without being discharged. His body was majorly dehydrated and his blood sugar levels were low. He'd been unconscious for the best part of three days and he had just learned that his act of heroism was actually the cause of death for everyone he had thought he was saving. Needless to say, it was beginning to take its toll.

The man sitting in front of him had slick black hair and a rugged, stern face. Tyrone could tell from the prominent wrinkles on his eyes and on his forehead that the man lived a stressful life, probably void of sleep and comfort. As he spoke, his tone matched his strict expression and Ty listened again to the words he had heard only moments before on his arrival.

"Tyrone Lindsey, my name is Detective Daniel Whitman, and this is Detective Ashleigh Buck."

The female detective had a much friendlier demeanour. A look of concern dominated her pretty face and she listened intently to the detective sitting beside her, bracing herself for the suffering man's confession.

"Mr Lindsey, I need you to start from the beginning because I'm finding it really hard to understand why you would lock those people inside a building for three days."

Tyrone held his head in his hands as the officers awaited his response. The truth was that he didn't know where to begin. His reasoning, his actions and his beliefs had all been thwarted the moment he had turned on the TV in that hospital bed.

The last thing he could remember was running away from those monsters and thinking he was going to die. He then woke up in hospital and the world hadn't fallen to pieces, he wasn't a character from The Walking Dead and the only thing newsworthy was that of the riot he had witnessed.

Everything had then come screaming back to him and he knew he had to get back there to find out what had happened and to make sure that the people inside were okay. Unfortunately, in doing so, he had offered himself up for an easy arrest, but being charged with imprisonment and murder? It was too much to take in in his current state.

"Tyrone?" The young bright-eyed detective was clearly playing the role of 'good cop' in this interview. "Tyrone, you need to tell us what happened. Look at it from our point of view. You locked a group of scared people inside a building for no plausible reason that we can understand and three days later, 21 of them are dead, and no one knew they were in there except for you."

Tyrone couldn't speak through his hearty sobs. He hadn't just condemned a bunch of strangers; he had locked his friends in there too and now they were all dead. They had found Kristie unconscious in the stairwell but she was fighting for her life and they were still searching the club for any survivors.

He furiously wiped his eyes and sat holding his hands to stop them from visibly shaking. He tried to steady his breathing before he started to speak but his words trembled all the same. "They were running…being chased. They were so scared…" His voice broke. "I just need a minute."

Whitman lost his temper. "Well, those people needed to not be locked inside a building!" He threw his chair halfway across the room, causing Tyrone to flinch and cover his ears. "They were innocent people for fuck's sake! Why did you do it?"

He slammed his hands down onto the table, making Detective Buck rise to her feet. She took him to one side.

"Dan, why don't you take five minutes?"

Detective Whitman stood with one hand over his mouth and the other placed firmly on his hip, wearing a look of frustrated, desperation.

"Dan?" Buck caught his gaze and ushered him out of the room before turning to face Tyrone who was now ever so slightly rocking in his chair, cradling his head.

"Tyrone, drink some water. You must be dehydrated."

He stared at the plastic cup filled to the brim with the clear liquid and shook his head rapidly, antagonising the already piercing ache that had taken up residence beneath his skull. He winced but he welcomed the pain. He deserved to feel pain. He had done this. He had been the cause of all those people's deaths.

He needed to feel how they felt: scared, trapped, and helpless. He could hear their screams like tiny landmines exploding simultaneously inside his head.

"Tyrone…" Detective Buck locked eyes with him and spoke softly. "I understand that this rabies virus has been exaggerated and over dramatized on social media. I know about the videos of supposed victims attacking hospital staff members or even family members. You've probably even heard about the fanatics killing people who have been given the all clear. This virus has got everybody shaken up and some genuinely do believe that this is the beginning of the end.

"When we arrested you, you told us that people were being chased by, in your own words, 'the infected'. I can see how it could have looked that way to you. They were advantage taking maniacs. Maybe they were even on some sort of narcotic. I get that you mistook the situation, but you need to talk to us. You're facing manslaughter, if not murder charges."

Tyrone began blinking aggressively. His whole body was twitching involuntarily and Buck could see his gaze shifting, uncontrollably so she beckoned for Detective Whitman to return.

As he entered the room, Tyrone began rambling. "She said they were all dead. I don't understand what happened." His head was beating his deafening heartbeat into his ear drums and his face turned to an ashy grey colour as his eyes glazed over.

"Mr Lindsey? Are you okay?"

"No," he stuttered. The room began to swirl around him. He tried to maintain focus, but his head was throbbing violently. "I need a minute."

Beads of sweat began pouring from his forehead and as his head got heavier, he felt his body drop off of the chair and onto the hard, cold floor. He started shaking aggressively and he could hear shouts of panic hitting his ear drums.

"Call an ambulance! Tyrone? Tyrone can you hear me? Look at me. Come on stay with me."

As Tyrone convulsed violently, he began frothing at the mouth. Detective Whitman hit an alarm on the wall and sirens began blazing in his desperate call for help. The door to the interrogation room swung open suddenly as an officer entered with a defibrillator and a first aid duffel bag. Buck and the officer began assessing Tyrone just as his body went limp.

"He's not breathing!" Buck began emergency CPR in an attempt to resuscitate the fallen suspect and on her thirteenth compression, Tyrone's eyes bolted open as he gasped for air.

The officer's breathed sighs filled with relief.

Detective Whitman leaned in closer to the man lying on the floor. "You gave us a scare there. Don't worry, you're…"

Tyrone shot forward and sank his teeth into the detective's neck, biting down hard as he screamed out in pain. The other officers began trying to restrain the once docile man, but his strength was inhuman. He threw Buck against the glass window and wrestled the other officer to the floor. Tyrone proceeded to punch the officer's face over and over as he failed to block the attacks and eventually lost consciousness. Buck managed to escape the room, locking the door behind her. As she cowered in the room behind the two-way mirror, she watched her colleagues slowly bleeding to death whilst the suspect continued to hurl himself at the locked door repeatedly.

Irritated, he turned his attention to the mirror and whilst unknowingly keeping eye contact with the young female officer, he headbutted the glass continually until his forehead split open and the glass began to crack.